# Another ONE

*Leatha, the lighter side of Aleatha*

**ALEATHA ROMIG**

New York Times, Wall Street Journal, and USA Today
bestselling author of the Infidelity and Consequences series
and Plus One

# COPYRIGHT AND LICENSE INFORMATION

## *ANOTHER ONE*

## Dedication

*ANOTHER ONE is truly a joint venture with my wonderful, patient daughter.*

*Many writer's roadblocks arose during the creation of Trevor and Shana's story. Sometimes it's difficult to get going in the world of make believe when real life is busy and full. I have no doubt that it was my many conversations with my daughter that steered this story back on track time and time again.*

*I couldn't be happier with the final result of A SECRET ONE and ANOTHER ONE.*

*I fell head over heels in love with this pretend couple. I'm so grateful to the readers who encouraged me to pursue Shana and Trevor's story, and mostly, I'm thankful to my daughter who during her own wedding preparations willingly added her advice. As a woman about Shana's age, her insight was beyond helpful and often comedic.*

*Maybe one day she will decide to follow her mother into the world of writing. Until then, I'm happy to have her at my side and as my constant support. May she, through life's ups and downs and friends and foes, have her HEA!*

*Thank you, Cass Romig. I love you and appreciate all you do, always.*

*-Mom*

# AUTHOR'S
*Note*

A SECRET ONE is a novella released prior to ANOTHER ONE.
This is the short story that explains the first meeting of Shana Price and Trevor Willis.
While it is not mandatory to read A SECRET ONE prior to ANOTHER ONE, I didn't want you, my reader, to miss this "free" ebook simply because you purchased the paperback.
I hope you enjoy A SECRET ONE, a novella.
Whether you do or not, once this is over, you will find ANOTHER ONE.
- Aleatha

# A Secret ONE

NEW YORK TIMES BESTSELLING AUTHOR

# ALEATHA ROMIG

LEATHA. THE LIGHTER SIDE OF ALEATHA

*Leatha, the lighter side of Aleatha*

## ALEATHA ROMIG

New York Times, Wall Street Journal, and USA Today
bestselling author of the Infidelity and Consequences series
and Plus One

# A Secret ONE

Standing beside my best friend, in front of family and friends, as she proclaims her love to her future husband, my mind should be on her. As maid of honor, I should be attentive and helpful.

I'm trying.

The problem is the man in the second row—her soon-to-be brother-in-law.

Trevor Willis is sweet and sexy with green eyes that hold my attention as well as my secrets.

For example:
How can his smile make my heart beat faster?
Why does his laugh turn my insides to jelly?
What is he thinking as his stare heats my skin?
And most importantly, how did I end up waking in his hotel suite bed on the morning of my best friend's wedding to his brother?

Learn the answers in *A SECRET ONE,* a prequel novella to *ANOTHER ONE!*

# A Secret One

*Leatha, the lighter side of Aleatha*

**ALEATHA ROMIG**

# CHAPTER
## *One*

**Shana**

*M*y incredible dream begins to fade as I wake to the embrace of strong arms and the strangely comforting aroma of day-old cologne—a mixture of spice and leather—combined with musk and cinnamon. Before I can fully process the possibility that my dream may not have been a dream, soft sheets kiss my skin as I'm pulled closer to a warm, hard body.

"Good morning. How are you feeling?" Trevor asks in a deep whisper, his voice dragging me from a dense, sleep-induced fog as butterfly kisses pepper the top of my head. His tone is thick with the gravelly stirrings of waking.

As I process his question and the reality that I'm in bed with a man I hardly remember, my eyes pop open to a dimly lit hotel suite. Pushing through the sensation of reality versus dreams, my pulse quickens as I slowly lift my chin, bringing my gaze upward from the bare chest before me, to a thick neck covered with a day's beard growth, and then all the way up to his green eyes, now open and filled with as much question as mine.

"O-oh," I stutter. "Oh my!"

I wiggle away from his comforting embrace as my mind fills with pieces of scenes from the night before. The memories are like a sliced-up film reel, the missing snippets now lying upon the cutting-room floor. With large gaps in my memory, I search for answers, for anything that will make sense of where I am, where we are, and how we got to this point.

*I'm* in a hotel, in Indiana.

*We're* in a hotel, in Indiana.

We're both here because...

The wedding.

The reality hits me with enough force to rock my already topsy-turvy world.

My best friend is getting married, and I'm her maid of honor.

She's getting married today.

*Oh my!*

"Oh no. What time is it?" My voice cracks with the desperation currently coursing through my bloodstream as I search the room, my eyes adjusting to the sliver of faint light seeping from around the thick curtains. "This isn't..."

It isn't my room. It's similar, but I recall hanging my maid-of-honor dress from the curtain rod after my flight and leaving my shoes on the chair. Since neither is here, I have the undeniable feeling I'm not in my suite, but in Trevor's.

"Hey," he soothes as he reaches for my hand. "Slow down. It's still early. No wedding obligations for a few hours."

"Okay." And yet my head moves contrarily to my agreement, shaking vigorously back and forth as I try to formulate my thoughts and find the correct words capable of leaving my dry lips. "No, this..." I motion between the two of us. "...what is this?" I sit up. "No matter what it is, we can't tell them. Not today. Not on their wedding day. Oh..." My temples seize up—from memories or possibly from alcohol, I'm not sure. Closing my eyes to the pain, I collapse, lying back onto the soft pillow. "Oh, what will they say?"

"Well, they might be happy for us. After all, they're happy. Why shouldn't we be?"

*Happy?*

Happy that the bride's best friend and the groom's brother had a one-night stand the night before their wedding?

Is that what happened?

Damn wine. No, it was more than that.

I lick my lips, the lingering taste of cinnamon a stark clue to what my mind forgot.

No, not just wine. Fireball.

*Oh dear Lord.*

I'm not a drinker. Why did I do it? And more importantly, what did I do?

My head continues to shake. "No. They don't even know we met."

"Oh, Shana..." He lifts my hand, his grasp sure and warm as his fingers surround mine. "I'm very glad to meet you."

"That's not... no," I say, more as a prayer than a testament to our meeting as I pull my hand away. Immediately, I miss the connection I hardly know and yet suddenly crave.

With my eyes still closed, I sense the shift of the bed, the way Trevor's weight settles closer to my side, his long fingers as they gently tease my messy hair away from my face. His soft yet sure lips as they once again kiss my forehead and hair.

Afraid to open my eyes—to see him or to remember—I swallow before asking the million-dollar question, "Oh goodness, Trevor, please tell me, what did we do?"

His laugh rumbles like thunder, rolling through the morning twilight. "That, my lady, could wound a man of less self-confidence. What do you remember?"

Slowly, I open my eyes and take in Trevor Willis. He's nothing like I imagined him to be from my best friend's description. The younger brother of her fiancé was rumored to be quiet and shy, an engineer who constructs roads and bridges. More of a thinker, she said, not as much of a people person, nothing like his gregarious entrepreneurial brother.

In my fevered memories, as I inhale his masculine scent, feel the warmth of his skin, and absorb the adoration of his gaze, nothing could be further from the truth. He's every bit as sexy. No, he's more. Much more. And there's a quiet reserve about him that I find reassuring. My gaze wanders downward.

The sheets from the bed where we slept are bunched near his waist, covering his legs and revealing his defined torso, broad shoulders, and still higher, the most mesmerizing shining green stare. His dirty blond hair is tousled in a sensual morning way, making my fingers itch to comb through his locks. His cheeks are high as his smile broadens. His strong chiseled jaw is covered in a day's overgrowth of blond.

If I didn't remember his name and our meeting—or at least the beginning of it—I wouldn't know he's my best friend's future brother-in-law.

If that were the case, I wouldn't realize that on the morning of my best friend's wedding, I'm waking in the bed of a man I met merely hours ago, with a terrible headache and more questions than answers.

Tentatively, I sigh and scoot up the large king-sized bed toward the headboard. As I do, I notice the clothes I'm wearing. They are clothes, but not completely mine. In place of a nightgown, I'm wearing a large button-down man's shirt and yes, my own panties.

At least I'm not nude.

The problem is that I'm not sure if that's a good or bad thing. I need the entire film. It wasn't the director who cut out important scenes, leaving them lying upon the editing-room floor, but Fireball. Trevor's cinnamon scent. Some of the memories are coming back. The problem is that they lack chronological order, creating a puzzle without shape. I can't see the whole picture.

"Trevor?" I ask, suddenly unsure if I can handle the truth. "Do you think we could get some coffee?"

His grin grows. "I already called. Room service is on its way."

"I'm a big hot chocolate fan, but right now, I think coffee sounds best."

"Anything else, my lady?"

I sigh again, dropping my gaze to my hands that are neatly folded on my lap. Looking back up through my lashes, I confess, "At the risk of injuring your self-confidence, can you tell me about last night?"

"Are you asking for a story?"

"I'm asking for the truth."

# CHAPTER
## *Two*

### *Shana*

*T*revor hands me a bottle of red Gatorade after untwisting the cap. "Here you go. While you were still sleeping, I went to the store off the lobby and bought you this." He shrugs. "I hope you like red. It's my favorite after a little too much to drink."

"You didn't happen to find something for a headache, did you? I'm going to be a terrible maid of honor."

From the bedside stand he grasps a small packet of over-the-counter pain relievers. "Before you're too hard on yourself, you only had three shots."

"Three?" Why does it feel like I drank the whole bottle?

"Three," he repeats before he shrugs. "Or four. How about you tell me what you remember?"

After a long drink of the Gatorade and swallowing the pain relievers, I lean back against the headboard and begin to recall. "My flight was delayed..."

I go on sipping the Gatorade and talking about my misfortunes while traveling from London, where I now live and work, to Indiana for Kimbra's wedding. It wasn't getting to the United States that was the problem, but getting from New York to Indiana. The direct flight was cancelled due to mechanical issues. After much pleading, I was put on a standby flight with one stop. Despite little to no sleep, I still made it to Indianapolis with two hours to spare for the rehearsal.

"You weren't at the rehearsal," I say, remembering the scene.

"No. Duncan asked me to be in the wedding, but I'm not the greatest brother."

"Really? You're here. Didn't you want to be in it?"

He shakes his head. "I did. And I'm here. It was that when the big event was being planned, I wasn't sure I would be." His eyes grow large. "It isn't because I'm not happy for them. I am. Kimbra's the best thing to happen to my brother, ever. It's that I'm working on a huge project in Washington." He waves his hand. "The details aren't that important, but there've been a few issues with construction. The project is behind schedule, and I was afraid that if I took too much time away, the foreman might be tempted to cut corners to speed things up. Let's just say, that wouldn't be good for anyone."

"So you're not in the wedding?"

"No. But Duncan understands work. He wasn't upset. I told him I'd be here. I haven't seen him yet, since I just arrived after ten last night."

I try to think back. "The bar." It was a revelation as well as the opening to my faded memories.

"You remember the bar?"

Slowly, I nod as a knock upon the entrance door echoes through his suite.

Trevor stands, the sheets falling away to reveal loose-fitting basketball shorts, hanging low on his hips, his trim waist disappearing in a V, and long muscular legs.

My bottom lip slips under my front teeth as I imagine what is not well hidden under the shorts and the way those legs would feel surrounding me. How could I know and not remember?

"Trevor?" I ask as he starts to move toward the door.

"Hmm?"

"We didn't... we didn't..." I can't completely finish the sentence. One-night stands aren't my thing. I mean, they never were. I'm a third-date girl. And since moving to London, I've been a not-in-a-million-years girl.

I love my job, but it's been all-consuming. I'm a buyer for Saks Fifth Avenue, overseeing the Junior line. The job title is everything I've ever wanted, and so is the responsibility. I love the excitement of a runway show and the anticipation of next season's fashions. It's the schedule that is daunting. I've dated a few different men since I moved across the pond, and if I am completely honest, it's usually their accent that hooks me or the way they use different words.

"We'll take the *lift*..." Or... "Shall we put your bag in the *boot?*" Yes. I crack a smile every time. The first time someone asked, I wondered how my bag would fit in a boot and why I'd want it there. The language idiosyncrasies are a never-ending source of my amusement. Lovely has become my favorite adjective. "I had a *lovely* time." "It was simply *lovely.*"

Nevertheless, even with the cute phrases, the attraction doesn't last—at least it hasn't. There hasn't been a spark with any of those men, not like the one I'm feeling right now.

Maybe it's the Gatorade or my undeniable attraction; however, just talking with Trevor, I'm beginning to feel better than I did when I woke.

"Did we?"

His head tilts in the most adorable way as he grins my direction. "Your coffee awaits, my lady. Then I'll tell you my story."

As he goes toward the door, I make my way out of the bed and hurry to the bathroom, my mind filling with scenes and more questions. After closing the door, I take a deep breath and turn on the light. Even through squinty eyes, the reflection in the mirror isn't nearly as bad as I expected. My blonde hair is a wavy mess, and my blue eyes have a bit of red, but it isn't anything that can't be fixed with a brush and a few eye drops. I quickly splash water on my face and reach for a toothbrush.

As my fingers graze Trevor's toothbrush, I decide that no matter what happened last night, I don't know him well enough to share oral hygiene utensils. Instead, I squeeze a dollop of toothpaste on my finger and make quick work of removing the tiny fuzzy sweaters that someone knit during the night and currently fit tightly around each tooth.

Don't let anyone fool you. Fireball is not your friend.

After another minute or two, I decide that just maybe I'll be able to pull off this maid-of-honor show. It's then that I notice my phone on the counter. It's turned off, and I pray it has some battery remaining. The charger is hopefully back in my room.

After a few seconds of pushing the power button, with a chime the screen comes to life. I swipe it and am met with multiple indicators of voicemails and text messages. Looking first at the text messages, I see that they're all from Kimbra. The first one asks if I made it to my room safely, followed by separate question marks, followed by the next one.

"TELL ME YOU'RE WITH SOME HAND-SOME MAN, OR I'M COMING TO FIND YOU."

Next: **"SHANA! I NEED MY BEAUTY SLEEP. GIVE ME A THUMBS UP—ANYTHING."**

Text number six: **"THE HOTEL WON'T TELL ME SHIT. GRANDMA HELEN CALLED, AND ALL THEY TOLD HER WAS THAT YOU WERE CHECKED IN. WE KNOW THAT. AT LEAST IT WAS MORE INFO. I THINK SHE SCARED THEM. LOL."**

Lastly: **"I'M STILL WORRIED. CALL ME BACK, OR GRANDMA AND I ARE COMING TO LOOK FOR YOU. IT'S NOT A SLUMBER PARTY YOU WANT."**

I check the current time—7:40 in the morning. Since it's not even eight, and Kimbra was texting until after midnight, I decide to text back instead of calling.

My fingers hover over the keyboard. **"SORRY I DIDN'T CALL OR TEXT. I WAS BUSY MAKING OUT WITH YOUR FUTURE BROTHER-IN-LAW."** ...Backspace and erase...

Starting over: **"DO YOU REMEMBER THAT TIME IN NEW YORK WITH THE FIREBALL? YEAH, NEITHER DO I. I ALSO DON'T REMEMBER LAST NIGHT IN INDIANAPOLIS."** (Smiley face emoji)

I contemplate hitting send.

Backspace...erase...one more try...

**"HEY, BABE. SORRY. I CRASHED LAST NIGHT WITH MY RINGER OFF. I'M ALIVE AND WELL. CAN'T WAIT FOR THE WEDDING. THE YOU, ME, AND GRANDMA HELEN**

SLUMBER PARTY WILL HAVE TO WAIT FOR
ANOTHER TIME. YOU KNOW I LOVE YOUR
GRANDMA! LET'S GET TODAY'S PARTY
STARTED. YOU'RE GOING TO BE THE MOST
BEAUTIFUL BRIDE."

Seconds after hitting send, my phone chirps: KIMBRA
flashes on the screen.

"BITCH. YOU HAD ME SCARED TO DEATH.
GRANDMA AND I WERE GOING TO DRIVE
BACK TO THE CITY, BUT SHE WAS WINNING
AT POKER AND KEPT SAYING ONE MORE
HAND. (Laughing emoji) DUNCAN EVEN TEXTED
HIS BROTHER, ASKING IF HE'D SEEN YOU.
HIS BROTHER IS STAYING AT THE SAME
HOTEL. INTRODUCE YOURSELF IF YOU SEE
HIM. HE LOOKS LIKE DUNCAN, BUT NOT AS
SEXY, WITH BLOND HAIR AND WELL, NEVER-
MIND. YOU'LL MEET HIM AT THE WEDDING.
DON'T FORGET HAIR AND MAKEUP AT NOON.
SEE YOU THEN. LOVE YOU."

I shake my head. Only Kimbra would start her text by
calling me a bitch and end it with "love you." I think for a
second about her description of Trevor. I could call her and
tell her that she's completely wrong about him, but that
would give away my uncomfortable situation. Maybe before
giving anything away, I should learn more about last night.

"Shana?" Trevor's voice calls from the other side of
the door.

"Yes?"

"The bellhop is here. He needs to see you."

"See me?"

His voice becomes softer, more of a stage whisper. "Apparently, he thinks I'm trying to get a key to your room for nefarious reasons. He will only give it to you."

"A key…"

The clue is a figurative light bulb to my lost memories.

Last night I couldn't find my key. My heart beats faster. It was more than just my key. It was my purse that I also couldn't find. I'd lost it. Oh God. My purse has my ID and my room key. They wouldn't give me one without the other. No ID, no key. No key and I can't get into my room. In my room is my passport. Without that, I can't get back to London.

My hands begin to shake as I search the bathroom for something to wear. I can't go to the door and speak to the bellhop wearing only Trevor's shirt and my panties. Just then, another soft knock taps on the bathroom door. The door opens a crack, and Trevor's hand comes into view, holding a soft white hotel robe.

"Thanks," I say with a grin.

The too-big robe swallows me as I cinch the tie around my waist. Doing my best to smooth my messy blonde hair, I take a deep breath and enter the suite. Standing just inside the room next to Trevor is an older man. He's shorter than Trevor and dressed in a hotel uniform; however, my eyes go to Trevor, who is now also wearing a T-shirt along with those sexy basketball shorts. I almost pout, missing the defined abs.

And then, my attention is diverted by an appetizing aroma. Saliva returns to my mouth as I notice on the table in front of the sofa a tray that holds a carafe of what I assume is the coffee Trevor promised, as well as two dishes covered with silver lids. Suddenly and loudly, my stomach rumbles in anticipation at the promise of food.

"Ms. Price?" the older man asks, his voice bringing back my panic over my purse.

"Yes. I'm Shana Price."

"Ma'am, I apologize for the mix-up last night. The employee is new; however, it's our policy to not dispense keys without identification."

I nod, remembering bits of the conversation. "The thing was that I misplaced my purse, with my ID. I lost both."

His eyes twinkle as he reaches inside the cloth bag I hadn't realized he was holding. "If you can give me the information on this driver's license, I believe that I can return your handbag, ID, and room key."

"Oh!" I reply, relieved to be able to get back into my room, my passport, and to the dress hanging on the curtain rod. After rattling off all of my information, the bellhop hands me the entire cloth bag. Peering inside, I let out a long breath, the mint of Trevor's toothpaste tickling my nose. Inside the bag is everything the bellhop promised. Opening my purse, I find all my cash, my credit cards, and my ID. Nothing is missing.

Handing him a tip, I say, "Thank you so much. Did someone turn this in?"

"One of our custodial employees found it last night after hours by the fire pit outside the piano bar."

My cheeks warm as pink undoubtedly rises to the surface, and I turn a bashful gaze toward Trevor.

The fire pit.

It's all coming back.

# CHAPTER
## Three

**Ten hours earlier**
### *Shana*

"Come stay out at the farm with me," Kimbra says as the limousine we all rode in from the rehearsal dinner stops in front of my hotel.

"I'm all checked in to the hotel. Really..." I give her a kiss on the cheek. "...sweetie, I'm exhausted. I will be a better maid of honor tomorrow if I sleep well tonight."

"Oh!" her grandma Helen says, the funniest little old lady who always seems to have more energy than I can muster. "We're not sleeping right away out at Judy and Oscar's. Nope! This is my first time in a limousine and I'm feeling lucky." She elbows my side and gives me a not-so-subtle wink. "Not that kind of lucky." She shakes her head. "The kind of lucky that will make me as rich as Kimberly Ann's man. I'm so confident, I'll spot you five dollars, and we'll all play poker. Five-card stud. Texas Hold 'em." She pouts her lips. "I'd win more if we could get Duncan to stay with us. Silly traditions. It's not like the man hasn't seen every part of you, Kimberly Ann. Tasted the milk, if you know what I mean." She grins at me. "I don't see anything wrong with that. I mean, as long as you both like the milk.

"Me," Grandma goes on. "I've been a big fan of milk. No lactose intolerance here!"

"Grandma!" Kimberly says with a shake of her head.

"Come on, Kimberly Ann, you should let your grandma have some fun. That man loses his shirt every time."

"Grandma," Kimbra replies as we all giggle at Grandma Helen's lack of filter, "he loses because you won't let him quit when he's ahead."

"Five dollars?" I say with a grin, hoping to get Kimbra off the hook. "That must mean it's not strip poker."

"Oh heavens," Grandma Helen says, "not with the people staying at Judy's. Besides, I'm too old for strip poker. I'd have to leave on my bra." She wiggles about as she pulls at her blouse. "And let me tell you, that baby is coming off first thing. My girls are tired of being locked up. Heck, I might not even wait until we get home."

The door to the limousine opens, and I give Kimbra another kiss. "The rehearsal was perfect. The dinner was fantastic. You and Duncan will be so happy. I'm going straight to my room and getting a good night's sleep." I tilt my head toward Kimbra's grandma. "I'll pass on the poker."

My best friend laughs. "With Duncan staying at my brother and sister-in-law's, I'm betting it's not a long game."

"Judy," Grandma Helen says to her daughter, Kimbra's mother, "I know. We can call the Peabodys down the way. Jeremiah is always good for ten dollars." She turns to Kimbra. "After your grandpa passed, he offered me some milk…"

Kimbra laughs as she steps out of the car with me. "Maybe I should stay here with you. The last thing I want to hear about is my grandma's dairy intake."

I smile wider. "She is a hoot! And you know, you're welcome to stay here."

She shakes her head. "No, I'd better keep an eye on them and make sure the game doesn't end up with Grandma's bra in the pot or more discussion on what could have been!"

We both snicker.

"Text me when you're settled," she says. "I wish you'd reconsider coming out to my parents' so we can stay together tonight."

"At your parents' house, in your childhood canopy bed? No way. I've heard stories!"

Kimbra gives me a hug. "Thanks for making it back for the wedding."

"I wouldn't miss it for the world!"

Cool air greets me as I enter the hotel's lobby and take a deep breath. Summers in Indiana are much warmer than in London. Then again, I grew up in Illinois, so this isn't much different. Somehow, your body forgets how 95 percent humidity feels. It's not just that, but also the transition to the cooled air as I step inside. My arms erupt with tiny goose bumps. Shivering, I ride the escalators up to the main level while taking in the entry. Marble floors reflect the large chandeliers as I pass the desks and make my way toward the lifts—okay, I really like that word for elevators. It's lovely. As I get closer, the ring of piano music fills my ears. Beyond the bank of elevators is an entrance to a small hotel bar, the sign in the hallway boasting the best jazz music in all of Indy.

My tired mind tries to decide if that's really a compliment. All of New Orleans...All of Louisiana, yes, but all of Indy as in Indianapolis? I'm not sure if the competition is that tough. Nevertheless, the longer I stand there waiting for the elevator, the more inviting the melody becomes.

Making a deal with myself, I decide I'll have one more

glass of wine—strictly for medicinal purposes to help me sleep—and then up to my room.

The bar is dark and chic with colored lights shining on the walls. One bar surrounds the piano, all the seats filled with couples laughing along with the pianist and singing slightly off-key. Instead of vying for a seat there, I make my way over to the sparsely occupied long bar near the side of the room. Its surface is shiny, reflecting the mood lighting. Easing onto a stool, I order a glass of cabernet. As I pay, a warm summer breeze skirts over my exposed skin, and I turn toward an opening door to what appears to be a patio.

"Is it warmer out there?" I ask the bartender.

"Yeah," he says. "Not too warm. The fire pits aren't on tonight. They're really nice on a cool night."

"I think I'll take my wine out there. I'm a bit chilled."

Outside is quieter but warmer, the night air heavy and filled with distant sounds of the city. Even though the fire pits aren't lit, there's a soft red glow coming from the glass embers, giving the illusion of fire without the heat. With my wine in hand, I sit by myself and relax for the first time since my trip began.

I'm finally here. I made it to the rehearsal. The wedding is tomorrow. Everything is good.

It's a mental pep talk, and after the last exhausting thirty-six hours, I'm beginning to believe every word.

"Excuse me," a deep voice interrupts my thoughts. "Is anyone sitting there?"

"Um, no..." I scoot over so the other side of the small sofa is available. "I'm not staying long if you need both seats."

He laughs. "I think I can fit in just one."

A blush fills my cheeks. "I wasn't..." I look him up and

down, recalling my affection for corn-fed Midwesterners. There's no reason to assume he would need more than one seat, not by himself, even with his broad shoulders—he has a trim torso and what appears to be a nice firm ass. My new home may be filled with great accents and fun words, but there's something about sexy men from my homeland.

The good-looking man sets his glass of beer on the edge of the fire pit and extends his hand. As he speaks, my gaze is fixed on his stunning green-eyed stare.

"I'm Trevor. Thanks for letting me crash your party."

My head turns from side to side, taking in my solitude. "Not much of a party." I accept his handshake. "Shana."

"They seem to be having one inside."

"Around the piano? Yes, they're having fun. Honestly, I'm here to relax. Besides, no one wants to hear me sing."

"Now don't sell yourself short. I bet you have a lovely voice."

*Lovely*. It makes me smile.

The conversation comes too easily. I learn that he's not from Indiana, but from New York. We talk about Manhattan and the places we love in the city. We talk about everything and nothing as I forget my need to sleep. It's when we go back inside for one more refill that things begin to get out of hand.

Across the top of the piano bar is a row of shots. When Trevor looks my direction, I shake my head. "No, I don't think that's a good idea."

"Hey, you two," a man who's sitting at the piano bar calls, "come on over. Have one on us. We're celebrating. My friend over here just got engaged."

Trevor and I smile.

"Come on. The more the merrier." The man gestures toward the piano bar where two seats are now available.

"Don't tell me you're against marriage?" the man asks.

When Trevor looks at me, I respond, "No, not at all. I'm in town for a wedding."

"Really?" Trevor asks with more than a little surprise to his voice. "Funny, me too."

"You are?"

"Come on over," the man says. "I'm Paul..." As he introduces the people around the piano, we take the two empty seats and learn that it's the younger couple who were just moments ago engaged.

Trevor hands me a shot glass. "To your wedding tomorrow. Too bad yours and mine aren't the same, or I'd ask you to dance."

We all drink.

"That would be nice," I say, placing the glass back on the bar and wiping my lips with the back of my hand. "But I'm the maid of honor, and I'm a little busy looking after the bride."

"I've heard those wedding dresses can be a real pain."

"Only if she needs to pee," I say and immediately cover my own lips. "Oh, I can't believe I said that."

"We'll blame the shot," he says with a laugh. "But now I'm going to blame you for making me think about that every time I look at my future sister-in-law."

"And I'll think of you each time I'm crammed in a stall with ten layers of lace in the air."

He leans closer, his warm breath on my neck. "At least you'll be thinking of me."

My skin heats. I'm not sure if it's from his closeness or the accuracy of his statement.

Just as quickly, his smile fades. "Unfortunately, I have a date coming to the wedding..."

Before he can finish, I start to stand. "Wait." Trevor reaches for my hand, his fingers surrounding mine. "Let me finish."

"Okay," I say, not sure why I want to let him finish. First, he says he wants to dance with me, and then, he mentions a date. Nevertheless, I tentatively sit back down.

"I'd much rather have you as my date. You see, the woman who is coming is a friend. And before you ask or think or anything...she really is...a real friend. The thing is that I couldn't show up at my brother's wedding stag."

The bartender hands us each another shot. I bring mine to my lips as Trevor continues, "We Willises have a reputation."

As he says his last name, I choke, cough, and almost spit as the Fireball burns its way down my throat.

His large hand rubs circles over my back. "Are you all right?"

"I don't think so." I lift my hand toward the bartender. "Another shot, please."

And that's how we learn the truth. Our wedding is one and the same. We could dance together. Except that Trevor has a friend from New York flying in the next morning. Apparently, Trevor's been working on an out-of-state project and wasn't even sure he'd make the wedding. If he'd accepted the best-man offer from Duncan, we'd be paired.

Now he'll be with a pretend date, and I'll be alone.

"I know," he says, "I'll call her and tell her not to come."

"No, you won't."

"Yes. She won't mind. She is coming here anyway, except..."

"Except what?" I ask, my mind filling with a thousand reasons why I don't want his friend who is a woman to be with him at the wedding.

"Her fiancé is a friend of mine."

My eyebrows arch. "Her fiancé?"

His shoulders shrug. "Okay, I'm about to share with you a Willis family secret. But first you must promise to never tell a soul."

"I don't know. My best friend is marrying your brother. Don't you think she should know the secret?"

"No, most definitely not."

The bartender eases two more shots our way. "I-I'm..." I wave it away.

"One more shot," Trevor says, "and I'll be brave enough to tell you what very few people know."

I never have been one to step back from a challenge. Whether it is moving from my small town to New York or from New York to London, I am driven to want more. That includes knowing family secrets. I lift the shot glass, fascinated by the way the Fireball no longer burns. Instead, it's a warm cinnamon liqueur much like a Christmas drink. Either that or my throat is now numb.

Trevor lifts his glass. Together we swallow our third, or is it fourth?

Slamming the glass down on the piano, I say, "Okay, spill."

He eases from his barstool and offers me his hand. Without hesitation, I place my hand in his. It fits in a way I've never felt before—like it's right. Like it's meant to be. Like fate brought me back to the hotel, to this bar.

The world wobbles as I step down from my tall chair.

Immediately, Trevor's arm goes around my waist. "Do you need to go to your room?"

The patio is just beyond the long bar and a few tables. I tilt my head that way. "Maybe some fresh air."

The fake red glow of the fire pit is the only illumination as the off-key singing and celebration from inside fades to a ringing in my ears. "Spill, Mr. Willis…" A laugh bubbles in my throat, growing until tears are falling from my eyes.

"What's so funny?"

"Mr. Willis. That's what Kimbra used to call Duncan."

"That's my secret," Trevor says in all seriousness.

I squint again, trying to see him better. "What's your secret?"

"Before Kimbra, Duncan was a lady's man like no other."

I shake my head back and forth. "From what I've heard that's only partially true. Women like to talk as much as men."

"I've never been able to keep up with him."

This time I lean back and take a prolonged look at Trevor Willis, his handsome features, and sexy, casual confidence. "That doesn't make any sense."

"It's true. I'm awkward around women."

"You don't seem awkward to me."

"You're different," he says as he moves closer.

"I'm a woman."

"Oh, Shana, you are definitely a woman."

My breathing accelerates as his lips near mine. Cinnamon fills my senses as we kiss. It's soft and fresh, growing warmer by the second. When we pull away, I smile. "Definitely not awkward."

"Cynthia, my pretend date, is engaged to my friend Eric," Trevor says. "He's also an engineer. We work for the same firm in New York. He's been working on a project here in Indianapolis. When I was talking to them about Duncan's wedding, Cynthia said she would be coming to town to visit Eric and would be happy to be my date. At first, we joked about it, but then it seemed like a good idea. Eric knows it's not real. Heck, he thinks it's funny. So, I RSVP'd for two.

"You see, Duncan and I are as different as night and day. We get along, yet there's always this brotherly competition. He went through some shit when we were young, but well, since then, he can never do anything wrong. It's not that I want to be like him. I'm happy. It's that I sometimes feel..."

"Don't tell her not to come," I say, reaching out and touching his arm.

Trevor covers my hand with his. "I am most certain that I'd rather be with you."

"I'd like that. But if you and Duncan are in competition, wouldn't picking up the bride's best friend be kind of a shitty thing to do on his wedding day? Or would I be that one person to up you in the competition?"

Trevor's eyes open wide. "Never." He turns our hands until our fingers intertwine. "This isn't about Duncan. I like you. I liked you from the moment I saw you, right here in the glow of fake embers."

We lean closer, our lips once again touching. "I like you too, but tomorrow is about my best friend. I don't want her thinking about anything but her big day and..."

"And?" he asks.

"Her crazy family." I giggle recalling Grandma Helen. "Seriously, she has enough on her mind."

Letting go of my hand, Trevor's warm palm skirts up and

down my arm. My flesh ignites as butterflies flutter to life in my stomach. And then, it's more. The Fireball, wine, lack of sleep, and irresistible attraction all move together, brewing a terrible queasiness inside of me.

"Oh," I say, jumping up. "I'm going to be sick..."

# CHAPTER
## *Four*

### *Shana*

y eyes close as I hold tightly to the cup of coffee and shake my head. "Oh dear Lord, I threw up."

Trevor laughs. "In the fire pit."

"All over the glowing red rocks." Setting the coffee cup down on the table, I cradle my head. "No. That can't be. I kind of go blank after that."

"Then you missed my finest hour."

Peering upward I smile. "That competition thing. According to Kimbra, if I experienced your finest hour, your brother wins. She says she couldn't forget."

"Oh, that's mean," Trevor says. "Believe me, neither would you."

"Right. Because nothing turns a man on like a puking woman."

"Hey, my competition with my brother has nothing to do with notches. Eat more of your toast, and let me fill in the blanks."

Pulling my knees up to my chest, I wrap the robe over my legs and nibble the edges of the toast as Trevor speaks.

"You were embarrassed about the little accident in the fire pit, so much so that you didn't want to go back into the bar. You made us leave through the hedges."

"Oh no. Really? I'm not sure I want to know more."

Trevor sits back with his cup of coffee and smiles. The way the green glistens in his eyes eases a bit of my embarrassment. "Are you sure? It's pretty good."

"Okay. I do."

"We slid out of the patio through the hedges, but the patio isn't on the ground level."

My blood races as I try to remember. He's right. I had to ride the escalator up to the lobby level. The same level as the bar. "I seem to remember that there was a parking garage."

His laugh rings through the suite. "And a fence, which I must say, you scaled very nicely in your dress and heels."

"My dress ripped!"

"Yes."

I peek under the robe. "That's why I have on your shirt."

"That," he says, "and because once we made it back into the hotel, via some questionable 'employee only' tunnels, your purse was missing. You went to the desk, but as the bellman said, they wouldn't give you a new key without your identification."

"That's how I ended up here in your suite."

Trevor nods as he finishes the last of the bacon.

"So we didn't..."

He stands and moves closer, each step predatory, his green gaze never wavering, until he is standing right in front of me. Offering me his hand, I take it and stand. His solid chest presses against my breasts as he reaches for my waist, holding us close until our hearts beat against the other. "Shana Price," he breathes my name. "We didn't make love. Not because I didn't or don't want to. It's that last night you weren't in a position to consent. If it ever happens—

which I'm still hoping it does—I promise, you'll remember."

By the way my insides flutter and pinch, I am most certain he is right about that. "What now?"

Trevor leans toward me until our lips connect. Bacon and toast, lingering cinnamon, and coffee may not sound like an intoxicating concoction, but it is. I'm lost as we melt together.

"Now," he says, "we have a wedding to attend. Tomorrow, time will tell."

"Tomorrow," I say sadly, "I'm headed back to London."

"And I'm headed back to Washington." Taking a step back, he lifts my hand and kisses my knuckles. "And if you think that distance is going to stop me from learning more about the most amazing woman to ever end up in my hotel suite, you'd be wrong."

"I would?"

"You would. And if you don't want the bride and groom to know, we'll keep it between us."

"Our secret night," I say, as much a statement as a question.

"Our secret one, my lady. However, you should know that each time I look at you during the wedding and at the reception, I'm imagining what our future could hold."

"How will I ever be able to concentrate on Kimbra?"

"She can have you today. I want what's after that."

"Time will tell."

### Not The End...Only The Beginning!

*Thank you for reading this short, fun novella.*
*Now it is time to enjoy ANOTHER ONE!*

# Another ONE

NEW YORK TIMES BESTSELLING AUTHOR

# ALEATHA ROMIG

LEATHA. THE LIGHTER SIDE OF ALEATHA

**Get ready to laugh out loud, swoon, and fall in love with this new, fun, and sexy stand-alone novel from New York Times bestselling author Aleatha Romig. Demonstrating her versatility in writing, Aleatha revisits her lighter side that you loved in PLUS ONE.**

A complete stand-alone, ANOTHER ONE is the next big summer hit.

*\*Shana\**

Trevor Willis is sexy, sweet, and oh so fun. He's also my best friend's brother-in-law. That should mean he's off-limits or that I should be off-limits to him.

Someone probably should have told us that before my best friend married his brother, before the morning of the wedding when we woke in each other's arms, before I woke with gaping holes in my memory.

They didn't.

We did.

The hilarious truth behind our crazy, secret adventure secured this handsome, off-limits man in my heart. But alas, life goes on. After our one secret night, we went back to our lives—our hardworking, solitary lives.

And then it happened.

My phone began to buzz. Each night with thousands of miles between us, we laughed, talked, and shared. And then the phone stopped ringing.

Before it did, I knew one thing...

**Our secret one had bloomed and blossomed, and now that our circumstances have changed, I want another one!**

*Trevor*

Shana Price is that one woman. You know, the one who suddenly makes the world more than a place to work, but also a place to live. Usually shy and awkward, in her presence I want to be more—*I am more*. I don't even have to try.

She's my one. I knew it the moment I first met her. What followed simply confirmed it.

The problem is the little hassle of the thousands of miles between us.

I tried to make it work, but each phone call made it harder. (Yes, that is a pun.) I couldn't take it anymore—and she became the one who got away.

Now, everything has changed.

Shana is back in the United States—all I have to do is make her see that her job isn't the only reason to stay.

That shouldn't be a problem, right?

**From a secret one to another one!: Try Aleatha's lighter side for a guaranteed smile—the perfect getaway.**

*Have you been Aleatha'd?*

**Aleatha's "Lighter Ones" are all stand-alone lighter romances guaranteed to make you smile, possibly shed a tear, and definitely enjoy the ride! They may be read in any order.**

**rologue -**

## Shana

"Can you believe I'm really married?" Kimbra asks, leaning as close to me as she can with her long white wedding dress filling the space between us.

"I'm so happy for you!" And I am. It seems like not that long ago we were roommates making our way through the big city of New York, the two of us against the world.

"If it can happen to me, I know your time is coming."

I don't want to burst her romantic bubble, especially on her wedding day, but if my time is in the next decade, the way my love life is going, I'll need some divine intervention. First, I'm not dating anyone, which is usually a prerequisite for marriage. And second, I'm now daydreaming about the man across the dance floor talking with his date.

Don't jump to conclusions. There's a lot more to that story.

My current obsession—or attraction—is new, exciting, and absolutely crazy. It began last night with an innocent drink near a fire pit, a few wrong decisions that included shots of Fireball, and continued into this morning, waking in the bed of said man.

No, I'm not into three-ways, and no, his date isn't real.

It isn't like she's a blow-up doll either, but she's a pretend date. She's even engaged to his other friend. The reasons behind his charade are not complicated. My best friend's new husband is Trevor's brother, Duncan. Before meeting my best friend, Duncan's history with women was, well, legendary. For that reason of sibling rivalry, Trevor said he couldn't attend Duncan and Kimbra's wedding solo.

Anyway, that's the story he told me and the one I want to believe.

"Let's concentrate on your big day," I say. "And your *big* night!"

Kimbra laughs. "I may be wearing white, but..." She looks out to find her new husband across the room. "I'm pretty sure that when it comes to tonight, I know all about what's coming."

"It'd better be you!" I say just before we both start laughing, sounding more like teenagers than adults. When we both settle, I admit to my best friend. "I may be a little jealous."

"Well, you can't have Duncan."

"I don't want Duncan. I just would like to..."

"I know," she says excitedly, reaching beneath the long table and lifting a gift bag. "You can have the gift from Grandma Helen."

I giggle into my own glass of bubbly. In the bag she's holding is a brand-new vibrator, color-coordinated to match Kimbra's wedding. "I don't know if that's sweet or gross or both. I'm sure it would be the most action I've seen in ages. But still, I'll pass."

As my best friend keeps talking, my mind goes back to this morning, waking in Trevor's bed, his broad chest and wide shoulders beside me and the warmth of his body against mine. Yes, we'd slept together. No, we didn't do more. It's a long story, but the most important part is that we both agreed not to tell Kimbra or Duncan what happened. We agreed to keep it our one secret night.

My lip disappears behind my teeth as I imagine Trevor shirtless, his morning beard covering his chin, and his hair all messed from sleeping.

"If you change your mind," Kimbra says with a grin, obviously misconstruing my concentration.

I lift my hand to wave her train of thought away. It may be hard to believe that the vibrator in question came from Kimbra's grandmother. But it did. Yes, you read that right. She's somewhere between seventy and one hundred years old, and as Kimbra says, her filter is broken and the warranty is expired. That means that you never know exactly what will come out of her mouth.

A few minutes ago, her grandma came parading to the head table and handed Kimbra and her husband Duncan a gift. I've heard stories of her doing the same to other family members. It seems that sometimes the gifts aren't wrapped. Thankfully, Kimbra's was in a gift bag. Even so, her grandma wanted the new couple to open it on the spot. The way Kimbra's cheeks filled with pink, I didn't have to ask what was inside.

It was then that Grandma Helen promised Duncan an entire package of batteries for the honeymoon. Their conversation makes me smile. "Besides, I don't think your new husband would approve. He sounded pretty excited about the entire package of batteries."

Kimbra shakes her head. "It's not like you don't have one."

"A husband?"

"No, silly. We were roommates for years." Her brows

waggle. "As my grandma would say, you weren't brushing your teeth at midnight."

"How do you know? I happen to believe in diligent oral hygiene." When Kimbra looks at me with that all-knowing grin, I go on, "Keep your gift. You're right. I have it covered." Yes, I have my own battery-operated boyfriend, but taking another glance into the crowd and seeing Trevor talking to his date, for the first time in a long time, I wish for the real live kind of boyfriend.

～

A few hours later back at the hotel, I've officially declared defeat, losing the fight I was having with myself. I guess that also means I won. Maybe I should declare victory. No matter the conclusion, my internal debate is still raging.

*Don't do it.*

*Then again, I'm almost there.*

At a little after midnight, instead of heading toward my own suite, I'm sneaking down the carpeted hotel hallway on my way to *his* suite.

I'm not sure if that makes me curious, attracted, or pathetic.

I don't want to overanalyze. All I know is that I'm attracted and yes, curious. (The jury is still out on pathetic.)

The way I see it, this is not 1960. A woman can initiate a conversation—especially with the man she woke beside—as well as a man.

*Why should I wait for him to make a move?*

Although my little pep talk is doing little to calm my erratically beating heart, I don't allow myself to stop moving toward my destination. Closer and closer with each step, I make my way to the suite of the man I can't get out of my head—the man whose deep voice and kisses woke me this morning. As I pass each door and the numbers grow closer to his, I'm contemplating my motive for this late-night walk.

*Why am I really doing this?*

It doesn't matter that I'm still wearing a long mint dress and crystal-studded high heels from the wedding or that my hair is plastered in place by a full can of hair spray guaranteed to open a hole in the ozone—or at least cause me to be most certainly flammable. I don't even care that my makeup is so thick that I could possibly get a gig at the local gentlemen's club.

All I can think about are the stunning green eyes that seemed omnipresent during Kimbra's wedding. Or how at the reception, each time I'd turn, our gazes would meet, and my pulse would race.

I wanted to go to him, to talk, to dance...but as the maid of honor, my role was beside my best friend. As the brother of the groom, his place was with his family.

Now, our designated roles are complete.

My best friend and her husband are off somewhere, and I don't even want to give them or her grandma's gift more thought.

*So what do I want to find when I reach Trevor's room?*

I don't know.

That isn't true.

I know.

I want to find Trevor Willis alone. I want to confirm that Cynthia, his date at the wedding, is as he said, a friend —a friend with a fiancé of her own, a friend whose fiancé is also Trevor's friend, a friend who helped him by being his pretend date and nothing more.

I want to confirm what my heart thinks it knows, to verify that the handsome, sexy, and honorable man I met last night is sincere and honest. I want to know that just because his last name is Willis doesn't mean he has kept par with his brother's reputation—per the rumors associated with Duncan before he began dating my best friend.

It wasn't so much that they *began dating* as they began pretending.

With each step closer to Trevor's suite, I hope that maybe, just maybe, tonight at the wedding of my best friend to his brother, we did the opposite of pretending to be together.

If there's a chance for anything more to materialize between Trevor and me, then maybe one day we can say it all began when we pretended *not to be* interested in one another at a wedding.

The idea makes my insides flutter as anticipation builds. I want that. I want this wedding weekend to be the beginning of a relationship with a future.

A relationship.

My mind tells me that a future is impossible. After all, I live in London and he's working in Washington State.

That scenario doesn't sound like the best setup for any kind of future, but after what happened last night, I want to try.

My heart wants what it wants.

Mind be damned.

As I turn the corner toward Trevor's room, he steps into the hallway, his suit from earlier replaced by chic casual attire. I'm stilled by the sight of him in nicely fitted jeans and a soft T-shirt. The cotton pulls tightly around his bulging biceps and wide shoulders while hanging looser at his waist. I bite my lip as I watch him. Closing the door, Trevor turns my way.

The other doors lining the hallway disappear as our gazes meet. Just like during the wedding, my pulse kicks up as my heart thumps loudly in my ears.

"Shana?"

# CHAPTER

*One*

**Nearly a year later**
**Shana**

"There are so many boobs—everywhere," Chantilly says with a shake of her head.

She's right.

We're in the middle of chaos—which if you don't know is filled with tall, beautiful women with high heels and perfect breasts—better known as the fashion show dressing room. Tomorrow all the models will have their makeup done and hair styled. Today they're simply here to make the last adjustments to the lingerie and final prep on the Saks Fifth Avenue semi-annual lingerie fashion show.

You may not think of lingerie as complicated.

I mean, it's something we wear under our clothes or to sleep.

Not here.

Not tomorrow with these models' bodies highlighting the latest in Saks intimate apparel. Not with my promotion on the line.

Today is the final rehearsal, the last chance to make this lingerie fashion show the best it can possibly be.

"So many," she whispers again.

"And our job is to be sure they're covered when they walk onstage."

We both eye the model wearing only a black lace thong

and matching bra that barely contains her C-cups. The padded half-moons of material push her boobs upward with the upper edge of her areola visible. My gaze narrows and lips purse as I turn back to Chantilly and fight back a smile with a shake of my head. It's the same battle we've been fighting for the past week.

Chantilly lifts a tube that resembles something like a bottle of roll-on deodorant or better yet, a glue stick from preschool. In reality, that's what it is, glue—body glue. By the time these models walk onstage their lingerie will be attached like a second skin.

"No wardrobe malfunctions," we say in unison.

"Shana."

"Shana?"

I'm turning and twisting in a million different directions as models and dressing assistants call my name with questions or simply look for my nod of approval.

That's who I am, the number-one point on Saks Fifth Avenue's semi-annual New York lingerie fashion show. It's one of the top shows for the company in terms of attendance. Not only will there be buyers from all over the world, but the show is also open to the public. That means interested parties from everywhere will be in attendance, possible buyers and investors as well as the competition and of course, just the curious attendee.

That isn't my choice. I like keeping shows professional. However, the added attendance is said to ramp up the excitement. According to Chantilly, who has been backstage for the last three shows, the enthusiasm radiates from the audience to the models.

As I fan myself with my clipboard, I wonder if we can handle more radiation. The temperature in the dressing room already feels like a hundred degrees and we still have hours of planning and refining.

Maybe the higher temperature is beneficial for the models. Since I'm not walking around in a bra and panties, my extra clothes may be part of my problem. No doubt that their lack of clothes could be an issue if they were cold.

Then again, too hot and body glue begins to melt.

No one wants that!

"Which one with the chemise?" Chantilly asks from across the room. "Thong or tanga brief?"

I eye the two swatches of white satin material she's holding in the air, neither looking as if they'll cover enough of the beautiful six-foot-tall model by her side to make a difference. However, with the way the white silk chemise hits the top of the model's thighs, unless this fashion show wants to be renamed a striptease, one is definitely going to be necessary. Yes, more than breasts are on display behind closed doors. "Tanga brief, but in black."

Chantilly's eyes narrow before her lips move upward. "I like that. Yes, through the white silk it will pop."

Models in all stages of dress and undress talk amongst themselves, moving about the crowded dressing room as they wait for their final assignment. I'm twisted in different directions with questions as I work to pin a too-long spaghetti strap onto the lace bodysuit.

"Shana!"

I turn my gaze as I poke the straight pin through the strap and into my finger.

"Ow," the model in my grips murmurs with a flinch.

"Sorry," I reply as my lip disappears behind my teeth and I assess the damage. I may have superficially nicked her, but damn, I practically stabbed my finger.

"Let me help," Chantilly says as she comes toward us. "I think you should stick to the clipboard and let the wardrobe assistants handle the sharp objects."

I lift my hands in defense, only a small dribble of blood visible. "You're probably right. She's all yours."

Yes, I also find it hilarious that the lead coordinator of a lingerie show is named after lace.

Brocade, guipure, knit, or alençon...I suppose it could be worse.

"Jenese," Chantilly says, reaching for my hand and assessing the damage, "needs your help with the French briefs." Her eyes meet mine as she tilts her head toward the entrance. "Band-Aids are in the cabinet by the door."

Did you know that Band-Aid isn't a universal term? I didn't know that until I was in London working. There they're called *fabric strips* or *plasters*. Simple things like that make me happy to be back in the States.

Nodding, I forget about the language idiosyncrasies and recall Chantilly's first statement. "Jenese needs my help with a pair of panties?" I ask, wondering what happened to miniskirts and lo-lace tank tops from the junior line.

I know what happened. Two weeks ago, while working in London, I received the call, the one offering me a chance to advance from juniors to ladies' lingerie. It is more than I ever dared to dream, and yet in the middle of this pandemonium that by tomorrow needs to be a finely tuned tranquility, I'm questioning my sanity as much as my ability.

Grabbing a *fabric strip*—which isn't even the Band-Aid brand— from the small cart near the door, I make my way through the sea of satin and lace until I find Jenese. As one of Saks's top models, she's stunning and at least ten inches taller than me—and that's without the five-inch heels she's currently wearing.

"See right here?" Jenese says with a frown as she points to the top hem of the French briefs.

"Yes."

"Maybe I should wear something else?"

"Why?" I shake my head. "Maybe I'm not seeing what you're seeing."

"The way it makes my skin bunch. It will be all anyone sees." Her tone and the way her words are clipped by her accent create a mix of irritation and disappointment.

"Jenese, your skin isn't bunching." Hell no. I don't think this woman standing nearly a foot over me has skin to bunch. If anything, I'd like to feed her a sandwich.

She sighs. "I don't know."

"They fit perfectly." I look up to my eye level and quickly move my head back. The black lace front of the bustier stretched across her breasts is sheer enough to be transparent, leaving two very large, round boobs inches in front of me. Chantilly was right—they're everywhere.

I take a step back as I return my gaze to Jenese's big blue eyes. "I don't think anyone will notice the briefs."

Jenese smiles.

It's then that I notice the edge of the bustier is precariously close to her nipple. "As a matter of fact." I speak louder. "Can someone be sure we have a little body glue on here?"

"They're not easy to contain," Jenese quips with a grin.

"Then maybe *a lot* of glue. Let's try our best to keep them covered today and tomorrow."

She gives me a wink as she walks over to one of the assistants already armed with the roll-on bottle.

"Ladies. Final number in ten," I say loudly, garnering everyone's attention. "I'm going out to talk to the sound guys. Does anyone have any questions?"

Every model's gaze stares my way, all wondering the same thing: will I be able to pull this off?

It's the million-dollar question.

"We've got it in here," Chantilly assures me with a smile. "Grab a Band-Aid on the way out."

"I already have one," I say, wiggling my wounded middle finger in the air. As soon as I do, I realize my unintended gesture.

"Hey!" Her smile grows.

Quickly, I wiggle all five fingers, waving as I step out of the room.

Opening the door to the stage, I'm met with the rush of cool air and at the same time, the heat of stage lights. It's a strange combination causing goose bumps and perspiration to materialize simultaneously. Wiping my brow while shivering, I'm now thinking about each possible piece of lingerie and how these lights and cool air will accentuate the models' attributes that won't be hidden with glue.

I make a mental note: nipple tape.

Skin colored, it stops the pebbling of nipples. Okay, it doesn't stop it. The tape hides it. Nipples harden. It happens. However, it's not always produced by endorphins as books make it out to be. A simple cold chill can change the way the lingerie hangs. And, like in the books, certain buyers can be all too easily distracted.

"Stephen!" I call out into the lights. "Remind me to check on nipple tape."

Since I can't see anything past the stage, I hope that I didn't just yell *nipple tape* to a room full of buyers. I squint into the sea of light. If I were a model, I think I'd appreciate the blinding fog. I could imagine that no one is out in the audience, that I am alone on the runway. After only a few seconds, the first few rows of seats become visible.

Moving forward, my flat ballet slippers slip on the smooth surface causing me to rear backward, nearly falling on my behind and losing my clipboard. A few windmill moves with my arms and I'm steady to go.

"Grace personified." My assistant laughs, his deep voice cutting through the light-induced fog until I see him moving toward the edge of the runway.

I can't help but laugh too. "Hey, I didn't fall."

"Lucky that quick move didn't land you on your nose or better yet, cause you to take flight."

"Fine. That's why I'm not a model."

"Yes, the only reason."

"Shut up," I quip. "And offer me a hand to help me down."

"I'm not sure that's in my job description," Stephen says, stepping forward and giving me a steady hand just as he's done ever since we met in London.

Nearly two years ago, I was transferred from New York to London and named as head of the junior clothing line of Saks Fifth Avenue. With that move, I acquired Stephen. As with Chantilly's help backstage, a great assistant can make or break a career. When I was offered the possible opportunity to move back to New York, to move up from juniors into lingerie, I made one request: I asked for Stephen to mirror my move.

Of course, I asked him first, and even though this is a trial run, he said yes. Thankfully, so did the powers that be.

Stephen is more than an assistant. Over the last two years, he's become one of my best friends.

Yes, you can have more than one.

"What was that about nipple tape?" he asks with a cheesy grin. "Max ran a marathon once and had tape to avoid bleeding nipples."

"Eww," I say, the image he's describing not what I need in my head right now, not with the memories of my injured finger.

"Yeah, but unless you've changed up the numbers or speed of the show—like the models are now going to run the runway—I don't see that being an issue here."

# CHAPTER
## *Two*

### *Shana*

*M*y nose scrunches at the thought of men I've seen running the New York marathon and the image of bloodstained shirts. Apparently, nipples aren't only a woman's problem. Shaking the unwanted images away, I say, "No. No blood. Yuck! The tape is for this cold air. We don't want the models to *look* cold, if you know what I mean?"

Stephen shakes his head. "Sometimes I question my life. You know, when I woke this morning, I never thought... *hmm, I hope that sometime today I'll have the opportunity to talk about nipple tape.*"

"You didn't?"

"Did you?"

"Well, it's more like when I wake, I wonder what crazy-ass stuff is going to be thrown my way. I'd say I'd rather avoid subjects like nipple tape, body glue, and boobs, but that would mean I don't love this." I wave my arms around. "All of it. And you know what?"

My best friend's smile broadens, lifting his cheeks and making the little creases appear by his eyes. "You love every minute of it."

"I do...nipple tape and all."

"Speaking of nipples and boobs and this..." He mimics

my Vanna White gesture showcasing the room. "How's the madhouse backstage?"

"Certifiable! Chaos at its finest. A second ago, I was telling someone to glue lace on boobs. There are so many boobs!"

Stephen laughs. "Boobs are good. Nipples bleeding or showing, not so much."

One more scrunch of my nose. "Not to the buyers and definitely not to the designers."

"No wardrobe malfunctions!" we say together, repeating what seems to be my current mantra.

"Honey, that's for sure," he says. "You don't need anyone going Janet Jackson on you."

I rub my hands over my arms, the air conditioning roaring from somewhere above. "Why is it so damn cold out here? We're showing lingerie not parkas."

"Tomorrow this place will be packed to the gills with shoulder-to-shoulder people and filled with bright lights." He points to the rafters where the rays of light shine at intervals. I squint as I follow with my eyes.

"Currently," he says, "only about half of the lights are on. When they're all shining, even without the people, it'll raise the temperature by at least fifteen degrees to at least seventy-five."

"Fahrenheit, I hope."

He laughs.

Different systems of measuring temperature were part of our adjustment to living in London. When an American hears the temperature will be thirty-eight, he or she thinks cold. It doesn't take long to learn that assumption is wrong.

"Better be," he says. "If it's Celsius, we'll be broiling the models, not showcasing them."

"I still think the tape is a good idea." My whole body shivers as we make our way to the light and sound booth. "Tell me you have everything set out here."

Stephen's head bobs on his broad shoulders.

"Have I ever told you how much I appreciate your confidence and decisiveness?"

"No, Ms. Price, you have not. Maybe you have. I'm really not sure." Sarcasm dripping from his friendly tone is why I've grown to love him. He can invoke humor in a way that takes off the edge while still being ever so competent in his job. If I had to narrow it down, I'd say that Stephen's ability to make me smile in the face of a challenge is why we work so well together.

For two years he's been my right hand. Heck. He's been my right arm and probably the right side of my brain. He's very creative yet also extremely well-organized.

Maybe he's my entire brain?

"So," he begins, changing the subject, "I'm finally going to meet my new bestie?"

I playfully punch his arm. "You can't have her. She's mine."

"Well, you're mine and she's yours...and I'm yours, so technically..."

Despite all the worries about the lingerie show, thinking about my two best friends finally meeting makes me grin.

When I was first transferred to London and overwhelmed with everything from the cute red phone booths and double-decker buses to learning how to navigate the tube, Stephen was right there beside me. Being also from the States—he was born and raised in New York—he's been there for me. I've been there for him. Together for the last two years, we've seen life's and love's ups and downs.

Recently, he ended his relationship with Max. Not as in Maxine, but as in Maximilian, a sexy investment banker with a to-die-for British accent and posh flat. Two months ago, I would have said Stephen and Max were perfect for one another. That was before Max did him wrong. Now, Max is pond scum.

That's what friends do. We adore those you adore and abhor those you abhor.

From "Oh, honey, he's perfect!" to "I never liked the guy. Have another glass of wine."

Pond scum is too good for the likes of Maximilian Cantel. He's lower than pond scum. That makes him fungi buried in the muck below the surface, the kind clinging to rubbish for survival.

Yes, the man beside me, my best friend and personal assistant, is a male fashion designer who happens to be interested in other men. It sounds cliché, but he's not. He's a whiz at fashion, knowing, predicting, and wearing. He has the looks and personality that draws both women and men. Though he's always been open about his orientation, the female models in juniors were always hanging on his every word. He's definitely handsome, charismatic, and fun.

He's also nice and considerate and incredibly efficient. With everything we've experienced, I think of him as the brother I never had. While he didn't need to make the attempt at this transition with me, I'm so glad that he did.

Now we're back in the States, in Manhattan to be exact, the home of my other best friend, Kimbra. I can't wait to see her again. While I've been off in London, she's been working her dream job and living the life of a newlywed with her sexy husband who also happens to be her boss. That's another story for another time.

Up until just recently, Kimbra and I haven't been able to make our schedules mesh. Even though Stephen and I have been in the city for over a week, our every waking moment and some of our sleeping ones have been dominated by this fashion show. Tomorrow it will be over, and tomorrow night the three of us are finally going to get together.

"Drinks tomorrow night at the Martini Club," I say. "She invited us to her place, but with the crazy schedule we've been keeping, I was afraid we'd be late or have to cancel. The club is in Lower Manhattan and not too far from our hotel." I'm really concerned I may fall asleep. Burning the candle at both ends doesn't even begin to describe my current state. "Tomorrow with the show as history, I figured we could relax. Besides, celebrating is better than crying. I'm excited for you to meet her. Just remember..." My volume lowers as my eyes widen.

Stephen waggles his brows. "Just remember...to fill in the infamous Kimbra on your little romp with her brother-in-law?"

I punch his arm again. "If you say one word..."

He presses his lips together. "You can be so violent! Sealed. My lips are sealed."

"I'm not violent. And it's also not that I want to be dishonest with her. This was a hard secret to keep. But I didn't tell her when it happened and now...well, now, it doesn't matter. Water under the bridge."

As you may have guessed, we're talking about my disastrous love life.

Disaster isn't the right word.

Disaster by definition implies a onetime catastrophic event with unimaginable consequences. My love life is more like a cataclysmic prolonged weather phenomenon better known as the century-long drought. Similar to both of my best friends, I like men. I like men a lot. I've dated some. I've even dated boys if you want to go back to my youth. But when it comes to long term, my relationship with Stephen is the longest one I've had with anyone with a penis. Not that I have seen Stephen's—or want to. But you understand.

And a *romp*, as Stephen called it, isn't exactly an accurate account.

However, when it comes to describing this man from my past as Kimbra's brother-in-law, that is one hundred percent on point.

Thus, the reason for secrecy.

Whatever Trevor and I had happened innocently enough. On the morning of Kimbra's wedding, I happened to wake in the bed of a handsome, sexy gentleman who later that day became her brother-in-law. It's a long story, but the reality is that it was simply that—one secret night. Even the next night as we grew more familiar, we didn't take it further. The timing wasn't right. I was headed back to London and he back to the state of Washington where he was overseeing an engineering project.

If romp implies sex, we didn't romp.

We had attraction—off-the-chart sparks—enough to ignite a forest fire with a side of some teenage making out—without the teenage clumsiness—but that was all. You could say that the lack of sex is another element to the drought I mentioned. Seriously, if things don't look up, my vagina may dry up and blow away.

After that secret one, we spoke a few times on the phone—off and on for a few months. While absence may make the heart grow fonder, distance sucks big hairy balls.

Living on two different continents separated by thousands of miles does little for a future. The spark didn't die as much as it was suffocated by the Atlantic Ocean.

While Trevor and I haven't spoken in months, now that I'm back in New York, I haven't been able to get him out of my mind. I imagine seeing his green eyes in a crowded restaurant or his wide shoulders in a packed elevator. I remember his dark blond hair that never seemed to stay in place, beckoning my fingers to comb through the soft tresses. I recall how protective he was and how we would talk for hours. Nevertheless, any hope for a future with him is simply my overactive imagination. Life has a way of inter-rupting dreams and even messing with our imagination. We both chose our careers. The last time we spoke, he was still working on a project on the other side of the country. Granted, that was a while ago, but still, Trevor Willis is water under the bridge.

That's what I keep reminding myself.

And now I'm here, back in New York, with a great opportunity to further my career. Not talking about that secret one helps to nullify its significance. Since only Stephen has heard my sad tale, I don't need to discuss it with anyone else. That way I can keep Trevor in the safe recesses of my memory, only to take him out when my mind slips to what could have been.

When Stephen meets my other best friend, Kimbra, he's forbidden from saying, "so I hear you have one sexy-as-hell brother-in-law," after introducing himself.

Life could be different if I were back here for good. However, there's no guarantee we'll be moving back to New York. Our promotion to ladies' lingerie is contingent upon the success of this fashion show and the work that follows. As it stands now, we're simply in the city for a trial run.

All at once, as Stephen and I enter the sound booth, the subject of our conversation changes. No more entertaining the memories of the one sexy man from my past. As the booth door closes and I'm faced with the empty stage, an array of lights, and plethora of buttons and switches, I'm back to work—no longer a lovesick woman but the possible new budding director of ladies' lingerie at Saks Fifth Avenue.

Mentally pushing Trevor aside, my mind is now consumed with beautiful women, sexy lingerie, and pulling off the best runway show this city has ever seen.

# CHAPTER
## *Three*

### *Shana*

o, no!" I say to Chantilly as I stare into her eyes. "Tell me this isn't happening."

"Shana, if I could, I would. Jenese is sick. Food poisoning, she thinks."

"Food! She doesn't eat."

"You know if she could be here, she would. It hit her hard last night. She tried to push through and early this morning she ended up in the ER."

"No. She's our top model. Everyone is expecting her, especially in the finale." I take a deep breath. "We have an hour to showtime...what are we going to do?"

"You could take her place."

I look at Chantilly as if she suddenly grew another head. Of all the possible solutions, this is quite possibly the furthest from my mind. To be honest, it wasn't even a consideration. "What? That's the most absurd thing I've heard in my life. I'm obviously not a model."

"It's not that obvious. No, you have never done it, but you know the routine." When I don't respond, Chantilly goes on. "Shana, you're a beautiful woman. The only thing stopping you from modeling is you."

"And my height, body, and, oh yes, inability to walk a straight line in flats, much less heels."

She looks me up and down. "Okay, you're not as tall, but

let's face the reality. It's too late to get a backup here and teach her the routine. That leaves you and Stephen who know every step for every model. Even I don't. My job is backstage."

I take a deep breath, afraid to listen to her reasoning.

"Shana, you can do this. Besides, think about it. Stephen won't fit into the lingerie."

I close my eyes, hoping that if I wish hard enough, Jenese will magically appear.

"The doors are open and people are coming in," Stephen says through an earpiece.

"The show, as you two have made it, isn't like it was when it first came to us," Chantilly goes on. "The changes are great, but *no one* else knows them, not like you do."

My head moves back and forth. "You do." I look her up and down. Chantilly is a pretty brunette with chocolate skin and big blue eyes. She's about my height, and as I take a closer look at her figure, I notice she has a shape that would easily be flattering in lingerie. "You say you were backstage, but you know everyone's place."

"Shana, I want this for you. I do. Putting me in heels out there is a mistake."

"What if we do some last-minute adjustments?" I ask, grasping at straws. "We can move Shelly to lead."

Chantilly nods. "That'll work. She's the tallest. Still, the finale will be minus one featured outfit. The finale is where the buyers take their last looks at their favorites. If you move Shelly to Jenese's outfit, the long negligee that Shelly is wearing won't make the finale."

I know that the designers pay a premium fee for place-ment in the show. Excluding even one piece from the finale will have far-reaching repercussions, ones that won't facilitate my promotion. I look down. "Chantilly, I'm too short to wear Shelly's long negligee."

She looks down at her iPad. "We have a petite in the back. It's white instead of the black Shelly is wearing, but in reality, that's a plus to show any style in two different colors. The designer is only paying for one."

My heart is thundering in my chest. This is a mistake. "Think," I say, clasping my hands together. "Give me anyone else. Please. Another option."

"We have other models." Chantilly lays her hand on my shoulder. "Even if one of them could be here in time for the show, she won't know the routine. I can get someone here for the individual runway, but not the finale."

"So no matter what, we need me to do the finale." The words come out flat as my mouth grows drier by the second, and my stomach does its own gymnastic routine.

"We do. Shelly can do both outfits during the runway. It saves us from calling in someone new. Then the only time you need to go out is the finale."

I process the show in my head. During the finale, each piece is reintroduced; the model makes one trip down the runway and back to a spot until the entire stable is onstage. And then it happens, the finale extravaganza, an intricate weave of models passing around one another, turning, repositioning as a team until one by one they exit. It gives each piece of fashion the same exact amount of time onstage to be seen.

*Why didn't I go with the simpler choreography?*

I changed the show to demonstrate that I could. I changed it to make the show special. To make it mine.

Last night, our final run-through was perfect. We stayed an hour later than scheduled, the models were exhausted, but the result was as stunning as a Broadway number. As my eyes closed on my pillow last night, I experienced a rare sense of accomplishment, and now that feeling is replaced with butterflies the size of dragons. Judging by the burning in my chest, the dragons are spitting fire.

"Let me think for a minute," I say, shaking my head as I lift the mouthpiece on my shoulder to my lips. "Stephen, I need you."

His reassuring voice materializes into my earpiece. "I don't think you want me backstage."

"I do, in a white lace-trimmed silk negligee."

"Talk to me."

Tears burn the back of my eyes. "Meet me in the sound booth."

～

"You can do it," Stephen says. "Let them shorten the hem so you're not wearing stilts. When they're all positioned, the outfit you'll wear is off to the side. Everyone will be looking at Shelly at center. You know this routine. You taught it to them."

My best friend blurs as the tears threaten to spill over my lids. "Stephen..."

His arm comes around my shoulders. "Stop it. You're our leader. Chantilly's idea is a good one. There isn't time to reteach."

"Maybe you're right and that negligee is off to the side in the routine, but I'll still need to make one trip all the way down the runway, and then manage not to knock out any other models during the last part."

"Boss lady," he says, his voice lowering to his reassuring

timbre, "I never told you this before because, well, it's not my style, but you're beautiful. The first time I met you, I thought HR had sent me to the wrong person. I assumed you were a model. Tell me you never considered modeling."

"I've never considered modeling."

Stephen's head shakes.

"Okay, maybe as a young girl, but I loved the fashions too much to simply wear them." I lower my eyes. "And the idea of everyone looking at me scares me."

Stephen lifts my chin. "Think about our junior models for a moment."

I do. Even though they model teenage clothes, most are adults in petite bodies.

"What about Becky?" he asks.

"What about her?"

"What does she do when she isn't modeling?"

The tips of my lips move upward. "She mostly studies. I think at last count she's only a few credits away from finishing her master's degree in finance."

"You went straight to the creative duties in fashion because you're smart. You've moved up in this company because you're quick on your feet and a problem solver. Those women back there are modeling because they are beautiful, and yet they also have other dreams and goals. You're doing yours in reverse."

"If I do this—"

He cuts me off before I can finish as he emphasizes his first word. "*When* you do this, you will overcome any fear you ever had about modeling. Not only that, but you'll be in a better place to do what you do because you will know what it's like to be out there. You will have experience. You will have conquered!"

"If I fall on my face, we're headed back to London. You know that, right?"

Stephen loosens his embrace, moving both hands to my shoulders. "Something came up last night, and I put a deposit on an apartment."

My mind isn't functioning fast enough. "You did what?"

"When you kill this show, they're going to see how amazing you are. We'll be moving back here, and I need a place to live. Would I have done that if I had doubts?"

My entire body begins to shake. "I don't know why you would do that. This..." I flail my arms about. "...isn't set."

"It is. Chantilly and I have your back. You said last night that you couldn't see anyone from the stage. Just imagine the only person out there is the one person you want to see you in a silk negligee."

My lungs try to fill with air. "The one person?"

"It's me, isn't it?" Stephen asks with a sheepish grin.

"It's *so* not you."

"There. You're smiling. When you walk out imagine that one person is the only one in the audience. It's just the two of you and you're walking to him—only him."

My nerves begin to calm as I imagine the green eyes I've been thinking about since our airplane landed on US soil. I look up to Stephen. "I really hate you."

He kisses the top of my head. "You love me. You, Shana Price, can do this. A leader, a problem solver, delegates when possible, and takes control when needed. We need you. You can do it."

"Thirty-five minutes," comes from Mike at the sound panel.

"Go," Stephen says. "I've got this out here. You need to

talk to Chantilly, and Shelly needs to know what's happening."

I narrow my gaze. "You really put down a deposit on an apartment in Manhattan?"

"Would I lie to my best friend?"

"In a heartbeat."

"East Village. It was too good of a deal to miss."

I close my eyes and bring up the image from my past. I envision the one person I'd like to have look at me in a negligee—the one man I've imagined since our secret night. I recall his gaze when I woke in his arms, his playful smile as he helped me remember what Fireball had tried to erase, and the way we kissed the last time we saw one another.

"Shit," I mutter to myself as I make my way backstage. "I'm going to need nipple tape if my thoughts go there."

"Shana?"

I turn to see my possible new boss. "Vicky!"

Her expression is more enthusiastic than her voice. "I heard about Jenese. I can't believe she isn't here."

"Things happen," I say with more confidence than I possess. "We will still make this work."

"I don't need to tell you that there's a lot riding on this show."

"You don't."

"And the designers paid for their spots."

"But not for the models wearing them. Every outfit will be spotlighted. The show must go on."

She takes a step back and nods. "Grace under pressure is an asset we can use in lingerie."

"I'm going to be backstage, but we can talk after the show," I say.

"Count on it."

# CHAPTER
## *Four*

### *Trevor*

*E*ric laughs as he settles against the cool vinyl of the booth and listens to his future. "You guys can't be serious? This sounds like *The Hangover* meets *Impractical Jokers*. This is my bachelor-party weekend. I was thinking bars and nightclubs. Last night was a good start." He shakes his head. "I wasn't thinking of crashing a fashion show. A. Lingerie. Fashion show." He says the last part staccato like it will change Max's mind.

"Deadly serious," our friend Max says. "I didn't travel across the pond to sit casually at some gentlemen's club. The fashion show is perfect. There will be beautiful women for you blokes and some nice eye candy for me. It's a win-win."

Max lives in the UK. How he became part of our inner circle is a long story. Suffice it to say, as an investment banker, his work with McCobb, the engineering firm where Eric, Matt, and I work, brought him to our New York offices many times. He has one of those personalities that is the complete opposite of most engineers: outgoing, gregarious, and fun. Yes, I'm admitting we can be boring. The thing that makes Max unique is that he brings out those traits in others. When I was in Washington and Eric was in Indiana working on different projects, Max used our apartment when he'd come to New York for work. Our interests may not all be the same, but we've become friends. While this weekend is about Eric and his impending wedding, Matt—the fourth of our foursome—knew inviting Max would keep the weekend lively.

It seems he was right.

As I try to smother the alcohol from last night in greasy eggs, potatoes, and thick bagel, I don't have the energy to argue. However, while taking a large gulp of good ole black coffee, my deductive reasoning is getting the better of me. "You don't expect us to just crash the Saks Fifth Avenue lingerie fashion show, do you?"

"Now, wouldn't that be fun?"

"You can't be serious. I'm sure there are tickets and shit. They don't just let four men off the street—"

Max holds up his phone, interrupting my only attempt to change our plans. The screen appears to have some sort of ticketing information. "Not crash. The dare..." He lowers his voice as his expression explodes with excitement. "...is to make contact with one of the models."

Eric shakes his head. "Are we twelve?"

"No," Max says. "Twelve-year-olds don't purchase tickets to see beautiful women walk around in lingerie."

"No, they sneak on to their father's porn sites," Matt says with a laugh.

"So we're too sophisticated for that. Besides, we can all afford our own viewing pleasure. This is different. It's unique and unusual. This fashion show only happens twice a year. How many times do you blokes get to watch lovely models parade in front of you?"

"Listen," Eric says, "I'm not doing anything to jeopardize my marriage to Cynthia."

"No one is asking you to," Matt says, joining the persuasion. He and Max have obviously worked the details out amongst themselves. "Make contact. That doesn't mean fuck or even touch." He shakes his head with a laugh. "Well, contact... no. Talk to, get a phone number, have a conversation. Unlike the show, the dare is not for all of us. One of us needs to be the judge. That, my man," he says to Eric, the groom-to-be, "is you. Max, Trevor, and I are the ones who have to do the dare. You choose the one who wins and the other two pay for this entire weekend...hotel rooms, drinks, and all."

I can't help but think that the overall expense would be less if Max had taken me up on the offer to use my apartment for this weekend.

Eric laughs. "No offense, Max, but I suspect the models aren't your type."

Max's cheeks rise. "No offense taken. As we said, fucking isn't the object. I've been known to be very debonair and besides, American women love a man with an accent. I can admire a beautiful woman as much as any one of you." He eyes the table where we're all slightly hung over.

Our eyes are undoubtedly bloodshot and none of us have showered. I know that because we all dragged ourselves out of our rooms with dry, messy hair and the lingering aroma of last night's drinks. Food and coffee were our primary objectives.

"Better than any of you blokes, actually," Max clarifies. "And as I said, it's about contact. The one who gets the most intel, the one who gets the closest wins. He then gets to spend the rest of the weekend at the expense of the other two."

We all look at one another and shrug. "I'm game," Matt says first.

"If I'm only the judge," Eric says, "I'm in."

They all look my direction. I narrow my gaze at Matt and Max. "You two were planning this. You know I suck at coming on to women. I should just throw my credit card on the table and call it a day. Hell, Max will pick up a model before I do."

The truth is that I have been on a rather dry spell. First, I'm not a lady's man. One-night stands aren't my thing. With my job that takes me from place to place for months or even years at a time, I find making commitments difficult. And then there is this one woman.

The unexpected surprise is that Eric's impending wedding has put her in the forefront of my mind. I met her at a wedding, well, the night before. It was my brother's wedding, and I'd gotten into town late. I told myself I'd have one drink in the hotel bar to wind down from the flight and let my body adjust to the time difference. With a beer in hand, I made my way out of the loud piano bar and outside to a patio.

There she was.

*Was she beautiful?*

Without question.

*Was I attracted?*

No doubt.

*Did I do something about it?*

For one of the first times in my life, I did.

I could blame my brother, but he wasn't there. The thing is that I'd spent the entire flight from Washington to Indiana thinking about my brother's wedding. I was and am happy for him. My sister-in-law, Kimbra, is a great lady. I'd gotten to know her before my job moved me across the country. It's just that there is this brotherly competition.

It started innocently enough when as kids we wrestled for the controller to our favorite game or the remote to the television. He was always good at football, so I excelled in wrestling. He made good grades. I made better.

I can't blame our parents. They didn't pick favorites or make either of us feel less than the other. It's simply part of brothers' DNA, an inherent need to one-up the other.

One place I always fell short was on the dating front. I'm not saying I'm not as good-looking. Hell, I know that isn't true. I'm way better looking than him!

Okay, granted, attractiveness is subjective.

If I were to truly analyze it, I believe deep down it's a confidence thing. Whatever the reason, I couldn't go to his wedding stag. I had everything all planned out—that's what I do. As a matter of fact, it was Eric's fiancée, Cynthia, who joined me as my pretend date.

And yet when I walked onto that bar's patio that night in Indianapolis, Indiana, I regretted all my planning. There on the patio of the piano bar was a vision. With long blonde hair and big blue eyes, she should have screamed untouchable to me. She's the type of beauty that honestly scares the shit out of me, but she didn't.

I don't know why.

I didn't question.

There was just something about her—an aura. Hell, I don't know. I just know that throwing caution to the wind, I approached her. We spoke.

It's not like I'm the guy on the TV show with the smart friends who becomes mute around women. I can talk. It's that when it's not about work or a project, the conversation feels forced. Nothing about communicating with this woman was forced.

We talked and drank.

It was later that night when we were coerced into partaking in celebratory shots inside the bar that things got out of hand.

I'll never forget her standing there, laughing. She was wearing this blue dress that hugged all the right places and heels that accentuated her shapely legs. She was laughing, and then all at once, her expression changed and well, the shots didn't stay down.

Yes, that's not an attractive scene, but what followed was better.

She was so embarrassed by what she'd done that she made us flee the scene.

Not leave through the door. No...that would have been too easy. She looked at the mess, looked at me, and yelled, "Run!"

We ran.

Scaled a fence, wandered through a parking garage, and finally snuck through tunnels.

It was the most fun I'd had in years.

It was as if instead of an engineer who planned everything in his life, I was spontaneous and free. She did that to me. With her hand in mine, I was someone else. Helping her escape while keeping her safe were my only thoughts.

From that moment on, I wanted her, all of her, but that night she wasn't exactly in a position to consent to more than my assistance. It wasn't that she fought me off, but then again, she wasn't coming on to me either. She isn't that type of woman. Her purse and room key were MIA after our little excursion. The hotel refused to provide another key without identification. Taking her to my room was all I could think to do. Once there, she fell sound asleep. Like

Sleeping Beauty from the fairy tale, it wasn't until morning when I kissed her forehead that she finally awoke.

I'm a thirty-three-year-old man who admittedly still has fantasies. Perhaps with the time I travel and read, you'd think I'd have daydreams—and night dreams—about a model or an actress, maybe my high school sweetheart or college crush.

No.

Shana Price, the beauty who made me feel alive, who woke a part of my soul I didn't know existed, who was within my grasp only to disappear...

She's the recurring star in my imagination.

She's the one who got away.

Even though we never did more than sleep—yes, the slumber type—kiss, and perhaps a bit of heavy petting, in my mind as I recall our short secret time, I imagine more. I've pictured her face on the pillow beside mine. I've imagined that kiss I gave her leading to more as I stand facing the shower wall, hot water streaming down and relief at hand.

It wasn't only our careers and distance that deterred a relationship but also our connection. She's my sister-in-law's best friend, her after-college roommate. Shana and I agreed not to tell Kimbra or Duncan about our secret time together.

Now sometimes I wonder if it really happened.

If it was real.

Did she exist or is she an unobtainable aspiration that will forever remain in my thoughts but never again in my grasp?

I reason that she's real because after that night, we spoke a few times on the phone.

Each time was harder than the last—yes, pun intended. The distance and inability to see her face-to-face became too much. With me on the West Coast and her in London, the time difference made even communication difficult. Finally, the calls ceased.

I thought to ask Max if he knew Shana since he lives in London, but what would be the chances? London is immense. An investment banker who's interested in men would have little reason to know or meet a Saks Fifth Avenue lead buyer for the junior line.

"Saks?" I say, looking back at my friends. Obviously, their conversation has moved on while I've been reminiscing.

"What?" Eric asks.

"Did you say this is a Saks Fifth Avenue fashion show?"

"Yeah." Matt's eyebrows waggle. "Lingerie line."

"Right." Lingerie. Perfect for a bachelor party but not for seeing the woman I want. Shana Price oversees Saks's junior line. Right now, she's most likely in London dressing teenagers and deciding on next year's best prom dresses.

# CHAPTER
## *Five*

***Shana***

*M*y heart beats so rapidly that I fear it may jump clear out of my chest. I'm confident the thin layer of silk covering me is jumping with each beat. I'm not usually concerned about my appearance. When it comes to my work, I'm confident and strong, yet in this negligee and about to walk out in front of hundreds of sets of eyes, I'm as insecure as a thirteen-year-old about to go to her first dance and sure she will spend the entire time in a circle of friends who no boy will ask to dance.

*How have I been able to send other women out onto the runway without considering this side of the journey?*

It's because those women are models. I'm not.

I'm dressed like one for a single reason—to save this show.

Even with my good intentions, every lie I've ever told myself, every thought of self-doubt, and every time I've compared myself—even subconsciously—to another woman...all the moments so many women can share are dancing in my head. As soon as Chantilly helped me slip into the white negligee, I saw the world of fashion from an entirely new perspective. It is one thing to be the one applying body glue. It's quite another to have the cool liquid rolled across my skin as goose bumps prickle and Chantilly yells for nipple tape.

I mean, nipple tape is a great accessory until it's applied to your breasts. I don't even want to think about removing it.

"You can do this," Shelly whispers as I slip my feet into shoes that could easily double as stilts.

"I'm not even sure I can walk in these."

"Did you take some painkillers? I have some Advil in my bag."

I'm lost on her train of thought. The way my head is pounding and nerves are stretched, painkillers aren't a bad idea. "Painkillers?"

"Oh, honey," she says in a stage whisper. "Every model knows the tricks. If your shoe size is seven, wear a size eight. And always take some over-the-counter painkillers two hours before the show."

"Two hours?" I say as a question. "Why?"

She shakes her head. "Let me get you some. It'll still help."

Before I can respond, Shelly rushes across the room and returns with a half bottle of water and two pills in the palm of her hand.

Eyeing her offering, I wiggle my toes. Immediately, I realize I've already agreed to the wrong size. Reaching out, I pop the two pills into my mouth, followed by a quick drink of her water. "Thank you. This is a lot easier from over there." I tilt my head toward Chantilly.

Shelly smiles, reminding me of that circle of friends from the middle school dance.

"Sometimes it's good to get a taste of both sides. You've got this. You and Stephen put this show together. You made it more than what we've done in the past. The audience is already going wild."

She's right. Since the show began, the electronic orders on every piece of lingerie shown are through the roof. The applause has been louder than I've ever heard at a junior's show. If I weren't about to ruin the entire thing, I might actually be happy about it.

Slowly, I stand, reaching out to Shelly's shoulder as I steady myself.

"Take two steps, then another one. You can do this."

As I start to move forward, imitating the grace of a baby fawn or maybe a newborn giraffe, she says what I've said to models for years. "Don't look down."

It makes a smile come to my lips. "Do you know how many times I've said that?"

Shelly just smiles knowingly back at me.

Taking a deep breath, I look over to Chantilly. Her grin widens as she nods her approval.

It isn't just the shoes and negligee. In the short time since the show began—with Stephen in my ear giving play-by-play—the backstage assistants have teased my hair and painted my face.

"That's it," Stephen says through the earpiece, the roar of applause coming from behind him. "Give me three and I'll make my announcement. Then it's time to wow them with the finale."

I want to respond, but I can't. Even with him still in my ear, my microphone is gone. And then I hear Chantilly's voice. "We're ready. Wait until you see Shana. She's gorgeous."

My gaze shoots her direction, but she's not looking my way.

*Could she possibly not know I'm still wearing my earpiece?*

"She can do this," Stephen agrees.

Before more can be said, I take out the earpiece and tuck it behind my things. I can't listen anymore. Their support means the world. If by chance something else was said, I'd never be able to go onstage.

"Ladies," Chantilly yells. "Get in position. It's finale time."

As Shelly's hand lands on my shoulder, I recall Stephen's advice from earlier. "Shelly?" I ask, "Can you see the audience? Yesterday during rehearsal, the lights were so bright..."

She smiles. "If you try hard enough, you'll see the first few rows. I recommend not trying."

"I don't want to," I laugh as much as say. "I want to pretend the room is empty."

"When I first started modeling, I imagined my family members were the only ones who could see me. And then I started modeling lingerie."

"I can see how that became awkward. *Now* who do you imagine?"

"No one. It's just me. It's like practicing walking in my apartment. Just me. I count my steps. I know my spots. I hear the music and the cues, but the people are gone."

I nod. "Good advice. Except I haven't practiced."

"Yes, you have. You know everyone's position. And as for walking, think back. Remember those cheap plastic heels most little girls wear for dress up?"

I do. I remember the pink sparkly heels with the stretched-out elastic band that held them to my feet. I also remember slipping my feet into my mom's shoes and walking around the house. "I'm afraid I wasn't too graceful."

She eyes me up and down as her eyebrows waggle. "But,

honey...now you're all grown up. If the *no people* idea for the audience doesn't work, make it that one special person."

"That's what Stephen said to do."

"What does he look like?"

"Stephen?" I ask.

"No..." We're now moving with the rest of the models like a well-oiled machine.

My rational mind reminds me that it was Stephen and I who made them this way—who choreographed and made this show our own. But they did the hard work. They put in the hours. I owe it to them to stand tall, move about the stage, and not ruin their success.

"That special guy," Shelly clarifies, bringing me back to reality.

Immediately, Trevor Willis's image comes to my mind. "Tall, not too tall, but taller than me."

"Even in those shoes?"

My grin widens, lifting my cheeks. Although, I'm suddenly afraid my makeup may crack, I think about Trevor. "Yes, even in these shoes. And his hair is light brown and a perpetual mess."

"Oh, sexy!"

"Definitely. And his eyes, vibrant green."

She shakes her head. "I'm imagining broad shoulders and just the right amount of facial hair."

"That's him."

"Strut your stuff for him. We're all counting on you."

Those butterflies that had been dancing around my stomach grow to the size of bats as we make our way past the curtain and onto the stage. The runway before me is brightly lit as if it were a landing strip, a place to land planes instead of showcase models. The lights from above flicker with color as I move forward. Doing as Shelly said, as I've told others to do, I count. Though the sound of the audience is there, I hear the music. I've listened to this arrangement over a hundred times. I've counted out each model's steps. I know it.

I'm lost in my own world, my body doing as it should when my gaze lands upon the first row. It's at that moment that I know I've found my Zen.

I'm not sure how my imagination could work so well, but off to the left of the runway, I see the green gaze from my memories. His disinterested smile morphs before me.

Appreciation.

Shock.

Bewilderment.

Approval.

My feet continue to move. I have one trip down the runway and back. Having Trevor in my mind, his are the only eyes upon me.

I can do this.

# CHAPTER
## Six

*W*hat the actual fuck?

My mouth opens, closes, and opens again. I consciously force my lips to close, afraid if I don't, I'll risk calling out her name or even make a bigger fool of myself by drooling.

*Holy shit!*

She's everything I remember and more.

Then again, maybe I'm hallucinating.

Maybe the vision before me is my imagination. Maybe it's induced by the alcohol we consumed last night. I'm sure after the quantity, there's still some coursing through my bloodstream. Maybe this is a mirage, a vision that doesn't really exist, one I've concocted out of desire. After all, Shana Price has been in my thoughts daily—and especially nightly—since our one secret night.

Whatever is happening...I approve.

This fashion show just got a lot better!

The rest of the models disappear as I concentrate on the blonde. She's not as tall as most, but damn, she's more beautiful. High heels move below the long flowing nightgown. Fuck that. It's not a nightgown. My grandmother wears nightgowns. This one is sexy and hangs perfectly from small straps over her slender shoulders with a lace trim that barely covers her breasts. The long skirt has a slit that allows her long and determined steps as she moves in sync with the rest of the models.

I'm certain this woman in the white negligee isn't the same model who wore the black negligee earlier in the show. I know it was black because when we entered, we were all given tablets with information on each showcased piece. Yet my reasoning mind can't come up with a plausible answer as to why they made the change. My heart tells me the woman of my dreams is onstage. The woman I can't seem to forget. The woman who stars in my fantasies. The woman who broke open my shell with only her smile.

The one I let get away.

Onstage is Shana Price.

*But how and why?*

I continue to struggle, my analytical brain searching for answers.

*Maybe the world is filled with doppelgängers?*

No. I'd know if it weren't her, and damn, I can't take my eyes off of her. She's beautiful and confident and fits right into the show without fanfare.

I'm awestruck.

As the realization settles in, murmurs of approval from the men around me fill my ears, filling me with dueling and equally powerful emotions. The first is pride mixed with amazement. It's not as if I know her that well; however, from what I do know, I can't fathom why the top buyer for Saks's junior department would be onstage for a lady's lingerie show, but damn if she isn't stunning. Like many others in the audience, I'm blown away by her presence.

It's the other people in the audience—their presence

and their eyes on her—that fuel my second strong reaction. Gripping the arms of my seat, my pride in her ability is the only thing tempering my growing need.

I'm overwhelmed with desire to rush the stage, wrap the woman of my dreams in my jacket, and carry her off like a prehistoric caveman. My skin heats at the thought that as gorgeous as she is, I don't want others looking at her. Yes, I know it's barbaric. I even have a split-second image of myself beating my chest and telling the world she's mine.

It may be insane, but nevertheless, it's real. Never before and with none of the other models have I felt such a strong urge to protect someone. It makes me wish that we weren't in a room filled with others. Instead, I wish I was the only one to see Shana in that negligee.

Whichever emotion I concentrate on, I'm mesmerized by the woman before me.

And then...she turns and looks my way.

Our eyes meet for the first time since our weekend so long ago.

Her expression changes for only a second, but as it does I know with everything within me that none of this is an illusion. The model in the white nightgown isn't a doppel-gänger. She isn't a mirage. Ignoring the rest of the women onstage, my gaze follows her every move as she works her way to the rear of the stage, mixing with the rest of the models. Her steps are flawless.

The music reaches its climax and all the models stop. Like statues of Greek goddesses, they stand perfectly still. People around us are using their tablets to mark the items they want to order. Even those of us who are here not as official buyers have the opportunity to order. It's one of the benefits of attending the show. Fingers fly on screens as sales rack up.

Yet the only thought in my mind has nothing to do with lingerie. My thought is getting to Shana Price.

# CHAPTER

***Shana***

*T*he show is over and as we all make our way backstage, I'm exhilarated like never before. It isn't only that the show is complete or that I didn't fall and make a total fool of myself—it's more.

An overwhelming sense of triumph.

Cheers fill the air as everyone makes their way into the dressing room.

From the sound of the crowd and the look on Chantilly's face, the fashion show was a shining success. Not only that, I overcame a lifelong fear. I did it. I walked onto the stage. For the first time, I was more than the woman behind the scenes. Putting the show ahead of my own fears, I did what needed to be done.

While allowing myself to be vulnerable, I kicked ass. At that second, I realize that sometimes it takes the first to do the second.

"To Shana!" Shelly yells above the roar of the other relieved models.

The backstage dressing room fills with applause.

"To each of you," I reply. "You did this, ladies. I'm so proud to have been a part."

Chantilly motions me toward her but not before I have the chance to step out of the tall shoes. When I reach her, she wraps a long black robe over my shoulders. "Before you change, there's someone who wants to talk to you."

For only a second, I imagine the person I pretended to see in the front row. "Who?"

"Stephen is outside. He has news."

Stepping from the room in my bare feet, I leave the roar of the models for the sound of the crowd beyond the stage.

As my eyes adjust to the dim hallway light, I'm wrapped in a bear hug. "You did it. I knew you would."

"Do you have numbers?"

Stephen nods ecstatically. "Through the roof. And they're talking about the late walk-on model. At first there were questions about Jenese."

"We knew there would be. She's Saks's top model."

"You, boss lady, are now the talk of the town. Everyone wants to know who wore the white negligee in the finale."

"They can keep wondering. I did it. I'll leave it to the professionals for the future."

"You know," he says, "if the promotion doesn't go through, you could consider..." Stephen's grin widens.

"If it doesn't go through, it won't have been for lack of trying."

"You can say that again."

Stephen and I both turn toward Vicky. Though her words sound encouraging, I can't tell from her expression what she's thinking.

"I'll leave you two alone," Stephen volunteers as he heads away from the dressing room door back toward the auditorium.

"Stepping in as a model," Vicky begins, "something that according to your résumé you've never before done, at one of the most important shows of the year, was your idea of making this work? Of thinking on your feet?"

I stand taller, remembering the exhilaration I felt only moments ago.

"Yes. The show had to go on. It did."

"We have an entire backlist of models—experienced models."

"And none of them would have known the show." I'm about to say it wasn't my idea, yet I supported it. Vicky was the one who'd given me the reins. In doing so, she supported my right to make the decision. The final product of the show is mine, no matter what she thinks now, no matter the consequences.

We both know that the show was essentially my interview for the new position. If she's upset, Stephen and I are headed back to London. That's her decision. Standing up for my show and my choices is my decision. I refuse to back down. "There wasn't time to get someone else in here, much less brief that someone on the choreography. You're right, I've never modeled before. I don't plan to do it again. However, as you said, the designers paid to have every outfit in the finale. We all know that it's during the finale that final sales orders are secured. I had a job to do."

"Delegation is the sign of a good supervisor."

"I agree," I say, straightening my shoulders and recalling Stephen's pep talk. "Delegation is essential. I delegated to Chantilly and Stephen. Stepping in when required is the evidence of a *great* leader. A true supervisor can do any job in their department. A true leader can't and shouldn't expect others to do something that she isn't willing to do. And one other thing..." I'm on a roll. "...stepping onto that stage was more frightening than taking the show you gave me and turning it into my own. Changing the mediocre and boring into exciting is what I love. Actually taking a part in performing that new show in front of a live audience is and was terrifying. I know from this experience that from now on, I'll also have a greater appreciation for the work those women..." I point toward the dressing room. "...do on that stage. It may look easy. It may look mundane. It isn't. It is both scary and exhilarating, and if saving this show's ass loses me the position, then at least I can walk away and go back to London knowing I did my best."

Vicky stares at me for a moment until the tips of her lips slowly rise as she shakes her head. "I can say that this is the first time I've had anyone give me a piece of her mind wearing silk lingerie."

I wiggle my toes on the cool cement. "I can see how being barefoot in a nightgown, I appear less fierce. But you gave me a job to—"

"No, Shana," Vicky interrupts. "You appear plenty ferocious and determined. The powers that be are upset about Jenese. Her name brings people in. Yet..." She lifts a tablet. "...the sales numbers don't lie. Orders are through the roof. Even Calvin Klein can't be upset that Shelly wore the chemise instead of Jenese. Orders for those, as well as the Vera Wang you are now wearing under that robe are higher than last season. Actually, having it displayed in two different colors seems to have been a positive reinforcement on orders. It's something we should consider in the future.

"Am I happy that things had to change? No."

I don't say a word.

"Am I impressed? Quite possibly."

Inhaling, I ask, "Vicky, what about our return to

London? Will the next ladies' lingerie show be something I need to consider?"

"You have a job to do in London that's still secure. You've shown your ability with juniors. Would you have decided to participate in a junior's fashion show?"

I can hear the accusation in her tone. "Was I more comfortable walking out in front of hundreds of people in a long negligee or would I be more comfortable in a prom dress or maybe a miniskirt and half top?" When she doesn't respond, I go on. "I've never been faced with the reality of participating onstage or disappointing investors. For the record, I'd do whatever needed to be done to make the project a success. Not just for me or even for Saks but for the women backstage who have worked their asses off over the last two weeks."

I feel the tears well and prickle the back of my eyes, yet I keep my steely expression unchanged. I guess at the very least, my little stunt didn't cause me to lose juniors. For that I should be relieved.

Vicky nods. "When we asked you here, it was for a month. The show was part of it. That part is done. For the next two weeks we'll see how you can manage at corporate, and take my advice..."

I wait.

"Wear something else to the office on Monday."

My jaw feels the pressure of my clenching, but before I can come up with a non-bitchy response, she turns and walks away.

*Shit!*

As the click of her shoes against the cold floor fades into the distance, I lean against the cinderblock wall and allow everything to sink in—the truth hits me. The show

I've obsessed over is complete. All the work. All the preparation. Everything is done.

It isn't though. Now our trial run continues as Stephen and I have a two-week working interview at corporate. It's where I used to work. Different floor. Different department, but the address begins the same: Saks Fifth Avenue on Fifth Avenue.

Suddenly, I'm exhausted. The adrenaline rush from the show is history as the repercussions of our conversation loom in the future. Part of me wants to go to the hotel, climb into the large king-sized bed, call for room service, and keep the real world away until Monday. Pulling myself away from the wall, I turn toward the dressing room door when I hear the slow applause.

*Clap. Clap. Clap.*

As I turn, my gaze meets Stephen's coming toward me. Instead of speaking, I lean into him. I know this isn't appropriate coworker behavior, but right now, I need my best friend more than my assistant.

"You told her," he says softly as my cheek falls against his shoulder, and he wraps me in a supportive hug.

I nod against the roughness of his suit coat as some of the tears break loose and spill down my cheeks as I fight to get the next breath.

Stephen holds my shoulders out to arm's length. "Ms. Price, you kicked ass out there. You hold your head high."

"What about your deposit?"

The tips of his lips kick upward. "We still have two weeks. I don't know what stick is up her ass, but the numbers are still climbing. The fashion blogs are touting the amazing show, the choreography, the designs, and the newest unknown face in modeling."

I close my eyes as more tears drip from my false eyelashes.

"Stop that. We're meeting the infamous Kimbra and going out and celebrating. This is a night to party."

"I was thinking a bottle of wine, a long bath, and maybe falling into a deep sleep."

"No!" Stephen proclaims. "There will be no room service tonight. We are in New York, and don't forget, I get to meet my new best friend tonight."

I let out a long sigh. "How could I forget? I was so excited to see Kimbra, but now..."

His head slowly moves from side to side. "No. Now, it's time to party. I love what you're wearing, but do you think maybe it might get a little chilly?"

"It's okay," I say with a renewed smile. "I have on nipple tape. No one will know."

Letting go of my shoulders, Stephen lifts a hand in the air. "Boss lady, sometimes it's just TMI!"

"If I can't talk to my gay best friend about nipple tape, who can I talk to about it?"

"First, I think there are some things better left unsaid. Then again..." His eyes widen. "...we're going to see Kimbra. Maybe we can get the scoop on her sexy brother-in-law and things like nipple tape could be left to discovery."

I squeeze his bicep. "Thank you. Thank you for being you and always making me smile. I'm sorry if I lost you your deposit."

"Nothing that happened today was solely your decision. I was one hundred percent behind you going onstage. You nailed it, and not in the Pinterest *nailed it* kind of way. No regrets. I'll admit, with your natural grace, I was a little nervous."

This makes me laugh. "I was more than a little nervous. But I did as you said. I walked onstage and imagined that one person."

"And it worked?"

"Well, I didn't fall on my ass."

Walking back into the dressing room to change, I'm a mix of thoughts and emotions. Despite Vicky's less than enthusiastic review, I accomplished a successful lingerie show. I did it—not alone, but with the help of everyone involved. It's then I see Chantilly.

"Hey," I whisper, causing her to turn my direction. "Stephen and I are meeting someone later. Would you like to join us and celebrate?"

She looks up from the tablet in her hands. "Celebrate...um, the numbers are really good."

I try to see what she's reading, but from the angle I can't. "Chantilly, is everything all right?"

Her lip disappears under her teeth for only a moment before she smiles. "Thanks."

"For?"

"I had more fun on this show than any in a long time. I think the way you and Stephen changed things up was great."

Why do I feel there's a *but* coming in her sentence?

I wait.

When she doesn't go on, I ask again about drinks. "We're going to the Martini Club on Houston. Come on by if you'd like. Drinks are on me."

# CHAPTER
## *Eight*

### *Trevor*

"$S$ o it didn't exactly turn out the way we planned," Matt says as he pops more peanuts in his mouth.

I want to disagree. The fashion show was much better than I ever imagined. I still can't come to terms with the fact that Shana was one of the models. I've decided it must be my imagination tainted with too much alcohol from the night before. Unwilling to give up on my illusions, I join the other three as we all drink, working to maintain that permanent *bachelor party* buzz.

No matter what else it was, the afternoon has definitely been entertaining.

We're now in one of those out-of-the-way bars, known mostly by locals, the kind that is ten feet wide and one hundred long. I may be exaggerating, but you get the idea. Our table near the front window gives us a view of the crowded street and if you turn a little, a view of the long, shiny bar. From my angle, I'm getting mostly heads, but it's a sea of people. Located in an upscale part of the city, this place is a longtime goldmine. Surrounded by more expensive establishments with fancier signage, I'd take this bar to the ones filled with tourists any day.

That's just part of what makes this place special. It's unique. Instead of dancing, there are a few pool tables near the back. Currently, we're waiting on one opening. A twenty-dollar tip helped move us ahead in the waiting order.

"I guess this means that we should take Trevor up on his offer of conceding," Max says. "I mean, it wasn't much, but I did talk to the one man from Christian Dior."

"You didn't get his number or his name," Eric reminds him.

"How do you know?"

"If you had, we'd all know!" Matt says with a laugh.

"Wait a minute, the night is young," Eric interjects. "I heard some people talking, and they said that some of the models like to go out and party after a big show. That's why we're down the street from the Martini Club."

In all of our planning, we hadn't considered the spring-time crowds. It's an epidemic. As soon as the temperatures rise and the snow stops falling, everyone is out and about. Max was in charge and should have made a reservation for the Martini Club. I'm a planner. Then again, I live in Manhattan now and could have volunteered. It might not be fair to think Max could have done it all from the UK.

"Remember, you're getting married in less than a month," I remind Eric.

"I am. I'm also the judge. And I think watching you three get turned down flat sounds like fun."

"I'm not conceding," I reason. "No one made a move on a model." I turn to Max. "You said models, not buyers. That means we're all still tied."

"We can up the ante," Max says with a grin.

"Forget the model. Anyone gets laid tonight and his expenses for the weekend are zero. Eric, you're exempt."

I shake my head. "I don't care if we have separate hotel rooms. We're not in college."

Eric takes a long draw on his beer. "You're right, Trevor. This weekend isn't about your dicks. It's about my wedding. I'm happy to keep drinking and know that tomorrow I'm going home to Cynthia and that none of you have a new number in your phone."

"Awfully concerned about the little woman, aren't we?" Max asks. "I believe there's a name for that."

"It's a phrase," Matt says with a chuckle, "and it begins with *P*."

"Second word begins with *W*," Max volunteers.

"Yeah," Eric responds to Max. "Just because you don't like pussy doesn't mean I don't." He turns to Matt. "And as far as the second word in that phrase, I remember a story about a college student who went to this BDSM club."

"Whoa!" Matt says, lifting his hand. "What happens in college stays in college."

"Good thing this isn't college!" We all laugh as more and more people make their way into the bar.

When our table finally quiets, Matt says, "I know I may be hallucinating, but when I went to sign us up for a pool table, I think I saw one of the models sitting at the bar. I know we talked about going to some other places, but who knows, maybe even Saks Fifth Avenue models know about our treasure here. There could be more on their way." He waggles his brow. "Maybe we don't have to give up on the models."

Eric looks at Matt's empty bottle. "We're in trouble. He's seeing models everywhere. Operation *stop Matt from sleeping with the first woman who talks to him*."

"That's the exact opposite of my idea," Max says.

Matt shakes his head before tilting it toward the bar. "No, I did. The blonde who was only in the finale, remember her? I swear that's who I saw near the end of the bar."

I immediately remember her—everything about her.

"You blokes keep imagining your models," Max says with a grin. "I'm stepping outside for a smoke."

While I listen to the conversation that ensues, I try to inconspicuously look down the bar. I haven't told anyone that I thought I recognized the blonde from the finale or that I was confident I'd awakened beside her at one time. These guys know me too well to believe my story. Yet with the bartenders and busy bar, my view is blocked. The stools are all filled, and there are people standing near the stools— blondes, brunettes, redheads, and even a few people with purple and green hair. I'm having trouble making anyone out until I zero in on a blonde near the end. She appears to be with a man. They're talking with their heads together. From this view all I can see is her hair.

*Could it be her?*

I tell myself that it's not. I don't want my imaginary Shana to be with someone else.

# CHAPTER
## Nine

### *Shana*

"I never expected the club to be so packed," Stephen says. Looking around, he adds, "Everywhere is packed. Even this place is filling fast."

He's right. There are wall-to-wall people and the buzz of the crowd is exactly what I need to get my mind off the show and on tonight. While the idea of room service and a bottle of wine had its appeal, this new and exciting chaos is just what the doctor ordered.

With all the work around the fashion show, we didn't think about calling the Martini Club for reservations. Thankfully, this hole-in-the-wall just down the street is a hidden treasure. Like a step back in time, there are no neon lights or exposed beams. Stately, dark mahogany paneling covers the lower half of the walls, likely having been in place since before the turn of the twentieth century. The top half is covered in photographs of famous patrons through the years. Most are black and white and many have large garish signatures obstructing a portion of the face. The wood floor is so worn. The illusion of a shiny finish was given up so long ago that in areas it actually bows. Tables and chairs have a slight lean, almost imperceptible were it not for the lines in the paneling. The uneven surface from years of traffic adds to the appeal. What the floor lacks in luster is compensated by the long, glistening bar. Going nearly the length of the building, the surface reflects the lights from the ceiling, with a leather edge that shows its years of use and care. The wooden stools known more for their functionality than comfort could easily be older than me. All in all, there's something about the establishment that feels comfortable and fun. It's like a forgotten island hidden within the upscale area.

"I love it," I say, taking in the positive vibes surrounding us.

Stephen touches my knee as he leans closer. "I do too. There's something about New York: the energy is everywhere."

Before I can respond, one of the bartenders, a handsome man with a deep voice, begins to sing along with the song coming from the speakers. All the patrons stop their conversations as the bartender's hands go into the air and his voice grows louder. I recognize the song as a tune from a recent Broadway hit show.

I smile and shake my head at Stephen who is suddenly enthralled with the man behind the bar. It doesn't take long before most of the customers begin joining in. The impromptu sing-along makes me realize how much I miss the arts of Manhattan. It isn't that there aren't amazing opportunities in London for culture: there are. I think it's the familiarity of New York that I miss.

When the song ends, the entire clientele breaks out in roaring applause.

"We need to go see a show," Stephen says, leaning close.

"Does that make us like tourists?"

"No. New Yorkers go to shows."

"We have two weeks. How many do you think we can see?"

"That makes you sound like a tourist."

"I'm not—" My rebuttal is stopped as my phone buzzes.

Kimbra: **I'M FINALLY HERE. SORRY. TRAFFIC.**

Me: **WE'RE AT THE BAR.**

I turn toward the door, peering over the heads of others as I wait for Kimbra. "She's here," I say excitedly.

Before Stephen can turn in the direction I'm looking, my smile widens as I see my other best friend's red hair. My mind fills with so many memories. I can't believe how much I've missed her. It isn't until she's within reach that I really allow myself to think about it. We lived together for years and since then, I feel like I've been separated from my sister from another mister—well, and another missus.

I know we've talked regularly—often on video-chat—but seeing her fills my heart with warmth.

And then the world freezes.

Stepping through the door behind her is Max: Maximilian Cantel.

It can't be.

*How and why would Stephen's ex be in the same restaurant in New York City?*

As Stephen starts to turn toward the door, I stop him. "Oh, can you get us all drinks while I go find her?"

His head turns from side to side. "Find her? Didn't you say she's here?"

I did. "Her text said she is here. This place is a madhouse. We don't want to lose our stools. How about you order us all another round? Kimbra will have the same as me: a lemon drop martini."

Before he can argue, I push my way through the crowd until I come face-to-face with Kimbra. Without a care for anyone else, we scream and hug, blocking traffic from moving all directions around us.

"I've missed you!" we say together.

I take a peek around her shoulders, wondering what happened to Max and if I imagined him. If that's the case, my imagination has been working overtime today. The bar is so full; I can't find the person I thought was him.

Surely, it wasn't.

*Why would he be here?*

I reach for Kimbra's hand and pull her toward Stephen. When he sees us, he leaps from the barstool and comes forward. Standing only a few feet back he shakes his head while smiling from ear-to-ear. "I can't believe I finally get to meet you."

"You must be Stephen," Kimbra says as she closes the gap and surrounds him in a hug. There's no handshaking for my best friend. She's one of the friendliest people I've ever known. Now that doesn't mean she can't tell you her mind. She can. But once she's done, you'll forget she was upset and be laughing about something again.

I look around once more, wondering why I'd imagine seeing Max.

"Who are you looking for?" Stephen asks.

"U-um," I stutter. "Duncan. Kimbra did you bring that man of yours?"

"No way! He'd be in the way. I miss girl talk."

Stephen grabs her hand and tugs her toward the bar. "That sounds right up my alley."

Within a few minutes, Kimbra and I are seated at the bar with Stephen standing between us as we all laugh like old friends. It's everything I hoped it would be. The two of them are telling their most embarrassing stories involving me, and I love every word.

"You should have seen her," Kimbra says. "We'd only lived here a few weeks, and we decided that the subway was the best way to get home. The problem was that neither of us knew the lines or stations. It's a miracle we made it back to our apartment."

"It was the homeless man who saved us."

"Now that's not a phrase you hear every day," Stephen says, listening to the story.

"No," I say. "He did. He asked us where we were going. He told us which line to take. He even rode part of the way with us to be sure we'd transfer correctly."

Stephen shakes his head. "And you weren't a little worried?"

"Why?" Kimbra asks.

"Is she always this trusting?" he asks.

"You could say we were both a little naïve," I admit. Looking over the rim of my glass, I go on, "I guess with your new hubby, you aren't riding the subway much."

"That's not true," she replies. "I'm proud I learned my way around the subway. And it's much quicker than the streets most of the time. If I'd have ridden it tonight, I'd have been here earlier."

"No shit! Have you gotten Duncan to try?" Her husband is kind of rich. I don't see him riding the subway or navigating transfers. Don't get me wrong. He's friendly and down to earth. It's just that he's more of a driver kind of man. It's true that he and his brother are about as opposite as oil and water. The only thing they have in common is good looks, and if my memory and imagination serve me well, Trevor exceeds in that category.

Kimbra grins. "I've gotten Duncan to try a lot of things."

Our heads fly back in laughter. This was just what the doctor ordered: a stress-free night laughing, cutting up, and reminiscing.

"Oh my goodness," Kimbra squeals after her second glass is nearly empty. "I can't believe it."

"What?" we ask together.

"I think I see my brother-in-law over there." She points toward the front of the restaurant where a group of men seem to be standing, giving up their prized table.

All at once, the air from my lungs evaporates as I choke on my last sip—or was it a gulp—of martini. No, these aren't as good as the ones down the street at the club, but after a few, they have become the best in the city.

As she pushes through the crowd, Stephen turns to me. "Does she have more than one brother-in-law?"

My eyes grow wide as she and Trevor embrace. I'm suddenly experiencing every emotion at once.

Excitement.

Nerves.

Tingles.

Queasiness.

Fear.

*How do I respond?*

I haven't spoken to him in months. Kimbra doesn't know anything about the weekend of her wedding. It's then I realize that I'm trembling. My hands are clammy, and my forehead is probably glistening with nervous perspiration.

"Damn, girl," Stephen whispers as Kimbra turns and points our way. "You have a great imagination!"

On Trevor's face—his handsome, sexy face—I read all the same thoughts flying through my mind. The top and most important is how much we will act like we know one another.

"He's better looking than the pictures you showed me when you were stalking him on social media," Stephen whispers.

"I wasn't stalking," I say, still unable to look away as Kimbra and Trevor begin to push their way through the crowd, coming our direction.

"You were *so* stalking," Stephen whispers, "but, honey, seeing him in person, I don't blame you."

My pulse kicks up to a dangerous speed as they come closer. I'm on a precipice.

*What do I do?*

For only a split second, I consider my options. Running to the ladies' room would still allow me to be seen. Fainting sounds like a reasonable alternative, but then it's too late.

They're both standing in front of Stephen and me.

Trying to drown out the volume of the crowd, Kimbra leans in so we can hear. "Stephen and Shana, this is my brother-in-law, Trevor Willis." She turns to Trevor. "Stephen and Shana."

Despite my friend's excitement about bringing us all together, my attention is solely on the man at her side. It's his green eyes that draw me in, just as they did a long time ago. It's their intensity that won't let me go. I'm a candle under the fire of his gaze and if I don't look away, I may melt.

I'll blame my reaction on the martini, but as we stare at one another, I am filled with hope. Not only is he real, but perhaps, there's hope for more. His hand comes out...then all at once his gaze is gone, focused now on Stephen.

"Hello." It's his first word since joining us and it's not directed to me.

"Trevor," Kimbra says, "do you remember Shana from my wedding? She was my maid of honor."

His lips quirk, but it takes a prolonged second before he turns to me. "Yes, Shana. Nice to see you again."

I can't tell what it is, but something in the way he's speaking is wrong. It's too formal or forced.

"Yes, Trevor," I manage to say. "Nice to see you, too."

I don't know if Stephen heard it—the tone in Trevor's voice—but, protectively, my friend moves his arm around my shoulder, drawing me closer to him.

Kimbra keeps talking. "Trevor recently moved back to New York. You'd think he'd come see his brother and sister-in-law more often, but no, I have to run into him in a crowded bar..."

Though she continues, I'm not hearing her. I'm not listening. My mind is screaming at me to take one of the options I didn't before. Fainting seems unnecessary, but running is still an option.

"If you'll excuse me a minute." I don't even mention where I'm going. I know it's the bathroom, but the closer I get, I find myself scanning the back of the bar for an escape. That hot bath, king-sized bed, and bottle of wine is suddenly very appealing.

I work out the details: a text to Kimbra, saying I was ill,

and one to Stephen, telling him to pick up pizza on the way to my room.

I'm almost to the ladies' room when I gasp as a strong hand grabs mine, pulling me until my back is flush against the wall. In the dimly lit hallway, Trevor Willis is all I can see. He dominates my vision as his presence surrounds my body.

He leans close, his words strained. "Are you dating him?"

The green eyes staring at me are the ones I've dreamt about, the ones I imagined to help me walk onto a runway, and the ones I've missed. Yet there's something different, something new, a fever burning within them, like golden fireworks exploding within the green sea, flashing and smoldering in the depths.

Despite the way his concentration takes my breath, I push back against his chest. "What the hell do you think you're doing?"

He doesn't budge. "I'm asking if you're seeing Stephen."

Anger mixes with my martini. A second ago, Trevor barely looked at me and now he's demanding answers. "Trevor, I don't know what to say. You quit calling. Obviously, you don't want to talk to me."

His voice grows deeper, more assertive and demanding than I've ever heard. "Just answer. Are you?"

The connections within my brain aren't firing. It's been too long of a day. Even though part of me wants to tell him to back the fuck up, another part of me—the part that's thumping in my chest and twisting my insides—can't believe that after all this time it's really him.

That he's here.

With me.

Surrounding me.

Pinning me against the wall.

The aroma of woodsy cologne fills my senses as multiple lemon drop martinis course through my bloodstream. Without reason I begin to giggle.

As my face falls in laughter, Trevor reaches for my chin, "Shana?"

I can't look away. I don't want to. "Dating? Stephen?"

"I've been thinking about you."

"Well, you haven't called in months. I figured you met someone new. Besides, there's no us, so why do you care whom I'm dating?" I'm not sure why I'm baiting him. Maybe it's the intensity of his stare or the way his body is pushed against mine. I couldn't deny how much it turns me on even if I wanted to. There's no doubt that as my breasts heave against his chest, my lady parts are waking from their long winter's hibernation.

Letting go of my chin, his tone softens. "You are supposed to be in London." It's as if he too is making sure it's truly me.

"And you in Washington."

He takes a small step backward.

"You'll think this is crazy," I begin, "but earlier today, I thought I imagined you." My gaze is no longer on his eyes, but his lips—his strong, full lips.

The ends quirk upward. "Then maybe we're both crazy because I imagined you, too. It was at a fashion show. You wouldn't have happened to have been at the Saks Fifth Avenue fashion show, onstage in a long white negligee, would you?"

Instead of answering that question, I go for the one he first asked. "Stephen is my friend. We work together."

Although no one is trying to walk past us at the

moment, Trevor leans his hard body closer, his warmth surrounding me and resuscitating every nerve that has gone dormant over the last dry spell. With his hands on either side of my face, I lean toward him. If only I were wearing the heels from the show. I'm not. I lift myself up on my toes until our lips meet.

# CHAPTER
## *Ten*

*Trevor*

*S*weet and tangy.

Shana Price tastes like sugar with a twist of lemon.

My mind tells me to go slow, reminding me that I don't have any right to this beautiful woman. My mind is saying to stop, yet her soft moan is all I hear.

My body has its own GPS with the destination close. Listening to my mind is out of the question.

Her petite body shivers as I tease her sweet lips. They willingly part as my tongue delves inside, wrestling with hers.

Not giving up its fight, my thoughts remind me how forward this behavior is and how it isn't like me. Trevor Willis is not a man who chases a woman down, pins her against the wall, and kisses her until neither of us can breathe or cares.

It's not me.

But, fuck, it should be.

I like it.

I won't blame the alcohol. I'll blame my need to know it's really Shana and to claim her for my own. I didn't do it last time, and I've regretted it every day since.

When her hands come to my chest, I seize them, lifting them above her head and pinning them to the wall. Shana doesn't fight; instead, her hips move against mine and our kiss grows more passionate. In the dark, crowded hallway, with my body pressed against hers, I swallow the soft moans coming from her throat.

At that moment, I want to be anywhere but a crowded bar in the middle of Manhattan. I no longer care about Eric's bachelor party or my friends. I don't even care about Kimbra back out in the bar. All I want is to whisk Shana away and do what we didn't do before, what her body and mine are ready and aching to do.

When we finally pull back, I release her hands. Slowly, they fall to her sides, yet her gaze remains locked with mine. I take her in under the dim lighting as her breathing deepens and her breasts brush against my chest. Her blue eyes are wide and full of wonder. Her cheeks are flushed and reddened by my facial hair. There are loose yellow strands framing her face, and her dark pink lips are beginning to swell.

She's absolutely the most beautiful woman I've ever known. Fuck, I'm still not sure if it was her on that stage, but damn, she should be a model.

However, I would rather have her model for an exclusive audience of one—me.

Brushing a strand of her long blonde hair behind her ear, I force my body to move away from hers. "I'm sorry."

"Why?"

"I don't know." I'm being honest. "It was that after so long...seeing you with him." I shake my head. "I know I don't have any right to be jealous. It's that I never expected to see you here, and now you're real. I've been thinking about you, and damn, Shana Price, you've been on my mind since our secret weekend. I've tried to move on, but thoughts of you are everywhere."

Her lips part and curve. I love the way she smiles. It isn't restricted to her puffy lips, no. It's her entire face. Her eyes lighten to a soft blue hue, and her cheeks become a deeper shade of pink.

"I was," she says.

"You were?" I ask, confused. "In my thoughts. Yes."

She shakes her head. "I was in a fashion show today. It's a long story, one that may not have a happy ending. I don't regret it. Getting on that stage was scary and exhilarating. I didn't know if I could do it." Her hands come back to my chest, splaying over the front of my shirt. "Stephen said that instead of seeing the audience, I should imagine that the only person who is watching me is the one whom I want to see me wearing the lingerie. I imagined you."

"Not him?"

She lets out a soft giggle. "Trust me. Not him. He's one of my best friends, but no. There's nothing between us." It's as if a light bulb goes off over her head. "Oh, no. Best friends. Kimbra is also my best friend. Have you? Her? Duncan? What are we going to do?"

I run my knuckle over her cheek as my grin grows. "I'm not sure there was a complete sentence in any of that, and yet I totally understand." Before she can respond, I go on, "No, I never told Duncan or Kimbra. Did you?"

Her lips form a straight line as she shakes her head again.

"What do you want to do?" I ask.

"Is sneaking out a back door with you an option?"

My knuckle trails down her cheek to her neck, purposely touching the soft skin behind her ear to see if she responds. All at once Shana shivers and I imagine doing more, planting kisses and running my tongue along the sensitive area. I lean in and deliver a soft one to my target.

Shana's grip of my shirt intensifies.

"Damn, my lady, I love the way you think. Maybe while we're at it, we could scale a few fences."

Shana giggles the most perfect melody. "Seriously, I'm in town for two more weeks."

"Are you suggesting we play it cool out there?"

"As much as I would like to do otherwise, and believe me, I would, but tonight is supposed to be about my best friends."

I also recall the reason why I'm at this bar. "Yes, me too. I'm at a bachelor party."

"Seriously?"

"I am."

"We seem to have a thing for weddings."

"Do you recall Cynthia?" I ask.

Her smile fades. "Your date at Kimbra's wedding."

"My *fake* date," I correct her. "Yes. Well, everything I told you was true. This weekend is her fiancé's bachelor party. If you remember, I said that he and I are friends. His name is Eric."

Shana nods. "I remember, the one working in Indiana."

I brush my lips over hers, fighting the urge to linger and taste more of her sweetness. "Damn. How are we supposed to walk out there and act like strangers when we have all this history?"

"Call me...in the morning? I wouldn't be opposed to repeating some of the history."

"Oh no, my lady. I want to make another one."

"Another one?"

"Another history. One where I don't let you get away."

I lean closer one more time. By the way Shana wiggles between me and the wall, I know I'm unsuccessful at hiding my reaction to being near her. That reaction is growing painfully harder every second. Yet I don't want to back away. I need to be close.

Like my body needs air, I want one last savor of her tangy lemon taste.

This time, her palm comes to my cheek. The soft touch lingers as our lips move ever so slowly. With a deep sigh, we both back away.

I cock my brow in question. "I suppose walking out to Kimbra hand in hand isn't an option?"

"Not yet. This would be awfully sudden."

"Is tomorrow too soon?"

"Hmm. Tomorrow, whatever shall it bring?" Her question hangs in the air like a whimsical melody.

Taking a deep breath, I inhale her perfume, hairspray, and presence. It's a concoction I could easily grow accustomed to. "It's springtime in New York. The possibilities are limitless."

Although I don't want to do it, I take a step back and allow her to pass. Before she does, she leaves one last chaste kiss on my cheek. Our fingers graze one another's as she gives me a final smile over her shoulder and heads into the ladies' room.

I lean against the wall and watch her disappear behind the restroom door.

Her loss is real, a hole in the depth of my soul. Nevertheless, it's easier tonight than it was the morning she flew back to London. This time I know the truth.

I can't let Shana Price go.

I won't.

Placing my hands in my pockets and bending at the waist, I think back to this afternoon. It was her on that stage. The revelation fills me with hope. Not only was it her, but while she was up there, looking incredibly hot and sexy, she was thinking about me.

It takes all of my self-control to not stay in this hallway and wait for her return.

If I did, I know what I'd do. I'd start as I did before, backing her against the wall. And then, grabbing that round ass, I'd lift her sexy-as-shit legs until they're wrapped around my waist, and finally, I'd wish to every higher power in the universe that she weren't wearing the tight jeans...that instead, she was wearing the negligee from earlier and nothing else.

I take a few more deep breaths. My current line of thinking is doing very little to ease my discomfort. But it has done something. It has made me more determined than ever.

I let her go once. I walked away thinking we would be better off apart than dealing with a long-distance relationship. I was wrong.

A day hasn't passed that she hasn't been on my mind in one way or another. Sometimes it's as simple as a fleeting memory...

Red Gatorade.

The aroma of coffee.

The mention of Saks Fifth Avenue.

A tall chain-link fence or a parking garage.

There are times when those innocuous memories blindside me. And then there are other times when her memory has been more difficult to deal with, as it is now. During those times I've had to take matters into my own hands.

This time, I swear to myself, will be different.

Making one last adjustment to my jeans, I begin to walk back out to Kimbra and Stephen. There's a slight possibility that I might owe that guy an apology. I can't even remember what I said to him. The only thing I can remember is seeing his hands on my girl.

Okay, she isn't my girl.

Not yet. The timetable is set.

I always have loved a challenge.

Shana Price will be mine.

I have two weeks.

# CHAPTER

### *Shana*

Standing at the row of sinks, I'm caught off guard by my reflection. While that image has been all kinds of crazy today—from lead in lingerie to model and back to friend—the reflection I'm currently seeing is my favorite. I tilt my head one way and the other. After only a few minutes with Trevor, my lips are pink and cheeks flushed. Even my neck is a light shade of red from the abrasiveness of his beard.

Closing my eyes, my chest heaves as I remember the possessiveness in his kiss and the determination in his stare as he asked about Stephen. Maybe it wasn't nice to not answer him right away, but the energy in his demand lit a spark that I didn't want to let die.

With the way I'm reeling, it's burning strong and bright.

I grip the edge of the sink, recalling his woodsy scent and the taste of good beer. That's what Trevor Willis is to me, the sexy aroma of spice and outdoors and the taste of craft beer, an intoxicating combination.

I could lie to myself and say that this unquenchable twisting deep inside me is from the martinis, but I know the truth. It's him. It's been him since the first night we met.

My world was sent out of kilter. For nearly the last year, I've tried to deny it. But the truth won't let me go. From his reaction, he's as captive as I am. While being held hostage by an undeniable attraction sounds somewhat frightening, I love every minute of it.

As I make my way back to my friends, I see Trevor and stifle a giggle as I contemplate our plan.

*Will it be possible to keep this secret for a little while longer?*

It's then that I remember that none of this is a secret to Stephen, only to my other best friend, Kimbra. My gaze narrows, as if it zeroing in my vision will help me hear their conversation. I love Stephen, but keeping secrets isn't his forte.

*What if he's already spilled the beans?*

I can't hear them over the music and other patrons.

With Trevor standing, Kimbra and Stephen have our barstools. It's as I approach that Stephen stands. I try to stay focused on my two best friends, but out of the corner of my eye, I catch the way Trevor's gaze turns sultry. The simple change in expression makes my chest tighten.

*Oh shit!*

This is going to be harder than I thought.

"What happened to your lips?" Stephen whispers in my ear as I move to sit on the stool he vacated.

My fingers come up to my mouth to assess what he means. "Umm, I think it's an allergic reaction to the lipstick they used today at the show."

"Oh my goodness," Kimbra breaks in. "Stephen was just telling us about the fashion show. Here." She hands me my martini. "The coolness will help your lips." She looks closer. "They don't look too bad."

Trevor also takes a drink of his beer, the glass barely hiding his amusement at my feigned allergic reaction.

Kimbra's voice grows louder. "Why in the world didn't you call me?"

"Would you have gone onstage for me?"

Kimbra laughs. "No. I would have been cheering." She turns and punches Trevor's arm nearly spilling his beer. "And you were there? Did you scream for her?"

"First, her name wasn't announced though she did have my attention. Besides, it wasn't exactly a striptease. It's not as if we were shouting catcalls."

"However..." Stephen asks suggestively. "If you could?"

Trevor smiles as his hand comes to rest on the back of my chair. "If it were appropriate, I so would have. Shana looked beautiful up there in that white negligee."

"Listen to you," Kimbra says, with a smile. "If Stephen hadn't just told us what she was wearing, I'd think you were smitten." Her mouth quirks for a moment. "Did you just say they didn't announce her name?"

"I'm a man. I notice beautiful women."

"Hmm," Kimbra hums. "Mr. Single-for-Life."

"It's a Willis thing," Trevor replies.

"Oh no," Kimbra responds. "No more generalizations. Your brother is cured."

"So there is a cure?" I ask, forcing my most innocent smile.

"Oh, ladies," Stephen interjects. "There is always a cure. And I personally believe I'm surrounded by two of the loveliest cures I've ever seen." He turns to Trevor. "Wouldn't you agree?"

My cheeks heat as I take another sip of martini.

It's everything I can do to maintain the conversation with the way Trevor is secretly drawing circles on my shoulder, running his hand through my hair, and teasing the place on my neck where earlier his lips made me shiver.

I want nothing more than to turn toward him and wrap my arms around his neck. But I can't because through it all, Stephen is dropping hints the size of grenades while Kimbra is chatting about everything, blissfully unaware.

"...we should have you all to dinner before you leave for London," Kimbra says. "You too, Trevor. This is fun."

"London is still up in the air," I say. "I mean, of course, if we get the job here we'll still need to go back to pack."

"Apartment in the East Village," Stephen says softly as he lowers his empty glass to the bar. "Next round is on you, boss lady." And with that, he steps away.

"What is he talking about?" Kimbra asks.

I shake my head. "It's not as if there isn't enough pressure, but Stephen put a deposit down on an apartment in the East Village for when we move back to New York."

"Is it that certain?"

I shake my head. "It's less certain after my little stunt today of going onstage. Even though I stepped in to save the show and showcase all the lingerie, the woman who would be my superior wasn't thrilled."

"Why?" Trevor asks. "I was there. It went off without a flaw."

"The sales are good, but the point of a fashion show is to showcase fashions. When the show is over, the fashions should be the headline, not pondering about the loss of one model and questions about her replacement."

"I don't know how you do it. Dealing in HR is enough for me," Kimbra says.

"Well, you seem to have an in with your boss, too. That doesn't hurt," Trevor says with a grin.

Kimbra shrugs. "Speaking of which—"

Before she can finish I hear a voice I never expected, one thick with a British accent.

"Willis, we're next in the pool-table queue. You're about up."

"Max?" I say, turning his direction. Stunned doesn't begin to describe my reaction.

"Shana?"

The good vibes I've been feeling since entering the bar disappear in a puff of smoke as Max Cantel's beady, cheating stare comes my way.

"You two know each other...?"

Trevor's comment goes unheard as I step from the barstool, all five-foot-six inches of me, poised and ready to fight. "Get the hell away from here before Stephen sees you."

"He's here?" Max asks, sounding less angry than I would have expected.

"Get out. How dare you track him down—"

"What are—" Trevor tries again to speak.

"Get the hell away." I frantically look to my left and right, wondering where Stephen went before turning to Trevor. "You know this man?"

"Yes, we're friends—"

Max reaches for me, but I pull away. "Shana, listen to me. There's been some misunderstanding. I haven't been able to reach Stephen for nearly a month. I've left messages and emails. I've even sent a courier."

My finger pokes his direction, getting closer and closer to hitting his chest with each word. "Keep your lame-ass excuses to yourself."

It's then that I feel another hand on my back. "I need to

leave," Stephen says.

I hear the anguish in his voice.

"Stephen," Max asks, "what the hell happened?"

When I turn, Stephen's back is as straight as a rod as he turns to Kimbra. "It was very nice to meet you. It seems I need to leave."

"Umm," she says, "I don't know what's happening."

I look from Kimbra to Trevor; both of their expressions are filled with question. "I need to go too. Call me." I stand taller. "Kimbra."

And with that I turn toward the door, my hand in the small of Stephen's back as I navigate our way through the crowded bar.

"Sorry, boss lady," he says as we step onto the sidewalk. It is then that my phone buzzes as his body trembles beneath my grasp.

"Let's get back to the hotel."

"Wine?"

"Copious amounts of wine."

Once we're in the taxi, I pull my phone from my purse, but before checking the screen, Stephen turns my way, his eyes glassy with pent-up emotion.

"Do you know something else I love in New York?" he asks.

"You mean, besides me?"

He nods. "Yes, besides you." When I don't answer, he does. "Pizza."

"Oh my God, I was just thinking the same thing earlier tonight."

I tap on the partition separating us from the driver.

Pulling the cell phone from his ear, the driver asks, "Yes, lady?"

"Stop at Underground Pizza on Hanover before going to our hotel."

"No good, miss. There will be no parking or standing in that area."

Stephen lets out a long breath. "Then drive me in circles until she has our pizza."

"Whatever you want. The meter's running."

I grin when I see Stephen smile.

"I'll cover the meter, you get the pizza," he says just before laying his head on my shoulder.

"Deal."

He looks up. "You really are my best friend. I don't know what's going to happen with this promotion, but whatever it is, I'm glad to be here with you."

I reach up and pull his head back to my shoulder. "This has been a crazy-ass night."

"Are you going to check your texts? Your phone's been buzzing since we left the bar."

I sigh as I swipe my screen. Three missed text messages.

"Two from Trevor and one from Kimbra."

"Crazy-ass night," he says.

"You can say that again."

# CHAPTER
## Twelve

### *Shana*

*T*he club clothes are gone; mine lie somewhere on my bathroom floor. I traded them for more comfortable alternatives: yoga pants covered in multicolored shoes and a big T-shirt. As soon as we made it to the hotel, Stephen did the same before coming to my room. His chic jacket and trousers are gone, and in their place, he's wearing jogging pants and a Yankees T-shirt.

Growing up in Illinois, I'm more of a Cubs girl. When I was younger, each summer my family would go into Chicago for a weekend of what my mom called *family time*. Most years we'd see a Cubs game. I love Wrigley, but my favorite part is Wrigleyville. Not only are the hot dogs and popcorn always the best, but it is one of the few times we'd get to see our parents relax and sit back with a few beers. They saved their alcohol intake for special occasions.

Another annual stop was usually a place my parents considered *educational*, such as the aquarium or one of the museums. While I always liked the *Museum of Science and Industry*, I think that while listening to my parents talk, I learned more in Wrigleyville.

Unlike my parents, I don't feel the need to limit my alcohol intake to family time. It's not that I drink a lot or every day, but life often requires a good glass of wine. Sometimes that's also a great time for a warm bubble bath or like tonight, just a good friend. Those are the ingredients for my special times since I don't have a husband or family of my own.

"Would you be my family?" I ask Stephen.

"Oh, girl. I've said it before; you're my sister from another mister."

"And another missus, but it still works."

I close my eyes and inhale the deep cabernet aroma. There are some people who can taste wine and recite a list of familiar flavors. I'm not one of them.

"I like wine," I admit.

Stephen laughs. "You'd make a great connoisseur."

"I could be one if I wanted to."

When he shakes his head, I sit taller, swirl the contents of my glass, and change my voice to something that sounds somewhere between a snooty librarian and Charlie Brown's teacher. Clearing my throat, I inhale deeply. Then I take a small sip. "Ahem, being grown in the Napa region of the valley, this full-bodied cabernet is dense in the darker fruits."

"You're dense," Stephen mumbles.

I ignore him as I take another sip and look at the bottle. "Hmmm, 2010. Yes, the blackberries were prominent that year, which is very evident. I also notice a hint of black pepper and do I taste...bell pepper?"

"I love bell peppers!"

"Next time we should get them on our pizza."

"Next time," he says, the excitement fading from his voice. "I'm not going to get drunk because of *him*. It was just that..." He swirls his cabernet. "...I didn't expect to see him and well, I wanted to hit him with a full-bodied bottle."

Perhaps the wine is getting the better of me, but the

more Stephen talks about Max, the more I think about Trevor. It's not that I wanted to hit him with a bottle. Well, maybe I did at first. However, after he chased me down the hallway, hitting him was the last thing on my mind. Besides, there weren't any hard bottles around—not within reach. The only hardness within reach...

"Shana!"

"What?"

"You're doing that thing again."

"What *thing*?"

"Sleeping with your eyes open. I'm not cleaning up full-bodied wine from this comforter."

I giggle. "I think it's called daydreaming and..." I grip the stem of my wine glass tighter. "...I'm not wasting a drop. Our bottle is empty."

It's not exactly the pity party I had planned back at the fashion show. Instead, this party is more about Stephen and less about me. We're sitting cross-legged on my king-sized bed. There's some old '80s movie playing on the television at low volume and an open grease-stained box at the end of the bed that very recently contained the most delicious cheese pizza ever created. Now don't think I'm exaggerating simply because I hadn't eaten dinner, had consumed three or four lemon drop martinis, and have now added at least half a bottle of red wine.

It takes more than that to make me exaggerate.

"How could I have known he was here?" Stephen asks.

I sigh, thinking through his question. "I agree. I mean, if the last time you talked to him he never mentioned moving back to New York, how would you know he's not a figment of your imagination?"

Stephen's eyes squint. "Max moved to New York?"

I wave my hand, realizing I'm talking about Trevor and try to hide my intention. "Hell, I don't know. I yelled at him. Did you hear me yell?"

Stephen covers his ears. "Babe, volume. You're yelling now. Let's not add getting kicked out of one of the nicer hotels in the Financial District—one, may I add, that's being paid for by Saks—to our list of crazy-ass things we've done today."

I fall back on the bed, kicking my legs out and nearly sending the pizza box flying. "Today. Just think about that. Twenty-four hours."

"Okay," he agrees less than enthusiastically.

I bolt up straight in the bed. "No, Stephen. Really. Think."

"I'm thinking."

I'm not sure I believe him. He's pulled the small folder containing the room-service menu from the nightstand and is covering one eye while he reads the open page. Stopping him, I reach for the folder.

"Wait," he protests, pulling it back. "I was thinking we should order one more bottle of wine."

"That isn't what I wanted you to think about. Think about all that has happened since this morning. The show is done."

He reaches over and squeezes my hand. "You did great."

While I appreciate his undying support, I'd rather hear it from Vicky. Instead of arguing, I simply say, "Thanks."

"Now that we're done thinking about today, because as amazing as you were, the show is over and well, the last two hours...no, two hours ago. Yes. That's when. The night sucked and not the good kind..."

His words trail away and I know him. I know he's falling

into a rabbit hole of memories, and if those memories involve sucking of any kind, I don't want to know. I don't want to hear about it. I must change the subject. "So what are we thinking about?"

"Right now..."

"No," I correct, "before that."

"Wine. I say we get more."

I shake my head slowly back and forth. "Not a good idea. My mom always says never drink more than you eat."

"Your mom is so smart. What else does she say?"

I shrug. "I don't know, some shit about marriage and babies and how happy she is for Kimbra and my cousin Kalli. And oh yeah, Pete, no, Patty...you know, that girl who works at the drug store who is now pregnant after years of trying."

"Pete is pregnant?"

"No, Patty," I correct. "She and I were in dance class together twenty years ago. She was also better at her pirouette than me."

"Oh, I'm sure you can do a pretty pirouette."

I start to stand and demonstrate my pirouette when the room begins to wobble. Just as quickly, I reach for the bed and hold on as the waves settle. "Maybe I can show you tomorrow?"

"That's a good idea. What I meant was, what else did your mom say about eating because on the menu it says that they have nachos."

"Nachos?"

"Yes," he says enthusiastically. "And you know what?"

"What?"

"I still have *his* credit card."

Of course, my mind goes to Trevor. We never got to the

credit card point in a relationship. To be honest, we never got further than what happened in that hallway. "I want a credit-card relationship."

"You want a what? Why? You have your own credit cards."

"No, don't you see? It's not about credit cards. It's trust. Max trusted you enough to share that information."

"Shit," Stephen says dejectedly.

"I'm sorry. What did I say?"

"You're making me feel guilty for wanting to charge his credit card for our room service."

"Why? He's a no-good, awful, terrible person. He doesn't deserve to have good credit. I say we charge the room and everything to him." I stand, holding onto the bed before making the full commitment. "I know. Tomorrow, we will shop!"

"I love shopping. That's tomorrow's plan."

"No, wait," I say, remembering Trevor for the one hundredth time in the last two hours. "I might have a date."

"A date? With sexy Trevor?"

"I'm sorry. I shouldn't be happy if you're not."

"I know what will make me happy."

"What?"

Stephen reaches for the phone on the nightstand. "Wine and nachos." He looks my direction and bats his eyelashes. "So you're good with another bottle of wine and a plate of nachos?"

"What will you say when he finds out?"

"I don't think he cares what I eat at nearly midnight. Hell, he doesn't care about anyone but himself and his pathetic assistant..."

I reach over, flop face-first onto the bed, and cover

Stephen's hand, thinking about what Trevor told me. "Maybe he just wasn't sure? Maybe he didn't know."

"You want me to tell him what I'm eating?"

I shrug. "Not what you're eating. But maybe talking to him is a good thing." Yes, I'm no longer talking about Max. Despite my best friend's heartache, I can't seem to get my mind off of Trevor. Then again, maybe there's some truth in this for both of us. "I think if there's any chance that in two weeks something can happen, communication is key."

"Why two weeks?"

"Because, no matter what, we're going back to London in two weeks. Either to pack or live."

"That could mean there's more than two weeks, depending on what happens."

I sigh. "I don't want the job to have anything to do with feelings."

"How can it not?"

I scoot around until I'm lying on the pillow. "I'm not a very good friend."

"You're a great friend."

"I can't think about Max when all that I'm thinking about is Trevor."

"I wouldn't be a good friend if I didn't know that. Now for the last time, wine and nachos?"

"Yes, but put it on our company charge. After all, we're recovering from the fashion show."

# CHAPTER
## Thirteen

### *Trevor*

*I* can't remember being more confused than I was last night. I didn't know what happened and obviously, my sister-in-law was no more informed than I.

One minute we're all standing around talking and laughing.

And while I was content to be part of the small group, I will admit that I was having trouble keeping my hands to myself. Shana was just too close and too beautiful. All the lies I'd told myself over the last year about how I could forget her flew out the window in that hallway. After that, I couldn't stop myself from constantly touching her shoulder, hair, or neck.

I did try to make it not too obvious, as I was trying to hide it from Kimbra.

I won't lie. That danger of discovery made it all the more exciting.

One of the great things about my sister-in-law is her conversational skills. I'm not sure how she and my brother will ever carry on the family name. I'm not sure she stops talking long enough for much more than wham-bam-thank-you-ma'am. Then again, I don't spend a lot of time considering my brother's sex life, only that his wife is beyond endowed with the gift of gab.

And then Max walked up to tell me it was my turn to play pool, and all hell broke loose.

Shana went full-out mother bear. I was lost.

It was kind of sexy seeing her all shouty and poking her finger at Max. The guy's been my friend for a few years and we've always gotten along, but I can see how sometimes he may come off as a bit of a pretentious ass. Then again, that wasn't what Shana was all up in his business about.

It was when Stephen walked up that the figurative pieces of the puzzle seemed to slide into place. I don't know what history there is between Stephen and Max—Max refused to talk about it later—but whatever it is, it does not appear to be good.

As soon as they left, I sent Shana a text, asking her what happened. I know Kimbra sent her one too. When she didn't respond, I sent another one that ignored the giant two-ton elephant in the room and simply asked if I could still call her in the morning.

She responded to the second one, saying yes and something about credit and cars. I took a screen shot of her reply and maybe one day I'll ask what it said. There were a few words that were merely jumbled letters and even one with symbols. As far as I know, they don't have any intelligible meaning. Maybe one day I'll find out. In the meantime, I sent back a smiling emoji and held out hope that in the morning she'd answer my call.

She did.

That's why I'm now here, at one of the girliest places I've ever seen.

Serendipity 3.

You see, I've replayed the scenes from the first time Shana and I were together over and over in my head. I've racked my brain to come up with something special, something to show her that I want to be part of her life. As much as I try to concentrate on those things, since last night, my thoughts slip back to the way she felt against my body while pushed against the wall and the pounding of her heart under that thin blouse. I can even imagine how her ass would have felt in the palm of my hands as I lifted her...

Yes, I'm more than a little aware that for our first official date, taking her to my apartment and doing what I wanted to do last night isn't exactly the most romantic of ideas even if I have thought about it every which way and a few ways I've never tried but would be more than willing to give it a go. That is why I'm meeting her at Serendipity 3.

I have two reasons for this location.

First, the name means the occurrence and development of events by chance in a happy or beneficial way—I looked it up. The way I remember the night that led her to my bed, it was completely a series of events of chance. I don't think it could be recreated if we tried. The other reason is that this restaurant is world-famous for its amazing hot chocolate. And even though the springtime weather is warm and sunny, I recalled something she told me.

The morning she woke in my bed, she mentioned she liked hot chocolate.

Now, as I wait, I hope she'll think this was a fun idea and not the desperate move of a desperate man.

I take a glance at my phone. As usual, I'm early. We didn't agree to meet for another fifteen minutes.

It's then that my phone rings. It's my brother.

I look around the restaurant and decide to speak quietly.

"Hey," I say.

"What the hell happened last night?"

"Great to talk to you too."

Duncan laughs in the easygoing way that should not be associated with someone like him. He's this big-time businessman who makes a fortune in shipping pharmaceuticals. It was a pretty ingenious plan that he and his friend devised. The idea was that as the population ages, medications will always be necessary. The production of medications, however, is too much work, not to mention time consuming and expensive. Instead, Duncan and his friend, Mike, decided the money was in logistics. Both the manufacturers and the distributors would pay big money for efficient shipping.

A man with that much on his plate shouldn't be laughing like he doesn't have a care in the world. Then again, that's one of the differences between the two of us. I'm the planner. It's what makes me a good engineer. Constructing roads and bridges can't be done on a whim. Apparently, starting a billion-dollar business can. Personally, I think his partner, Mike, is the true brains. Duncan is the charismatic one who keeps the investors and employees happy.

"Kimbra," he says, "was going on this morning about Shana and her friend Stephen. It was something about them leaving the bar upset."

"It was odd, I know. Kimbra and I spoke about it before she went home. I offered to call her a cab but being your wife, she was taken care of."

"I'm all for her strong will. Hell, I love it," he says. "But seriously, if she had her way, she would have come home alone via the subway."

It's my turn to laugh. "You know what, brother?"

"What?"

"You deserve her."

"I'm hoping that's a good thing."

"It is," I confirm. "You've always liked a challenge."

"Oh, Kimbra is definitely a challenge. One I'm glad I have."

Of course, my mind goes to Shana.

"So you don't know what happened?" Duncan asks.

"I got the impression that my friend Max—Maximilian Cantel—and Shana's friend Stephen have some history that isn't good. All I know for sure is that Shana laid into Max and after they left, Max refused to talk about it. He said the weekend was about Eric, not him."

"Hey, I'm glad you and Eric are still friends."

I'm ready to end this conversation, but his comment has me curious. "Why wouldn't we be? I've known him since college."

"But weren't you dating the woman he's marrying? Isn't she who you brought to my wedding?"

"What? No... oh, well... Um. We're good. They're better together. You know me...not much with the ladies."

"That brings me to the other reason I called," Duncan says. "Kimbra said something else about last night."

It's then that I look up and see Shana walking toward me. Immediately, I notice the flowing long skirt she's wearing, and my thoughts go back to my fantasies about the hallway last night. Those damn sexy jeans would have been a problem. I'm suddenly a huge advocate for skirts and dresses.

Her smile lights up the room as she comes closer.

"Duncan," I say, "I need to go. My date...umm, the person I'm meeting just arrived."

"Trevor, wait. A date? Who is it? Kimbra said she was getting a feeling—"

"Bye, Duncan. Talk to you later."

I hang up just as Shana makes it to the table, just in time to stand and pull out the chair for her.

# CHAPTER
## Fourteen

### *Shana*

$\mathcal{I}$t's been so long since I've been on a date—one that I actually care about, one that I want to succeed—that I am second-guessing everything, from my choice of clothes to the way to wear my hair. I know it's silly to act like a schoolgirl at twenty-seven years old, but I can't seem to help it.

This morning after copious amounts of coffee, Stephen gave me a pep talk, which was sweet because I could tell he is still upset about seeing Max. He's also not feeling too well. I think it's because he fell asleep before eating many of the nachos. I, on the other hand, made sure the plate was clean before placing it out in the hall. I won't tell my mother, but I think the nachos saved me. Even though I wasn't one hundred percent behind ordering them, I admit that I was feeling a bit tipsy before they arrived.

The fact that they also arrived with a new bottle of wine is simply another element added to my total alcohol intake for last night. Despite what some may think, I'm really not that much of a drinker. It's just that some situations call for alcohol. Celebrating a stranger's engagement and supporting your best friend are two that come to mind. I can't even relegate the fashion show to a cause for imbibing.

The sales were better than expected. Last night, after Stephen and I ordered the second bottle of wine, I checked my emails. There were two from Vicky. Neither was complimentary, yet they did have links to the sales spreadsheets. All of the chosen outfits had better-than-expected sales and according to sales in real time, the white negligee I wore had increased sales during and after the finale. Her last email said that all of the designers were content with the numbers.

If I were the one sending out the emails to my assistants in juniors, I would probably be over-the-top with adjectives describing my enthusiasm for both their hard work and the show.

This morning I sent one to Chantilly and the other assistants telling them how much I enjoyed working with them and thanking them for their time and energy in making the show a success.

It is my word: success.

I've decided to embrace it until I learn otherwise. After all, when my job is boiled down to the nuts and bolts, it's about sales. The sales were up. That equals success. So my drinking last night wasn't about the fashion show, but in support of Stephen.

That's my story and I'm sticking to it.

Each martini, each glass of wine...

No matter the amount or substance, I was there for Stephen. And he was there for me, following my mother's rule. Don't drink more than you eat. Last night's lesson, regardless of the alcohol source, was that there's something about gooey cheese, corn chips, and shredded chicken that apparently is very absorbent.

All in all, I may have gained five pounds last night, but I didn't wake with a hangover.

In my book, that's a win.

Now, I'm on my way to Serendipity 3, an iconic restaurant on the Upper East Side of Manhattan. It's where Trevor wanted to meet for lunch. I'm not only excited to see him, but to also see Serendipity 3. After years of living in the city, this will be my first visit. Maybe it is like Stephen and I said. Maybe I'm once again a tourist.

As the taxi approaches my destination, stopping and starting in city traffic, I reread my text messages from last night, thankful that I didn't respond to the first one Trevor sent. After all, it's not fair to be mad at him for being friends with Max. Last night, I was just too shocked and shaken for Stephen and his feelings to comprehend how we all ended up together.

I did send a text to Kimbra finally, apologizing for our abrupt exit and promising to get together, just the two of us, before I head back to London.

It was as I scrolled that I found one more text message that was more than a bit confusing. I'd like to say it wasn't from me, but unfortunately, it was. I suspect it was sent between pizza and nachos, around bottle two of wine.

It was sent to Trevor, and this is what it said:

**"YES, I STEAL WANT TO SEA U. 3ECAUSE OF YOUR @$$ AND FIVES. DO U THANK WE CAN CREDIT CARS?"**

Trevor's response was a simple smile emoji.
*What does that mean?*
*What exactly does my text mean?*

I suspect it has something to do with seeing him, liking his ass and thighs, and a question about credit cards—loosely translated to trust. While those are my thoughts, I hope not to have to discuss it.

*Why can't text messages be deleted the next day?*

It's a feature I believe would be well accepted by the majority of the population.

The cell phone companies could call it the gaslight feature. I know it would cost extra. I'd be willing to pay.

A simple message would replace the one that was deleted.

**"NO MESSAGE WAS EVER HERE. IT WAS YOUR IMAGINATION. GO BACK TO SLEEP AND STOP TEXTING."**

I smile as I consider the possibilities of this new feature. That is, until I recall my message that I can't take back. Once there, my mind returns to his ass and thighs, and I'm a little frightened that he might bring it up. I think the answer is clear: the combination of martinis, wine, and text messages is never a good idea.

The warm spring air fluffs my skirt as I step from the taxi onto the street. Looking all around, I see the Queensboro Bridge within sight and am reminded once again about my love for the city. Despite the time of day, there's already a line forming at the restaurant, and I hesitate to send a text, asking if Trevor is inside.

If I do and he didn't see the other one, I'm caught.

Instead of thinking any more about the texts, I look up at the Serendipity 3 storefront.

I can't really believe this is my first time here. Even though I've never visited the restaurant, of course, I've watched the movie. It's what I immediately think about as the gentle breeze blows my hair and I take it all in.

In the movie *Serendipity*, Jonathan and Sara have a chance meeting at Bloomingdale's.

Glancing down the street in the opposite direction of the bridge, the sight of the famous store makes me smile. The setting and scene really are as they were portrayed.

In the movie, the time between Jonathan and Sara's first meeting to their second is ten years. The first was a chance meeting brought on at Bloomingdale's over a pair of gloves. Trevor's and my first meeting was at a piano bar by a fire pit. It was brought on by us both being in Indianapolis for a wedding, the same wedding, which took us a little while to figure out.

Momentarily, I recall last night, in the hallway of the bar. The way he followed me. The dark hallway. His kiss. The tips of my fingers go to my lips, the phantom feeling is fleeting as my heartbeat quickens. Ten years may be good for a movie. For me, in real life, one year has been long enough.

Taking a deep breath, I step past the line and say a prayer that Trevor is already inside. I guess the only way to see if Serendipity is real is to test it.

"Excuse me," I say as I make my way toward the hostess stand.

The decorations within make me smile. They are exceedingly girly, bright, fun, and over-the-top. Tiffany lamps litter the ceiling in an array of colors and styles. The tables are close together and all seem to be occupied.

"Do you have a reservation?" the girl at the stand asks.

"I'm supposed to meet someone here," I say to the hostess.

After asking my name and the name of my party, the young girl leads me a few feet to a hidden corner with a small round table occupied by a man who seems too large for the scene. All at once, my entire body warms.

It's him.

In the split second before he notices me, I'm both amused and attracted. Though he's relaxed and talking on the phone, his presence here seems completely out of character. I can't help but wonder why he chose this restaurant. And then it happens.

His vibrant green eyes meet mine as the tips of his lips move upward and he stands. Almost immediately, he ducks as his height nearly collides with one of the lamps.

Damn, Trevor Willis is sexy surrounded by garish colorful lights. That's not something just any man could pull off. As I get closer, his stare fills me with something new. The butterfly wings in my tummy come to flight. It's as if he's lost sight of the rest of the world. It's as if his entire being is standing and seeing only me. I hope I'm right because at that moment I feel the same way. The bright decorations could fall and the chandeliers could crash to the floor, and it wouldn't matter because we're seeing one another.

I can't take my eyes off of him. His shirt pulls tightly over his broad chest. There's a casual sport coat draped from his broad shoulders, and it takes all of my control not to stare at his trim waist and perfectly worn blue jeans. I recall with vivid detail the way he pushed me against the wall in the hallway. My insides twist recalling the way his hardness pressed toward me.

I move my gaze upward and smile at his sexy, messy hair. I've seen Trevor Willis dressed up for the night or a wedding, and I've seen him when he first wakes, with basketball shorts and his thick thighs. No matter the occasion, his hair is definitely something I adore. It always seems out of place, as if it's in need of my fingers to comb it away from his stunning green eyes.

"You made it," he says happily as he ducks under the lamps and pulls the chair out for me.

"I'm not late? Am I?"

"No, I'm just anxious," he says with all honesty as he pushes in my chair and gives me a kiss on the cheek. It's romantic and chivalrous and reminds me how a gentleman is supposed to treat a lady.

While some may find it old-fashioned, I like it.

That's how our first official date begins, with niceties and gestures, with simple conversation that flows too easily yet is capable of tying my stomach into knots. Everything about Trevor Willis is sweet, sexy, and funny.

We are too interested in one another to even look at the giant menu. Finally, after the waitress leaves for the second time, we both decide we need to take a look.

"We have to get the frozen hot chocolate," I say, finally peering at the scrumptious-looking pictures. "I saw a few on my walk back to the table. They look amazing."

"Frozen hot chocolate with two straws," Trevor tells our waitress when she returns for the third time.

Once she's gone, I turn to him. "I'm a little surprised this is where you wanted to meet." I gesture about. "It's a little...small. I almost feel like you don't fit."

He chuckles. "It is a little smaller than I expected. But don't you like it?"

"I do."

"The real question is...do you believe in serendipity?"

My grin grows. "I was just thinking about that same question when I arrived and the taxi dropped me off."

"You were?"

"Have you seen the movie?" I ask.

"There's a movie?"

I giggle, shaking my head.

*Men.*

"Yes," I say. "Oh my gosh, you wanted to come here even though you haven't seen the movie?"

He shakes his head.

"Then what made you think of here?"

"You."

"Me?" I ask, genuinely curious. "Why me?"

"The morning of Duncan and Kimbra's wedding, I ordered us coffee and you told me you like hot chocolate."

My mouth opens, but it takes a minute before words come out. "What?"

"Now, don't tell me that was still the Fireball talking. I mean, I hope I'm not sitting in an explosion of Tiffany lamps at a table too small for me when in reality you hate hot chocolate."

"No," I say quickly. "I love hot chocolate. I just can't believe you remember that."

He reaches over and covers my hand with his. "Shana Price, I remember every second we've been together."

Warmth fills my cheeks. "I can't say the same."

His laugh is deep, rumbling through the air from him to me. Soon, I'm laughing too.

"That's what makes it special."

"I mean, I know what happened," I explain, "because you told me. And well, the holes in the memories from that first night aren't as large as they were the morning I woke."

He releases my hand as the waitress returns with a large glass bowl of frozen hot chocolate overflowing with whipped cream and complete with two straws.

"It's huge!"

Trevor looks at me and grins. "It's taking everything within me not to say what I'm thinking."

I waggle my eyebrows. "Oh, come on. *That's what she said.*"

"I only care about one *she*. Hopefully, one day I'll learn what *she* says."

"Shall we?" I point toward the frozen hot chocolate.

"I'm ready whenever you are."

As I move forward, pursing my lips over the straw, I wonder how long we could take this conversation before we were too inappropriate for some of the young patrons sitting nearby.

"It's thicker than I thought," he says after a few drinks. "You really have to suck."

I can't take it anymore as I grab my napkin and hope I won't spit frozen hot chocolate through my nose as I laugh. It's contagious and soon we're both sucking and laughing and dropping terrible double entendres. Somehow, we manage to finish our hot chocolate and each eat some lunch.

Once we're finished and extremely full, Trevor asks, "I'm hoping I can occupy more of your afternoon?"

I was hoping the same thing. That's why I told Stephen not to wait up for me. Before I can answer, Trevor goes on.

"It's a nice day out there. Have you had much of a chance, with the fashion show and all, to see the city?"

"I've had no time."

His head tilts a bit. "Well, my lady, do you have time now?"

"I'm free until work tomorrow...Wait, I don't mean..."

Trevor reaches for my hand and lifts it to his lips. "Then let's go see the city."

# CHAPTER
## *Fifteen*

### *Shana*

The sun has risen higher in the blue sky. Once we're past the growing waiting crowd, Trevor starts to head west, and I hope I know where he's taking me. "Are we going to the park?"

"Unless you want to stop at Bloomingdale's?"

"Only if we can both try to buy the same gloves."

"You don't need gloves." He retakes my hand. "I'll keep your hand warm."

Even though that wasn't what I meant and he totally missed the movie reference, I like his alternative.

The city is alive with people hurrying from here to there. On corners, the music of street performers fills the air, temporarily masking the sounds of traffic. It's New York City and I'm finally glad to be here.

"You know," I say as we near the park, "it's nice not to worry about the fashion show any longer. It's done. Now only time will tell."

"I couldn't believe it when I saw you up there."

I shake my head. "What are the chances you'd be there?"

"Probably about the same as being in that bar the night before the wedding."

"Serendipity."

Trevor nods.

"You know," I say, "if you would have called me recently, you'd have known I was going to be here in New York." I'm not sure what made me say that, but the words are out and I can't take them back.

Trevor leads us to a bench near the entrance of Central Park. Once we sit, he says, "Phones are funny things. Mine rings too."

"Oh, I deserve that."

"Can I be honest with you?"

"I'd prefer you never be dishonest with me."

He squeezes my hand. "You scare the shit out of me."

"Me?"

"You, Shana Price. I told you something about me the night we met. Do you remember?"

"I do, but I'm not sure that was truthful."

"I promise it was."

"You said you are awkward around women?"

"That's it."

"Do you remember what you did after you told me that?" I ask, hoping he does.

Trevor doesn't answer; instead, he leans toward me until our lips touch.

On a warm afternoon with people milling about, the world disappears. It's not the fervent explosion of last night.

It's more.

It's sunshine and freshly cut grass, bicyclists and horse-drawn carriages. It's a walk in the park and sharing a giant frozen hot chocolate. It is the careful tending of a fire, the diligent care that is needed to keep the flames burning, their intensity growing with each moment we're together.

When our kiss ends, we both stare into one another's eyes. Finally, it's Trevor who speaks.

"That was what I did. Now, do you remember what happened next?"

I take a deep breath and close my eyes. "Can we please forget that part?"

"Nope. Never. When it comes to you, I don't want to ever forget a second. And I want to keep learning. Tell me something about you that I don't know."

"I love New York pizza."

He shakes his head. "No way. Cop-out answer. Everyone loves New York pizza. It's the best in the whole world. Tell me something else."

"Well, I have family in Illinois who would wholeheart-edly disagree. Chicago has pretty good pizza, too."

"That age-old debate was obviously settled from your first answer. Chicago's pizza is deep-dish. Real pizza comes from New York."

I grin as I take a second and decide to tell him some-thing that even I'm unsure about, something I don't want to admit. "I'm afraid that I messed up my chances to get the job in ladies' lingerie. I don't regret what I did, going onstage. The show had to go on. But now I am afraid."

"What's the worst thing that can happen if you don't get it?"

I swallow, thinking about his question. It's a good ques-tion. I like that his response isn't false reassurance. Instead, he's making me think about the possibilities. "I guess the worst thing is that I don't get to move back here...*and we will be apart again*." I don't say the last part.

"Don't you like London?"

"I do. I really do. I think I'm a little lonely."

"How can you be lonely with Stephen? He seems like when he's not upset, he could be a lot of fun."

I scoff. "He's even fun when he's upset."

"Is he helpful?"

"Yes. He's the best at...well, most everything."

"I was wondering if he could help me with something."

"Stephen? My Stephen? What do you need help with?"

"I was wondering if he could help decipher a text message I received last night."

"Oh my gosh!" I lean forward until my chest is flush with my knees and cover my head with my hands. My words are muffled against my skirt. "I was hoping you wouldn't mention that."

"Can I take the funny symbols to mean you like my ass?"

I peer up at him. "Seriously? You're going to call me out on one drunken text?"

His smile grows. "If it means you like my ass, you're forgiven. I have a secret that shouldn't be too secret."

I sit back up and look him in the eye. "I already know you're not great with women. Which isn't true, by the way. What other secret do you have?"

"I like your ass."

I shake my head. "Is that all?"

"Oh no. I like your ass and..." He takes his finger and traces my cheek. "Your eyes. Your smile." His finger continues moving downward. "The way you shivered as I kissed your neck."

"I'm ticklish."

He keeps going, his touch moving along the side of my breasts. "Your tits."

"They're not that impressive. Have you seen my best friend's?"

Trevor laughs. "I didn't think Stephen's were that remarkable. Yours are definitely more impressive."

His response makes me giggle.

"I love your laugh. And in this dress and even in the jeans last night, you have shapely, sexy legs." He looks back to me, our gazes set on one another. "There's a part of you that I haven't experienced, somewhere between your tits and legs, and believe me, I want to."

"Rather direct for a man not good around women."

"That's why you scare the shit out of me. When I'm around you, I say things I'd never say. I want things, things I'm willing to do anything to get. I also want to be everything you deserve. That means that even though my first idea for this date was taking you to my apartment and getting to know that part of you that I'm missing, we drank frozen hot chocolate and are about to walk around Central Park."

I stand and hold out my hand to him. "Come on. Let's walk. Remember, I'm free until work in the morning."

Trevor's eyes sizzle, golden flakes exploding like fireworks as he reaches for my hand.

Hand in hand, we walk along the main path, taking in the crowds of people, all most likely brought out by the nice weather. New Yorkers are a hardy bunch. Winter doesn't stop them, but spring brings them out of the woodwork. Like rats in the subway, and yes, I mean that favorably, sunshine, flowers, and budding leaves awaken the masses.

"Can I ask you about one other thing that's been bugging me?" Trevor asks.

"Sure."

"Do you want to steal cars or is there something about credit?"

I twist and play punch his shoulder. "Stop. My autocorrect was having problems last night."

"Oh, we're blaming autocorrect?"

"Yes. That's my story and I'm sticking to it."

After nearly two hours of walking and one pedicab ride, we're back to the entrance.

"May we continue this date on to dinner?" Trevor asks.

"I want to." And I really do.

"I sense something else."

"It's Kimbra. Since I arrived in the city, I've only seen her last night, and as you know, I kind of left abruptly. She's sent me a few hundred text messages this afternoon and wants me to come over to her apartment."

Trevor's smile grows. "I think she's setting you up."

"What? Why?"

He pulls his phone from his pocket. When he shows me the screen, he too has multiple text messages from Kimbra and a few from Duncan.

"When you came into the restaurant, I was talking to my brother. I mentioned that my date arrived. Since then, the two of them have been blowing up my phone. I had to put it on silent. Kimbra thinks she sensed something between us last night."

My eyes widen as I chew momentarily on my bottom lip. "You mean we aren't as good of actors as we thought?"

"Apparently, neither of us should give up our day jobs for Broadway."

"Well, there goes that backup plan."

"Right?" he asks. "All those voice lessons down the drain."

"You sing?"

"Only in the shower."

My cheeks rise and heat as they undoubtedly fill with pink.

Trevor reaches for my hand and hails a taxi. "That's it. I'm taking you to my apartment to hear me sing."

"Trevor..."

When the taxi stops, he gives the driver an address that right away I recognize.

"Wait a minute. You don't seriously think we should show up at Kimbra and Duncan's together. Do you?"

Before he answers, I willingly get into the back seat.

"My lady, I'm tired of keeping our history a secret." He turns my way as the taxi moves forward. "We can change our destination. We can go to my apartment or you back to your hotel. But no matter where we go, I'm not making the same mistake I made before. This will not be our only date. I want another one and another one. I think coming clean to Duncan and Kimbra is the first step."

"What if they're upset?"

"It won't stop us. Nothing will stop us." He leans close and kisses me.

I've never wanted anyone to be more right about anything.

# CHAPTER
## *Sixteen*

***Trevor***

*O*f course, my brother and his wife live in the penthouse, their apartment complete with an amazing view of the Empire State building. "Have you been here before?" I ask Shana as the elevator moves upward.

"Once."

"Good."

Shana turns my way and smiles. Today's walk in the sun and wind has left her cheeks pinkened. Her hair is pulled back in a long ponytail, the ends twisting into long curls and her eyes are wide. "Is there a reason we're now talking in one-word sentences?"

"I was just thinking that it was a dick move to bring you here before my apartment."

"Why?"

"Now, who's using one word?"

Thankfully we're alone in the elevator as it continues its climb. To access the penthouse, you must first check in on the lobby floor and the doorman must enter a key, unless of course, it's your penthouse and then you have a key.

"Okay, why was it a dick move?" she asks, leaning back against the wall of the elevator.

I look at the numbers changing above the door and know there's no way I have time to explain that my apartment pales in comparison to Duncan's. Instead, I lean over and kiss her cheek. "Because I would rather be back at my place serenading you."

Shana squeezes my hand. "If you can't carry a tune in a bucket, I'm going to be very disappointed."

"No, my lady, when we're together in my shower, I promise you won't be disappointed."

Shana takes her free hand and reaches out to the elevator's control panel, her finger poised to push something.

"What are you doing?"

"I'm looking for the turn-around button."

"I don't think—"

We both still as the elevator comes to a halt and the doors slowly open.

The entry before us is an expansive foyer with two large doors leading to one destination.

"Once, before they were married," Shana explains, "Duncan was out of town and I was in town. I stayed here with Kimbra for two nights."

Before I can respond, one of the grand doors opens and both Kimbra and Duncan are standing in the open frame. Their expressions are a mixture of emotions that seem to be waiting for us to comment.

"Hi," Shana says, stepping forward and hugging Kimbra. "Sorry about last night."

"Come on in," Duncan says.

Once the women are ahead of us, he pats my shoulder. "Sly, I like it."

It's no secret that I'm not overly thrilled to get dating advice from my older brother.

Their apartment is luxury at its finest—marble floors, fireplaces, and floor-to-ceiling windows. I think back to when Duncan first bought the penthouse. With his reputation as a lady's man, I expected it to be the ultimate bachelor pad, a place with a revolving door where the doorman allowed only one woman up at a time—unless instructed differently.

To his credit, as far as I know, it never was.

With my experience in architecture, I could better describe the penthouse by assessing the square footage and mentioning the twelve-foot-high ceilings or custom woodwork and molding. While that's all impressive, what really matters is that it's fucking huge with a to-die-for wraparound balcony. And despite all of that, for years this beautiful apartment was simply the place where he slept.

Kimbra really has changed his life.

Looking around now, I see the subtle differences since they married: color and accents. If Max were here he might call them *homey touches* such as pictures of the two of them, as well as other photography of the city and artwork that was never here before.

Through the years, my brother and I haven't always seen eye to eye. There's the natural brotherly competition, and yet for some reason as I stand here at this second, I see him differently.

With our history, this is a welcome revelation.

"Wine?" Kimbra asks.

"I'm fine," Shana replies.

The difference in Shana's demeanor from the park to now makes me uncomfortable. I don't want to be the cause of any problem between her and her best friend, even if that best friend is my brother's wife.

Taking a deep breath, I jump in with both feet. "Wow, I bet the two of you..." speaking directly to Duncan and Kimbra, "...would never believe that Shana and I ran into one another in the lobby?" I look to Shana whose eyes are wide. "Actually, it was our taxis that arrived about the same time. Right?"

"Umm," Shana says, "we did arrive at the same time."

"Because?" Kimbra prompts, not letting us off the hook.

Shana rushes toward Kimbra. "I'm sorry. I wanted to tell you, but I didn't know how."

I can't help but notice Duncan's large smile. Soon, his wife is smiling as widely. "That's it," Kimbra says. "Spill. I know darn well that you didn't accidentally bump into one another in the lobby or sidewalk. I want all the juicy details."

As Kimbra speaks, Shana and I sit and our hands come together. From the strength of her grip, I know that she's more nervous about this then she's let on.

"Oh my goodness, you're holding hands." Kimbra says, practically bouncing on the edge of the sofa facing us. "Last night...your lips!"

"What?" Duncan asks.

"It wasn't an allergic reaction. Was it?"

"We should have told you," Shana confesses, blowing my well-contrived lie out of the water. "It's that we didn't want to complicate your wedding."

"Whoa, our wedding?" Duncan says.

"That was nearly a year ago," Kimbra remarks as if the wheels are turning in her head. "You two...this has been going on...for a year?"

Shana's big blue eyes turn my way and I begin our story. "Yes and no. You're right. We arrived in the same taxi and how about before we give you all the details, we take you up on that offer of some wine?"

"Only if Shana will help me find the glasses," Kimbra says standing and beckoning Shana away from us.

Before she goes, I give her hand one last squeeze.

Instead of talking, Duncan leans back against the sofa and stares. I can't tell if it's his CEO look or just his cocky *I'm better than you* attitude. With each passing second, his grin grows until I find myself debating about yelling at him or jumping up from the sofa and punching him. Because that's what brothers do or what being with my brother makes me think of doing.

"Stop," I finally say.

"No way. I'm enjoying this."

"What?"

"Seeing my little brother smitten."

"Smitten?" It seems like I've heard that recently. "What kind of word is that?"

Duncan shrugs. "It's what Kimbra calls it. I like it. It means—"

"Bro, I'm the one with the master's degree. I know what it means."

Instead of flinging back with a comment on how my education hasn't given me the empire he's built, Duncan stays calm, cool, and collected. "It looks good on you," he says, moving his head up and down. "You know, better than that brooding loner thing."

I exhale. "You're not mad?"

"Fuck no. All I want is for you to be happy."

"Whatever this is," I say, "started the night before your wedding. After that, I let her go, and I've regretted it for a year. I'm not letting her go again."

"Then don't fuck this up. Kimbra loves Shana like the sister she never had. That makes the woman who was holding your hand like family." His nose scrunches. "Okay, that seems weird, but whatever. Whatever you do, don't piss off my wife."

"I've seen your wife pissed."

Duncan laughs. "Christmas last year. Who knew a delivery company could be persuaded to deliver on the holiday?"

"She didn't give them a choice."

We both laugh, remembering Kimbra's persuasive technique.

"Yeah, no one wants her upset." I turn the direction of the kitchen. "They're taking a while to get glasses."

Duncan tips his head toward the other side of the room. Nestled near the fireplace and built-in bookcases, there's a small bar area with a large wine refrigerator and stemmed glasses hanging below the shelf above. "Especially since the glasses aren't in the kitchen."

We both chuckle as the ladies come out of the kitchen empty-handed but thankfully, smiling from ear-to-ear.

"No glasses?" I ask.

"Actually," Kimbra says with a smirk, "we were checking on dinner. It's still baking but should be ready in a half hour. In the meantime..." she goes to the wine bar and reaches for the glasses. The crystal clinks as she brings four large round goblets and places them on the table between us. "Red or white?"

Once we're all properly equipped with our glasses, I begin.

"The night before your wedding, at a small piano bar in the hotel in Indianapolis, I happened to go outside to the fire pits and saw the most beautiful woman—"

"Wait," Duncan interrupts, talking to Kimbra, "...the

*most beautiful*...I thought you spent that night at your parents'?"

Shana and I laugh as Kimbra slaps his chest. "I love you. Now, shut up and let Trevor talk. I just adore stories with happy endings."

My gaze meets Shana's as she begins to speak.

"The ending isn't set, but right now, we want to see where this takes us."

I clear my throat. "Well, the strangest thing happened with that beautiful woman; I was instantly..." I think of the right word. "...smitten."

"Smitten?" Shana asks.

Duncan smiles as Kimbra bounces and says, "See, I told you!"

Two hours later, the four of us are laughing and talking as we finish the remainder of dessert. "Damn," I say, "Kimbra, my brother definitely doesn't deserve you. Not only are you beautiful, but you're also an amazing cook."

Her cheeks grow pink. "Confession time."

"What?"

"The chicken Marsala was mine and being from Indiana, I make a killer green-bean casserole; however, the cannoli, not so much. They came from that great little bakery on Mulberry Street." She turns to Shana. "I had Duncan go pick them up for you."

"Oh shit," Shana says as she begins to giggle and her face drops a little. "You're a bitch."

"But you love me."

"What's going on?" I ask.

Duncan looks to Shana. "Kimbra said that you like cannoli, and she wasn't sure when the last time was that you had really good New York cannoli."

I can't figure out what's happening. All I know is that now both Shana and Kimbra are laughing.

"Am I the only one who doesn't know what's going on?" I ask.

"No, bro, I'm pretty clueless." Duncan speaks to Shana. "Don't you like cannoli?"

Shana's voice is all strained from laughing as if she's gasping to breathe. "I love cannoli as much as the next woman. Right, Kimbra?"

"I definitely love cannoli, the bigger the better." She lifts her wine glass to her lips before adding, "I especially love the cream filling."

It's then that Duncan's hands go into the air. "Seriously? Are you kidding me? You sent me to a bakery across town to get edible penises?"

I spit a little as I look down at my empty plate. "Shit and you let us sit here and eat them?"

Kimbra's entire face is almost as red as her hair because she's laughing so hard. "I wanted Duncan to get them yesterday. You know, so they wouldn't be as fresh."

"So they'd be hard," Shana adds, almost choking on her laughs.

My lady isn't the only one who's laughing. All four of us are cracking up.

Finally, I stand. "I'm getting some water. Would anyone else like some water to wash away the cannoli?"

Duncan raises his hand as the two women look at each other and break into another fit of laughter.

"Hey," Kimbra calls as I make my way toward the kitchen. "Spitting is for quitters."

When the night finally comes to an end, we stand near the elevator as Kimbra hugs Shana.

"I know the future is unwritten, but I just want you to know that the two of you have our full support."

Duncan nods.

Kimbra goes on, "And if you, Trevor Willis, hurt my friend, I will hunt you down."

Duncan nods again, this time chuckling to himself.

"Yes," I say, "I've been warned." I reach for Shana's hand. "All I can promise is that I will do my best to not let that happen."

Duncan's hand lands on my shoulder. "That's good. I don't want to be the one to tell Mom and Dad that my wife made me an only child."

Kimbra crosses her arms over her chest. "But I would do it."

As I hug her goodbye, I whisper, "You're kind of scary."

"Don't forget that," she replies as she kisses my cheek.

When the elevator doors close, Shana leans toward me. "I got the feeling you weren't looking forward to that."

"I wasn't, but I think it was the best time I've had with my brother in...well, in a long time." I reach for her hand. "Now, my lady, shall we discuss Italian pastries?"

Her cheeks fill with pink before she leans in and kisses my cheek. "How about I go back to my place tonight and maybe we can meet for dessert tomorrow night?"

"As long as I can accompany you to your hotel." Before Shana responds, I add, "Only to the door, my lady. I can't let you ride across town alone."

"I think I'm..."

I shake my head. "You're capable. I just want to be sure you don't share a drink with anyone at the piano bar. You know, there are some men out there who may try to take advantage of you."

"I guess that means that I found the right man." She tilts her head. "But maybe soon, he'll decide that taking advantage wouldn't be such a bad idea."

"Oh, he already has given that some thought."

"Good."

# CHAPTER
## *Seventeen*

### *Shana*

*M*onday evening, Stephen and I walk out of Saks and onto busy Fifth Avenue as the traffic picks up its pace. In New York City that means the volume increases as the speed decreases. Across the street, tourists as well as employees buzz in and out of Rockefeller Center. The city is filled with electricity, yet the traffic and iconic buildings are merely blips on my already-full radar. I'm thinking, instead, about the ongoing discussions I've been having most of the day up on the tenth floor of this famous store.

According to Vicky and others in our meetings, the sales from the fashion show were even better than the earlier emails indicated. Nevertheless, fashion headlines are still mentioning the change in models. What I'd hoped would go virtually unnoticed is trending with the following hashtags: #mysterymodelmayhemwhoisthatgirl #sakssexysub and #sakssecretmysterymodel.

It wasn't mayhem. It was orchestrated and constructed. That's what I spent a better part of today reminding myself —and others.

"Don't let her get to you," Stephen says as we take a moment to enjoy the warm breeze.

I don't want to think about it anymore. I've been the

good and strong salesperson through it all. Now with just the two of us, the emotion that has been building all day is boiling just below the surface and if I talk about it, I may break down. "I'd say that it's probably too late for that advice."

"Nine more days," Stephen reminds me. "We have nine more working days here before the final decision is set to be made. I say we make the most of it. I say we enjoy the city."

"I'm sorry...I thought I told you that I have plans for tonight."

He waves his hand. "Oh, boss lady, you did. And even though I could get my feelings hurt that you're leaving me again..."

"What if I told you that there's a very good reason?"

"I'd say that I met him and I know!"

I force a laugh, and then as my mind moves from Saks Fifth Avenue to Trevor, the laughter flows, no longer forced. I shrug. "It's simple. I find myself famished for Italian pastries."

"I love that Kimbra remembered that. Personally, I'm a cannoli man myself and when I move into that apartment in the East Village, I plan on indulging."

I arch my brows.

"Veniero's are truly the best." He laughs at himself. "Maybe I should call Kimbra to hang out. She's hilarious."

I shake my head as we both slide into the taxi taking us back to the hotel. "I can't believe she did that at her dinner party. What made it even funnier was that neither Trevor nor Duncan had a clue."

"Doesn't your man need to work?"

"He is working today. The engineering firm he works for is here in the city. Yesterday, he said something about following up on some bids for a few new projects and proposing others. I guess it is a merry-go-round of stages when it comes to what he does." I shrug. "Not a lot different from us."

"How do you figure?"

"Well, we work on next season's fashions while figuring out how to sell this season's. It sounds the same with him. They find projects, bid projects, and then, if accepted, the next step is construction.

"There's a lot more to it, but right now, he's in the bidding part of one he's particularly interested in." I shrug. "He's very smart."

"I'm sure that's only one of his good qualities," Stephen says with a sly smile.

I shrug. "I mean, I learned about most of this when we used to talk on the phone. It amazes me how he can look at a space and see what isn't there."

"Maybe he can also see what is?"

"Like?" I ask.

"Like a woman who I think has one of the best minds in fashion yet is genuinely interested in boring things like bridges and roads."

I tilt my head toward the window. "Think about it. They aren't boring. They're simply taken for granted. Whether here or in London or in some small town, roads and bridges have to withstand the stress and tension of tons of pounds of force. Think of the Brooklyn Bridge or the Queensboro."

"Will it hurt your feelings if I tell you that I don't want to think about a bridge?"

"Trust me. It's more exciting when Trevor talks about it."

Stephen pats my knee. "I'm sure it is. But really, don't

worry about me. I'm meeting up with some old friends tonight. We're headed to dinner and drinks in the village."

Though I can't say how happy I am to hear that, I wouldn't be surprised if the relief shows. After all, I'm the one who dragged Stephen here to New York. It's because of me that he ran into Max. I hate the idea of him sitting in his hotel room all alone while I'm out with Trevor.

"I guess with the last two weeks being so consumed with the show, I forgot that you're from here too."

He looks out the window as we pull up to the hotel. "I am, originally from upstate. My parents want me to go up there over the weekend. I was hesitant, not wanting to leave my boss lady alone in this big old bad city." He winks. "I don't think I need to worry any longer."

After paying the driver, we both pause on the sidewalk outside the hotel. The evening breeze has picked up and the sunshine is obstructed by the tall buildings. I wrap my arm around my midsection as goose bumps appear on my arms. "I'm sorry."

"For?" Stephen asks.

"For everything. For dragging you here. For what happened Saturday night. For messing up our chance of staying here—close to your family and friends."

"Don't say that."

"I think it's pretty obvious that you want to stay here. You have a deposit on an apartment."

"I'm thinking you might have a reason you want to move back here too. And it has nothing to do with an apartment."

I shrug. "I don't know yet. I'll admit that it was fun to hang out with Duncan and Kimbra as two couples, and yesterday when it was just the two of us, I had a great time."

"And...?"

We step aside as people pass us.

"And...I'm nervous. I've worked too hard and too long to change my career for a man, one I barely know."

"How long did you two talk on the phone?"

I look up to the blue sky, wishing the sun were directly overhead as I think about his question. "For a few months, off and on."

"What did you learn about Mr. Trevor Willis during that time?"

My smile broadens. "You mean besides bridges and roads?"

"Yeah, girl, give me something juicy."

"Everyday stuff. He likes comedies and action movies. He's always reading some book or another. His favorites are thrillers, but he also reads boring nonfiction—biographies and stuff like that." I tilt my head as I recall some of our conversations. "And when he talks about those boring books, they aren't boring. He even listened when I told him about what I was reading or about the latest trends in prom dresses or midriff tops. Not just nodding—well, because we were on the phone—but actually listening. He remembers what I say and asks questions."

"Why did the calls stop?"

My shoulders droop as I lean against the building, unsure why we haven't gone inside. "I blame him for not calling—or I did—but honestly, it was me too. I found myself rearranging my schedule to be home when he called. The time difference was a bitch. I decided I couldn't do it anymore."

"So what happened?"

"He called and I didn't answer."

"Purposely?" he asks.

"A few times and then I'd forget to return his calls. I'd blame it on the time difference even when that wasn't the reason."

"What was the reason?" He leans close and cocks an eyebrow. "It was the bridges and biographies, wasn't it?"

"No. I think the whole thing scared me. I was growing accustomed to it. I didn't even notice when men were hitting on me. I mean I would, but later. My mind was too full of Trevor. It felt wrong, like I shouldn't give up me to be with him. Besides, I wasn't with him. We were on two separate continents."

Stephen puts his hands in his pockets and spends a minute digesting my response. "Is that what you think? A relationship means giving up who you are?"

Once again, I shrug.

"It's not like I'm an expert, and my recent run is pretty shitty, but when I'm in a relationship, I find that the more I think about him, the less I think about me, but it's not like I become less because when the other person is the right person to be in your life, they're doing the same thing. Together you're more than either could be alone. It's not taking or losing. It's complementing."

I feel tears begin to prickle behind my eyes. I'm not sure if it's because I want so badly what Stephen is describing or if it's because I have never had that. Then again, maybe the tears are because I want that relationship for Stephen too.

He gives me a hug. "Come on, boss lady. No crying."

I nod as he leads me to the large revolving door. A few moments later while we're waiting for the elevator, he says, "I think you're a lot braver than you think."

I scoff. "Are you kidding? I just told you that I'm scared."

"Hell no, I'm not kidding. Admitting fear is actually brave. And I'll give you another example: you went out on that stage in a white see-through negligee because it was what needed to be done. You walked out there proudly, nipple tape and all."

By the time he stops talking, my mouth is agape, and we're getting sideways looks from more than a few people. "It was not see-through."

"Oh, right."

My mind fills with the memories of seeing myself in the mirror. There was lace that went down between my breasts that prohibited a bra, but I know for certain that silk was body-glued to my skin. I turn toward Stephen as we wedge into the elevator and whisper, "How did you know I had on nipple tape?"

His laugh is his only answer.

I'm not sure if I should be upset or worried or laugh along with him.

"It was not see-through," I state matter-of-factly.

My comment does nothing but make him laugh more.

When we finally step out of the elevator, our rooms being on the same floor, I punch his shoulder. "You're mean."

Stephen leans in and kisses my cheek. "No, I'm not. Have fun tonight and don't wait up for me. I could end up spending the night with friends in the village. I promise to be at the office bright and early with two cups of steaming Starbucks."

With that, he disappears down the hallway toward his room.

"You are mean," I repeat, but only at a volume that I can hear.

# CHAPTER

*Eighteen*

### *Shana*

*T*he restaurant high in the sky is filled with customers, every table an island among the sea of flickering candles within the ocean of windows offering the most spectacular view of New York City. Our conversation pauses as the waiter returns with Trevor's credit card. I take in the stunning view as he signs the final bill and closes the small folder.

This is our second real date, third if you count the first night at the piano bar in Indianapolis. The thought makes me smile. Three dates in the course of a year. No one can say that we're rushing things. As soon as he places the pen on the tablecloth, I lean forward and speak. "Dinner was amazing. You really don't need to buy each time. I do have a spending stipend from Saks to cover my meals."

Trevor just smiles.

"You know," I offer, "I also know how to cook."

"And does your hotel room have a nice kitchen?"

"I could invite you back to see it. Really, it's amazing for a suite. The microwave oven is out of this world."

His smile grows. "I like the invitation. I could even bring some microwave popcorn."

I lay my hand on my stomach. "I'd say yes, but I believe I'm stuffed. One piece of popcorn and I may explode."

Trevor stands and reaches for my hand. The warmth

envelops me from my fingers within his grasp all the way to my toes. However, as I stand our connection breaks, and we casually move as a couple between the tables. And then, within a few steps, his hand returns, this time covering the small of my back.

I struggle with myself to admit that I like the way it feels to have him with me and how easy it is to fall into his lead as if we're connected as one.

"Where to?" I ask as we stall just inside the large glass doors on the ground floor. Outside, the sidewalk is crowded with people as taxis and horns fill the street.

"That, my lady, is up to you. I know you had a big day at work today, and I wasn't sure what you'd be up for doing."

"Would you like to see my microwave?"

The gold flecks sparkle as he knowingly returns my grin. "You know, I have a full kitchen in my apartment."

"No?"

"I do. I admit I don't use it much, but I too can pop some scrumptious popcorn."

I lean close and throw caution to the wind. This is our third date and no matter what the powers that be at Saks decide, I'll be headed back to London in less than two weeks. "How about my microwave tonight and your kitchen tomorrow? I could stop and pick up some groceries after work and wow you with my culinary skills."

"Or you could allow me to show you that I can cook something besides popcorn?" He stands tall and puffs out his chest. "After all, I've survived for thirty-plus years. I can make more than microwave meals."

I lift my eyebrows, widening my stare. "Yes, Trevor, I'd say you've survived quite well." I reach out and splay my fingers across his chest. "Probably not a lot of desserts."

He reaches for my hand. "If you are asking if I can make a cannoli, I already have one."

Heat fills my cheeks as my smile turns bashful. "I know."

When he looks at me with a questioning expression, I go on, "I could tell the other night at the bar."

"Shana?"

"Trevor, I'd like to have you come back to my room." The words sound sure but saying them cranked up my pulse until I'm worried that if he doesn't answer soon, I may faint.

His hands move upward and gently palm my cheeks. Slowly, he moves closer until our lips touch. When he pulls away, my eyes open wide to his. I'm lost in the golden flecks within his stare until he speaks.

"If I go to your hotel, I don't want popcorn."

I let out a soft giggle. "What do you want?"

"Shana, I want the same thing I've wanted since the night before the wedding. I want you." He leans back and takes me in. The heat from his stare is like a flame on my skin as his eyes scan from my shoes to my eyes. "All of you. I want all of you."

"I guess that's good."

"You guess?"

"I don't have any popcorn."

One more kiss and we step hand in hand out onto the sidewalk as the doorman flags us a taxi.

Other than the outside noise, the ride is quiet as we both silently watch the world pass by outside the windows of the taxi. The streets never seem to care if it's day or night. The traffic remains. My mind and body twist with eager anticipation. The overwhelming expectancy is like a warm fog surrounding us, filling the taxi with its sweet scent. It's as if we're floating instead of driving to our destination.

Subconsciously, I nibble upon my lip as I overanalyze what we're about to do. It's not like I'm naïve. I'm a grown woman who knows exactly what she just agreed to have happen, and yet in some ways, I feel as though I'm at as much of a loss as I was my first time.

Don't misunderstand. I'm not a virgin, and I know the fundamentals. It's just that it's been a long time since I've had what Kimbra and I used to refer to as mind-blowing sex.

As I think back on my not-very-impressive list, I'm beginning to wonder if I ever really had it. I contemplate the elements necessary for taking a relationship to this next level. First, there's usually a physical attraction. I mean, no one usually jumps into bed with someone they're not attracted to. As I think back, I wonder if sometimes the surface is the only element.

There's no doubt that when it comes to Trevor, I'm extremely attracted. I have been since the first time we met.

Turning, I take in his profile, his nose, strong chiseled jaw, and neck, the way his Adam's apple bobs. Against the lights of the city, riding along beside me, in some ways he seems larger than life. From his wide shoulders to his thick arms, I have fantasized about him. I recall his wide thighs from a year ago and the hardness of him against me at the bar.

The first element is definitely there and growing stronger with each block the taxi moves through the city. It's the *more* that I'm unsure about. I like him. I really like him. I like his company, conversation, and presence. Just being beside him fills me with a reassuring warmth and contentment.

In only three dates and nearly twelve months, I trust him. I trust him in a way I've never before experienced. After all, three dates can happen within the space of three days. In those instances, there's no denying the attraction. But with Trevor, it feels different.

I've never known a man as well as I know Trevor before making love.

In most cases, that knowledge and understanding came later, if it came at all.

This new direction is uncharted territory for me, and I'm worried it's turned around.

*What if in getting to know one another we have unrealistic expectations? What if he doesn't want me the way I want him?*

Without warning, that voice in my head scatters seeds of self-doubt that were better left unplanted. It isn't until we pull up outside the hotel that I recall my talk with Stephen earlier in the night.

I'm brave. That's what he said.

I don't feel brave, but then again, what did he say?

Stephen said that this isn't about losing me; it's about adding Trevor to the equation, about being more, not less.

As the taxi stops, Trevor lifts my knuckles to his lips. "You've been very quiet."

"So have you."

"Have you changed your mind?"

Again, I speak without worrying what it may bring, facing Trevor and giving him my most honest reply. "I guess I'm worried. I want to know if you really want me."

With only the light of the overhead canopy, Trevor's

eyes open wide and he leans close. His voice is thick and filled with desire like I've never heard from him. "My lady, I could take this hand..." He splays my fingers against his. "...and place it somewhere else. If I did, you'd know that wanting you has been my only thought during this entire ride. Right now, I'm so fucking hard that I'm not sure I'll be able to walk."

It may not be the kind of talk that every woman wants to hear, but every word is music to my ears.

"How about I check that situation once we get upstairs?"

"How far up? I'm not sure I'll make it."

# CHAPTER
## *Nineteen*

**Shana**

*W*e both laugh as Trevor hands a twenty-dollar bill to the driver and we get out of the taxi. It takes all of my restraint not to look at the front of his trousers, wondering if what he said is true.

As we wait for the elevator, a few other couples join us, and I give up the fantasy of a scene from one of those hot romance movies. You know the one I mean, the one in an elevator?

I had it all in my mind, just the two of us as we recreate the back hallway at the bar the other night: his body against mine as we float higher and higher toward my suite.

As we step into the elevator, Trevor moves to the back wall and while facing the door, pulls me to him. My back falls firmly against his front as I unknowingly let out a gasp.

*Oh shit!*

He wasn't lying.

I close my eyes as his undeniable erection probes against my lower back. With his hands steadfastly on my hips, moving away from him is out of the question. He has me trapped, and I'm overwhelmed. My breathing catches as my body trembles and heat floods my lady parts. In that instant, every movie scene I've ever seen disappears.

Reality is so much better.

His lips lower to my ear, his warm breath tickling my neck. "I told you."

I wiggle against him as much as I can as the heat between my legs radiates to my breasts and beyond. Every nerve is on alert. I want nothing more than to turn into Trevor's arms, but with the way he's holding me, all I can do is sway slightly from side to side. "The twentieth floor," I say to the person by the buttons.

"Twenty?" Trevor whispers through clenched teeth. "Are you fucking kidding me?"

That heat from below fills my cheeks as I assess that I'm the only one who can hear him. Or at least I hope.

The elevator comes to a stop on the second floor as Trevor's fingers grip my hips tighter.

"Two, really?" he whispers.

All I can think is *stairs*, buddy. You could have walked.

We stop again at seven, ten, and again at fourteen. Each stop intensifies his grip upon my hips, his fingers holding tighter and stronger until I'm biting my lip to keep from calling out. It isn't that he's hurting me; it's that his desire is so strong that I want nothing more than to feel that same intensity inside me.

We still aren't alone when the elevator stops at twenty.

"Our stop," I say, waiting for his grip to loosen.

"You first."

I take a step and then another, realizing that he's not letting go. It isn't until we clear the threshold to the empty hallway and the doors to the elevator close that he finally releases me, and I spin to face him. With my heart beating out of my chest, the world is filled with haze. Yet his green stare keeps me focused. "I'll never doubt you again," I say, leaning into him.

His gaze is a mixture of lust and urgency. "If you tell me you lost your key again—like in Indianapolis—I'm taking you right here."

Quickly, fumbling in my purse, I tug his hand and lead him down the maze of a hallway until we make it to the door of my suite. Once there, I lift the key card high in the air. "Not lost."

His voice is thick and deep. "Open the door."

It's not a request.

As soon as the door opens, Trevor pushes me inside, and with a quick turn he shuts and bolts the door. When he turns back around, the temperature of the room rises. Like before, the heat is coming from his gaze. It reminds me of the cartoons with the creatures that can literally burn with their eyes.

He's the flame and I'm the kindling.

Under his stare, I'm on fire.

Not wanting to wait any longer to see and hold what I've only felt, I boldly reach for his belt.

His hand covers mine. "No, my lady, I wasn't joking. I need you now. Later, we'll investigate."

"Now?" My breathing hitches as my insides twist.

"Right. Fucking. Now."

Trevor Willis takes one step and then another until my back hits the wall.

In my mind, it's Saturday night at the bar all over again, and I'm right where I want to be, trapped by this mammoth of a man. "Trevor?"

A quick kiss of my lips and neck and the next thing I know, he's gone. When I open my eyes, Trevor is kneeling before me. It only takes a second as he lifts each of my feet and removes my high heels, one by one. And then, our eyes meet as his warm hands circle my ankles, heating my skin as they graze slowly up my bare legs. Each inch is sweet torture as he leans in and begins kissing in the wake of his touch.

My knees wobble as I struggle to stay upright, reaching back to the wall for support.

Along the smooth wall, there's none.

It's then that he latches on to the sides of my panties and pulls them down. I'm at his disposal as he guides my movement until my panties are lost somewhere on the floor. A scream escapes my lips as his tongue laps my sensitive skin.

"You taste amazing."

Words no longer form as his lips latch on to my clit and tease. "O-oh..."

"I promise we'll do this sweet, but not right now."

I fight to articulate. "Please, I don't want sweet," I pant as he stands and unbuckles his belt. "I want you. Take me." I shudder as he releases his cock, and for the first time, I see what I've only imagined. He's big and thick. And before I can contemplate more, he reaches for my behind and lifts me in the air, spreading my legs around his waist and opening me to him. With my hands on his shoulders, I lock my ankles.

Though the tip of his cock is near, it's his fingers that first find my opening and make me whimper.

"Shana, you're so fucking perfect." His fingers continue to thrust. "So wet and tight."

I can't help but rock to his movements as he spreads my essence.

"Shana?"

"Please," I scream out. "Please, take me." My fingernails

threaten the weave of his jacket as he pulls me down, sheathing himself with me. It's all I can do not to scream again as I bite the jacket covering his shoulder.

He suddenly stills. "Are you all right?"

"Yes," I pant, nodding as I move a little, each wiggle helping me adjust to his girth. It's the most amazing fullness I've ever known. Once I'm there, I kiss his neck. "You feel so good. Please don't stop."

He doesn't. Thrust after thrust, he does exactly what I've asked, taking me, marking me, and making me his. Nothing else in the world matters as we become one, in body and soul. Our movements, our breathing, and even the beating of our hearts are in sync as he takes me higher and higher. Like a spring twisted tighter and tighter, one about to snap, I'm losing control.

It's been so long since my body has been this fulfilled; I'm gripping his shoulders for dear life, afraid that if I let go, I may fall without experiencing the ecstasy that is within reach. The room fills with the sound of our bodies against the wall, marked by whimpers and moans that sound vaguely familiar. It isn't until I'm almost to the figurative edge that I realize it's my voice I've been hearing.

With my orgasm almost within reach, Trevor's lips find that place on my neck—the place he'd kissed Saturday night —and all hope for control is gone.

The world tilts on its axis. Stars in the sky collide. Up and down no longer exist. Directions cease to have meaning. My entire body implodes.

If this is what the big bang was like, no wonder it created the universe as we know it.

I'm spiraling out of control when Trevor's body stills, the room filling with his deep powerful roar, the sound reverberating from him to me as he fills me with his warmth.

My forehead falls to his shoulder as aftershocks continue, and I ride out the best orgasm of my life. In his arms, I'm floating on the comforting sea as wave after wave washes through me. It isn't until our eyes meet that I'm convinced I'm not lost in the monsoon.

His gaze is different than what I expected, silently encouraging me to say something. "Trevor, God, that was amazing." I wince as we separate, and he moves me from his waist to my feet. Despite our separation, I hold on to his shoulders. "I'm not sure I can stand."

With a chuckle, he lifts me in the air and carries me to my bed. It's then I realize that except for my shoes and panties, we're both fully dressed.

"I'm sorry, Shana."

*Sorry?*

"Why?" I ask.

"I have condoms in my wallet. I just wanted you so badly, I didn't even think."

I crook my finger and bid him closer. "I'm not sixteen. I have condoms too." I shrug. "I bought them today during my lunch break. It's not all your responsibility."

"I swear, I'm clean. I haven't been with anyone in a long time." He flashes his classic grin. "As you may have noticed, we didn't exactly set any endurance records."

"I'm clean too. I won't bore you with how long it's been, but let's just say that my checkup has come and gone a few times. You don't need to worry. I have the birth control insert. It's still good." I cock my head to the side. "And as for endurance, I'm not complaining."

"That's good to hear."

I reach for the lapels of his jacket. "Now, Mr. Willis, unless your plan was to ravage me and leave, I'd say you're overdressed."

After easing out of his jacket, Trevor reaches for the buttons on the front of my dress and begins to slowly unbutton each one, opening the front to my bra. "We're both overdressed because ravaging you was only the beginning."

"There's more?" I ask with a smirk.

"My lady, the night is young."

# CHAPTER
## Twenty

*Trevor*

*I* wake to the warmth of Shana's body against mine, or more accurately, mine against hers. While waking with a hard-on isn't unusual, having the woman of my dreams in bed beside me is. Reaching out, I run my fingers through her beautiful sex-mussed hair on the pillow beside me. In the morning light, the golden hue catches my attention while beneath my fingers, the soft curls remind me of spun corn silk. It's my fantasy come to life.

I don't try to suppress my smile as I recall how Shana's hair became tousled.

It's as my mind goes back to last night that my body responds. I shouldn't want her again, not after all we did, but I do. Closing my eyes, I recall everything after our initial sonic connection. I remember carrying her to the bed, the way she stared up at me with her big blue eyes. My fingers twitch to touch her smooth skin as they remember unbuttoning her dress...

Last night...

*Fuck!*

*Shana's smile lights up the hotel suite as she willingly gives me access to each tiny button on the front of her dress. It's like opening a package you've anticipated, one where you know the contents, but yet the reality is exceedingly better than the description.*

*The tiny lace cups pushing her tits upward have a small clasp between them. Without a word, I unlatch it, opening the package and moving aside the packaging. Perfect and round, I lean forward, sucking one and then the other between my lips. Each time I trace her hard nipple with my tongue, her back arches and the best soft mews fill my ears.*

*Slowly, I ease the dress from her body, leaving the unfastened bra as the only piece of remaining clothing. "Miss Price, I believe you're still overdressed."*

*Her head shakes from side to side, her long golden hair billowing against the pillow in waves at each movement. "And I'm going to stay that way until you join me."*

*"Oh, my lady, I'm right here."*

*"No, Trevor. I've been dreaming about you since Indianapolis. I want to see all of you, from your wide chest to those sexy thighs."*

*I lift my brow. "Thighs are sexy?"*

*Her giggle fills the suite. "Oh, come on. You know women have turn-ons as much as men."*

*As I stand and remove my shirt, Shana's grin brightens as her beautiful blue eyes search my torso and below.*

*Following her line of vision, I see my not-fully-erect penis. It's not that I'm not game. It's that we just were going at it pretty hard. A man needs a moment or two to regroup.*

*"Give me a minute," I say with a shrug.*

*She reaches up and palms my length, the blood immediately returning as I harden again under her grasp.*

*"Fuck, Shana."*

*"That's right. And you will," she coos. "First, I want those pants gone." Her gaze drops to the floor beside the bed. "And your shoes. Seriously, you're still wearing your shoes?"*

*"What can I say? I was a man on a mission."*

*She crosses her arms behind her head, the movement pushing her tits higher. And while I'm distracted by all of her lain out before me, it's her gaze that has me captivated. "I'm waiting," she says with a smirk.*

*"You made me hard again. Maybe we should fuck first and reveal what's under these pants later."*

*"Oh no. I want to see all of you."*

*I shake my head as one by one my shoes, socks, and finally my trousers and boxers find their way to the floor. It feels odd and yet right to be standing fully naked in her sight. "I hope you like what you see. It's the only Italian pastry I have."*

*Again, she reaches toward me as she sits up. I close my eyes as she runs her hand up and down my length, adding the second hand as her grip fully surrounds me. "Fuck..."*

*I open my eyes as Shana moves to her knees and crawls to the edge of the bed. Before I can comment or say a word, she leans forward, taking me between her lips. Looking like a goddess, her long hair creates a veil around her. I can't see her face, but holy fuck, what she's doing behind her hair with her hands and lips...my knees are about to give out.*

*It's the best damn blowjob of my life, but I can't let her take me all the way. It has nothing to do with finishing. It has everything to do with needing to be back inside her.*

*I reach for her face. The room fills with the sound of a pop as she comes off me, and her eyes meet mine. "You're absolutely perfect."*

*Her smile grows.*

*"But, Shana, I really want to be inside you again. I want to do it right so you'll fall asleep knowing I was there."*

*She scoots back. "If what you just did was wrong, then please, never do it right."*

*When she lies back, I crawl on top of her. "Not wrong, my lady, different. I want to take you slowly and completely." I let my cock tease her entrance as she wiggles beneath me, spreading her legs farther... "I want to take you to that edge and ease you back until you scream my name, until your only relief is me." My eyes close as I slide inside her warm, soft glove. Our earlier lovemaking has left her ready as her body arches and I bury myself.*

*"Yes."*

*Ever so slowly, I move, taking time to kiss her slender neck, her collarbone, and nibble her perky tits. Each ministration is torture for us both. I'm using every trick I've ever known to not wildly ravage her again. She feels too good. I'm on the edge. My restraint is waning when her face contorts, neck strains, and her perfect lips form an "O."*

*"Baby, are you there?"*

*Her head nods quickly as I ease out.*

*"W-what?" She looks up at me.*

*I shake my head. "Not yet."*

*"Trevor?"*

*Her gaze disappears as I taunt her breasts and move slowly over her stomach.*

*"Trevor, no. I can't wait."*

*Her protest falls on deaf ears as I lower my lips to her swollen core. Her objections grow louder, turning quickly from disapproval to approval as I tease, suck, and lick. She's sweet and creamy, the best dessert on this planet. She and Kimbra may joke about cannoli, but fuck, my lady is better than any warm glaze.*

*My grip upon her strengthens, holding her in place as her hips begin to buck. It's as her legs grow rigid and her toes begin to curl that I move over her, thrusting deep inside as she screams out my name.*

*I'm lost to the waves as her pussy grips me, squeezing me until I'm over the edge. I hope she's right about the insert, because, damn, there's no way I can move as my orgasm continues filling her with my seed.*

*Once our breathing settles and we finally move apart, Shana lays her head on my shoulder. With my arm around her, I smooth the strands of hair away from her beautiful eyes.*

*"Thank you," I say.*

*"I think I should be thanking you. I'm completely wrung out."*

*"Is that a good thing?"*

*"Oh yes, Trevor, it's a very good thing."*

*Easing her head to the pillow, I lift mine higher. "Tell me about this weird thigh fetish."*

*Shana's laugh rings through the suite. "It's not a fetish. I don't scope out guys' thighs. Tell me what you notice on women."*

*I trace the side of her face. "I notice smiles. A sincere smile is sexier than lingerie."*

*"Hmm. I thought you liked me in that white negligee."*

*"I think I like you even better out of it."*

*Her eyes open wide. "Was it...I mean, could you... see... was it transparent under those lights?"*

*"What?" I lean back. "Are you fucking kidding me? Once I realized it was you, it took everything to not get up on that stage and cover you with my suit coat. If it had been see-through, I would have probably been arrested."*

*Her facial expression relaxes. "Good."*

*"Did you think it was? Why would you go out there?"*

*"No. I didn't think it was. It was just something Stephen said. I think he was trying to boost my confidence."*

*I shake my head. "You seem very confident to me."*

*"And you, Trevor Willis, are the least awkward man I've ever known."*

*I lean down and kiss her lips. "Maybe we bring out the best in one another?"*

*"I think we do," she says as her eyes close and she snuggles closer.
"Trevor, can you stay the night?"*

*"I don't want to be anywhere else."*


The morning light seeps around the blinds as Shana's wondrous eyes blink open. Just as quickly, her lips curve upward into a lovely smile.

"You stayed," she says, her voice gravelly with sleep.

"I did. I need to leave soon, but I didn't want to go while you were asleep."

"If I pretend I'm asleep, will you stay?"

"I'd rather you be awake."

As she snuggles closer, my erection makes itself known. "Oh, I may not be able to walk today at work, but I just found the best way to wake."

I laugh. "It wasn't exactly a treasure hunt."

"Hmm. It was..." She reaches for my length, stroking the tightening skin. "...and I found the treasure."

I bite my lip as she takes me to that place between heaven and hell. My goal is heaven and she's right beside me. "Shana, I'll take it slow, so you can walk."

Her blue eyes shine as she releases me. Lying back, she shakes her head against the pillow and beckons me over her. "Walking is overrated."

# CHAPTER
## Twenty One

### *Shana*

riday lunch and Stephen looks at me over his glass of iced tea, his gaze narrowing as he assesses what he sees. "Take a step back," he says. "I like you better all giddy and sexed up than bitchy and mean-spirited."

I toss my plastic fork into the plastic bowl filled with a green leafy salad that I've barely touched and stare at the man who is supposed to be my best friend. "First off, I'm not bitchy."

"Right."

"I'm not. I'm not bitchy." I lean back, crossing my arms over my chest, and assess the people walking by. Our small bistro table isn't anything special. It isn't like we're in Paris or Rome. Stephen and I are simply at a small round table on the sidewalk outside a local deli hidden down a less-traveled street.

"I know," Stephen says, "this attitude of yours is because you want to go with me upstate tonight and spend a glorious weekend with my parents and siblings. Boss lady, you're welcome. You know my mom loves you. I just thought you'd rather keep up this bunny-rabbit sex thing you've had going on for a few days now."

My lips come together as I shake my head. "I hate you."

"You love me."

"I want you to go to your parents. I want you to see them. Because as far as our work is concerned, this has been a week from hell. If I have to listen to Vicky talk about Saks Fifth Avenue standards one more time, I'm going to cut the bitch, and then you're going back to London alone and I'll be in an American prison."

Stephen sets his cup of iced tea on the table between us and reaches over toward me. I know he wants my hand, and maybe I'm being petty, but damn it, I'm in a bad mood.

And, for the record, a bad mood is different than being bitchy.

Perhaps, not technically, but I'm pissed at the way Vicky has been acting. I'm upset that despite the good sales, she seems unwilling to relent on the whole me-stepping-into-the-fashion-show thing. I keep coming back to the fact that I saved the show. The designers are happy and the numbers are good. From what I've seen, she's the only one with a stick up her ass. Yes, she says she's speaking for others, but we're here at corporate and she's the only one raining on my parade.

Therefore, instead of reaching out to Stephen, I keep my arms crossed over my chest. "Stephen, I'd let you hold my hand, but if someone saw us, I'd probably get repri-manded on proper supervisor-assistant behavior. Here's the thing, orange washes me out. My complexion is just too fair. It's a known fact that blondes don't do well in bright orange or pale yellow, for that matter. Since most prisons use orange jumpsuits, yellow currently isn't my concern."

He wiggles his fingers, beckoning my hand. "So the selfies I took sleeping in your bed the other night? I should take those off my social media?"

Instead of holding his hand, I reach out and hit it.

Not really a hit. It is more of a tap.

"Ouch! I think that violates something too. Where is HR when you need them?"

"Kimbra is HR for Duncan's company. Maybe you should contact her and find out if you have a case."

Stephen laughs. "You want me to ask the HR associate who blackmailed her boss who is now her husband about sexual harassment in the workplace?"

"Yes. And while you're at it, find out if verbal assault is as bad as physical because knowing me, when I snap at Miss Witch Vicky, it'll start out as verbal."

Stephen rubs his hand that I tapped. "Lucky me. I'm so glad that you've escalated to physical only with me." He leans across the table. "Seriously, my dad used to work with this guy. I'm pretty sure he still has the connection. Let me give you one saying...concrete shoes." He nods as his lips come together. "Okay, two...swimming with the fishes."

"Stop."

"No. It's a real thing. Where do you think Hollywood got its material? And judging by the heels that woman wears, she loves shoes. You could consider it a gift." He shrugs. "It might even be a tax write-off. But I'd check with your accountant first."

"It would be a gift for the world."

"Now you're talking."

Letting out a long sigh, I lean back and try to think of something else as the air fills with the sound of horns. "Why do horns make me happy?"

"Because everyone in New York uses theirs."

"I've never understood it. It's not like honking will make a stoplight change or intersection suddenly become clear. Yet as soon as the stoplight changes, there's a chorus."

"If you're trying to change the subject, you can think about the bunny-rabbit sex." Stephen shrugs. "It's a good subject. Sex always makes me happier."

"Bunny-rabbit?"

"It means a lot—a lot of sex. You know, rabbits do it all the time."

A smile breaks my stern expression. "I really haven't researched the mating habits of woodland creatures."

"Think of it as Disney's education. There are always rabbits...*Snow White, Cinderella,* and even *Bambi.* Why do you think they named him Thumper?" He smiles at me. "I'll give you a hint. It wasn't because of his foot tapping. And did you notice how big his feet were?"

I try to get the image of animated rabbits out of my mind. "Trevor and I do other things," I say. "For example, the other night I went to his place and he made me dinner."

"So he cooks and is great in bed?"

"And don't forget about the roads and bridges," I volunteer.

"At least those thoughts are making you smile."

"I just feel like since the show, I can't do anything right. We were in this meeting this morning and had this big campaign all spread out with many of the fashions from the show. Since it's spring, we're working on the fall campaign and started talking about the holidays. Every suggestion I presented was shot down. Maybe I've lost my touch. I just don't know anymore."

"Did I tell you the apartment in the village is a sublet?"

Just the mention of his pending apartment combined with my terrible week at work makes the little bit of salad I've consumed churn. "No."

"It belongs to a friend of a friend. He's going to be in

California for six months and doesn't want to pay double rent. He also doesn't want to lose his place here. It's a two-bedroom and the location is prime."

"Stephen..."

"Shana, the point is that I can back out. Nothing is set in stone. He'll find someone else."

"But you don't want to back out," I say, knowing I'm right.

Stephen shrugs. "I didn't. I'm not sure anymore."

Tears fight to move forward, stinging the back of my eyes. "I'm surer than ever before that I want to stay here."

This time when Stephen reaches across the table, I do too, and our hands clasp. "If we go back," he says, "it won't be like it was before. The two of you—obviously with the rabbit thing—have gotten to know one another better than before. Last time it was infatuation. This time, there's more to it. You'll make it work long distance."

I lift my cup covering my grin. "There's a little more to it."

"Oh, please. It's not like I need measurements or anything, but boss lady, you wouldn't be floating into work every morning if it were *a little*." His eyebrows waggle with his last two words.

"That's not what I mean. Besides the Disney education, Trevor is doing more. He's keeping me sane."

"If sanity is all we're discussing, I think I should have a little credit."

"Okay, you get *a little*." My brows do the same dance as his. "Trevor gets a *big part* of the credit."

Stephen's head shakes. "I'm more than happy to continue this with the penis innuendos. However, you and I..." He motions between us. "What we have is bigger than that, and I'd be happy to give you a list of references who will attest to this..." He motions to himself. "Is not *a little*, nor do I take—"

"Whoa! Way too much information."

"Tell me about Trevor's part in your sanity?"

I shrug. "For the first time, I understand the dream. I can see it. And I want it all. I want the relationship that comes with simple things like making someone's favorite meal. I also want the career where I'm appreciated and feel essential."

"So he made you pizza?"

"No," I say with a giggle. "He made me chicken tacos."

"With guacamole?"

"Yes. He called Kimbra and asked what I liked to eat besides pizza."

"So," Stephen says, "you have a nice guy. That career appreciation thing... would that be like in juniors?"

"I don't know. I was completely satisfied there until this opportunity came along. It was all so fast. The call, the flight. Boom, we were here. It's been a whirlwind. I don't know if it's being back here that I was excited about or if it was more the idea of moving to lingerie. I want the career and the relationship. The thing is that I don't want to compromise one for the other."

"Has he asked you to compromise?" Stephen asks.

"No. Trevor would never do that."

Stephen looks down at his watch. "We need to get back. I just wanted to be sure you didn't want to go upstate with me. I'm taking the four o'clock train."

"I think I'll stay here and assess the mess that is my life."

"Assessing is good. I've been doing some of that."

We gather our plates and cups, throwing them into the nearest trash bin. "What are you assessing?"

"How about I keep you posted?"

"Now I'm curious."

"That's good. The next time Witch Vicky gets you all bothered, think about my secret. Don't let her have all of your attention."

I nod as we turn onto Fifth Avenue. "I have a secret too." Before he can question, I go on, "I received a call from Neil today."

"Neil Butler? In London?"

"Yes, our other boss. He asked about you."

Stephen shakes his head. "Oh no. You and me, we're a team."

"You could do it, Stephen. You were amazing in juniors. You understand the styles and clients. Your predictions are spot on. The designers love you and so do the models. I'd be a fool to think I'm not where I am because of you."

"Stop it, Shana. We stay here in New York together, or we go back to London together. We're a package."

This time I reach out to him, taking his hand in mine. "Thank you, Stephen. I really don't hate you."

"Oh, boss lady, I know."

# CHAPTER
## Twenty Two

### *Trevor*

"**Y**ou and Shana Price?" Max says with a shit-eating grin as he smiles at me over his glass of bourbon. "I guess that means you won the bet, her being one of the models and all. Hell, I can't believe I didn't recognize her."

"You really didn't?"

"No, not until later. I think it's that thing where someone is out of context. I wasn't expecting to see her here, much less onstage wearing a negligee."

My mind goes back to that moment. I understand what he means. I was flabbergasted and shocked all at once when I realized it was her. Then again, I think she was the most beautiful woman on the stage. I'm surprised that every man's vision didn't immediately gravitate to her.

"So how much do I owe you?"

I wave my hand. "No one won, and meeting up again with Shana had nothing to do with a bet."

"Fair is fair," he says.

"We all chipped in. Everything is even. Besides, the gamble would have been less if we'd just have stayed at my apartment as I suggested in the first place."

"Your apartment used to be Eric's too, and that's not exactly bachelor-party excitement. And..." Max's voice trails a bit. "...two bedrooms and four men. That scenario only works with a different crowd." He leans back against the bar and surveys the room. "Not that I'm on the hunt for that crowd."

I'm not exactly sure what he means, and I don't know if I want to know. Before I can respond, he speaks again.

"She's a fiery one."

His assessment of Shana makes me smile. "What can I say? I like to be burned."

"Well, that little tirade she gave me the other night...you'll be in for worse from Stephen if you hurt her."

"Apparently, according to my brother, Stephen would need to stand in line. My sister-in-law will also kick my ass."

Max shakes his head. "Man, you're on a hit list."

"Only if my intention is to hurt Shana, and it's not."

Max shrugs as he turns back toward the bar and reaches for his glass of bourbon. After swishing the contents for what seems like too long, he mumbles something about intentions and how they can be misconstrued.

"What?"

"Nothing. I'm no expert at relationships, but all that bullshit people spew about communication...there might be something to it."

"Umm. Okay. Hey, I'm not trying to change the subject," I say, doing exactly the opposite of what I said.

"Yes, you are. Go ahead."

"I was surprised when your firm said you were still the contact here in the city. I thought you were leaving after the bachelor party."

"That had been my plan. But you're right. I'm not here as a friend but as an investment specialist. I almost forgot this is a business meeting." He looks at his watch. "Now, what was it you wanted to discuss?"

I pull out my iPad and bring it to life. "This proposal has been out to..."

While I feel a little guilty talking to Max without letting Shana or Stephen know that he's still in town, this really is a business meeting. When I contacted Max's firm to question what was happening with a proposal I'd generated, I never expected to see Max.

I'd said goodbye to him, Matt, and Eric on the Sunday morning after the party.

We'd managed to keep Shana's little blowup away from Eric. Through it all, the groom-to-be seemed to have a good time. Less than a month to go and he'll officially be a married man. The wedding is a destination thing with an exclusive guest list of his and Cynthia's family. Last weekend was our time for his friends to be together to send him into the world of matrimony with memories.

Now that Shana and I are kind of together, I'm not too sad about missing the wedding.

It doesn't take a genius to figure out that Max and Stephen have history. And even though neither Max nor Stephen has given me any information, I've managed to get a little bit here and there from Shana. In a nutshell, she thinks that one of my good friends is worse than pond scum. She mentioned something about fungi below the depths.

For that reason, inviting her to Eric's wedding where Max would be if it weren't a small family wedding would probably not be a good idea. Oh, and then there's the whole thing about my taking Cynthia to Duncan's wedding. Yes, the bachelor party was our friend send-off for Eric to the world of married bliss.

Though my information regarding Max and Stephen is

mostly self-generated, it isn't difficult to connect the dots. Shana and Stephen have been living in London. Max lives in London. The chances of their paths crossing in a city as big as London is probably statistically similar to the chances of their paths crossing in New York City—given the variant and taking subcategories into consideration.

Their connection skews the median results.

It happened.

In both cities.

As we're about to leave the bar, I realize why I'm surprised Max is still in town. "You've been in the city all week and haven't stayed at my place? Eric has moved out. He's now with Cynthia. I still have the extra bedroom."

Max's hand lands on my shoulder. "No, I haven't. After Saturday night, I figured you were probably busy, you know..." he says with a grin, "getting burned."

*I was. I am.*

"Still, friends are always welcome..."

"Trust me, I've been busy too."

"Are you heading back to London soon?"

"The flights are a mess right now. The royal wedding has caused ticket prices to soar. Since my plans changed, rebooking will nearly take selling the royal jewels. When I negotiated my itinerary change, I told my firm that I'd stay here and take care of a few matters we have pending. In the long run, I'm saving them money. I'm sure they'll remember that when it comes to bonus time."

"You have my number," I say, "if you need anything or if you hear about the proposal."

"I do. I'm going to be out of the city..." Max looks at his watch again. "...as a matter of fact, I need to get to the train station. I have a four o'clock. I'll be back on Monday and let you know what I hear—if I hear."

"Thanks. I appreciate knowing I have someone on the inside."

Max's expression stays the same, yet his eyes cloud in a way that makes the enthusiasm I felt while explaining my proposal disappear. "Hey," I say, "I understand, there's a limit to friendship."

"No. The limit's not on the friendship. I'll do what I can. The limit is on my influence over other people's decisions. Investment is a slippery slope. I know McCobb Engineering is worth it. I've seen your work and dedication. All I can do is make the proposal. Pushing too hard isn't in anyone's best interest."

"Only shear...but pulling, that's tensile." I place my glass on the bar and look for some acknowledgment of my comedy. When I don't see any, I explain, "Pushing and pulling...engineering humor."

Max shakes his head. "I hope you wooed Shana with something other than your stand-up comedy."

"Yes, as a matter of fact, she's fallen for my singing."

"You sing?"

"Only in the shower."

Max shakes his head as his phone and mine buzz at the same time.

"Thanks again, Max," I say as I look down. "Please keep me posted."

Shana: **"I'M FREE FOR THE ENTIRE WEEKEND. PLEASE TELL ME YOU CAN TAKE MY MIND OFF SAKS UNTIL MONDAY MORNING."**

Me: **"OH, MY LADY, I HAVE A CONCERT PLANNED."**

Shana: **"A CONCERT? WHAT BAND?"**

Me: **"IT'S A PRIVATE SHOW. VERY INTIMATE."**

Shana: **"WHAT CLOTHES SHOULD I PACK?"**

Me: **"NOT NECESSARY. NUDE VENUE."** (Smile emoji)

Shana: **"THEN I'M PACKED!"** (Blushing smile emoji)

# CHAPTER
## Twenty Three

### *Shana*

*B*ack in my hotel room, as I prepare for my escape weekend with Trevor, I contemplate what to throw into my carry-on suitcase. There might have been a time when I would have felt guilty about leaving two hotel rooms in the Financial District of Manhattan unoccupied for two nights on Saks's dime, but as I take a deep breath to expel the negativity from the last week working with Witch Vicky, I'm filled with nothing but anticipation.

Even though Trevor told me the concert venue is nude, I throw a few tops, a pair of jeans, and even a skirt and blouse onto the bed. It's then that I see the black Saks Fifth Avenue bag with the small black and white bow that brings a much-needed smile to my face.

The negligee inside isn't exactly like the one I wore on the runway. That one is for next season's sales. This one caught my eye as I was leaving the offices on the tenth floor this evening—the mannequin near the elevators was wearing it. Reaching nearly to the floor, the sleek satin fell loosely from its shoulders, held in place by delicate spaghetti straps. What caught my attention were the lace accents strategically arranged for optimum viewing.

It was Stephen who encouraged me, telling me to go for it. "This is our weekend," he said. "Last Saturday, you wore lingerie for Saks. This weekend, do it for you."

When I shrugged, he whispered, "This time, you'll not imagine those sexy green eyes. All he'll see is you."

"Do you think it's a little forward?"

For the first time since leaving the offices, Stephen smiled. "Girl, bunny-rabbit sex is forward. That right there..." He tilted his head toward the mannequin. "...is wrapping. It's anticipation...it's—"

I placed my hand on his arm. "Stop. I'm going to need nipple tape if you say any more."

"Go get it." The door to the elevator opened. "Bye, boss lady. I need to get straight to the train station."

It was as the doors were closing that I realized he wasn't packed for a weekend with his parents. "Where are your things?"

Stephen winked. "Not to worry. A friend is bringing them."

"A friend...?" The doors closed.

Now, as I'm packing, I remember that at lunch he told me he had a secret.

Damn, I'm a bad friend. Instead of thinking about work or daydreaming about Trevor, I should have asked. Lifting my phone, I send a quick text.

Me: **"I KNOW YOU'RE ON THE TRAIN. TELL YOUR MOM AND DAD I SAID HI. ALSO, WHEN DO I GET TO KNOW YOUR SECRET? IT ISN'T NICE TO MAKE ME WAIT."**

I hit send, fully expecting to not hear a word back from him until Sunday or at least tomorrow.

As I'm about to finish packing, my phone rings.

KIMBRA is on the screen.

"Hi," I say.

"Are you really leaving next Friday?"

Letting out a long sigh, I sit on the edge of the big bed. "Stephen and I have return airplane reservations for next Friday night leaving out of JFK. We're headed back to London, no matter what happens with the position. Either we need to pack and get juniors squared away or we are simply moving back home to our places in Shepherd's Bush, just a tube ride away from our jobs."

"Am I a bad friend if I don't want London to be your home?"

"No," I say with a grin. "I think that makes you a good friend."

"So what are your plans for your last weekend in the Big Apple—until you move back here?"

I recall Trevor's comments last night as we dined at yet another fabulous restaurant in the sky. "Well, I've been told that I have and can make no plans."

"Oh! I like that. And how are you supposed to pack for this no-plan weekend?"

I giggle. "I was told the venue is a strict no-clothes zone."

"Well, hot damn. Quiet Trevor needs a new nickname."

I laugh, thinking I could give him a few. Of course, none are ones I'm willing to share.

"Shana?" Kimbra says when I get lost in my own erotic thoughts.

"Sorry. Yes, he's definitely not quiet or shy or any of the other adjectives you've mentioned."

"Babe, I'm so happy for you and for him," she adds. "I don't want to impose on your weekend, but can we see the two of you?"

"I guess I better pack clothes."

"Yes, that's a good idea. The thing is that on Sunday afternoon Christopher and Beth are coming over for dinner. They're in the city for a concert. That's a good thing because they can't stay too long. Duncan and I were thinking this would be a good time for them to meet you."

My mind is filled with names and people. I think about friends I used to work with here in New York. I've seen a lot of them here at the offices. I try to recall people from Kimbra's circles. "I'm sorry, I'm drawing a blank. Who are Christopher and Beth?"

"Oh shit. Well, you met them once."

I shake my head. "Can you give me another clue? I've been a little crazy lately."

"First, tell me if you can come over Sunday?"

"I need to check with Trevor. Remember, he said no plans. Now my curiosity is growing. When did I meet these people?"

"At my wedding," Kimbra responds.

"At your wedding?"

"They're Duncan and Trevor's parents."

I fall back onto the bed, landing on the pile of clothes waiting to be packed as I let out a long breath. "Kimberly Ann!"

"It won't be bad. They're great people. They're much saner than my family, and you've survived them. Besides, I may have mentioned to Beth that Trevor was seeing my very best friend in the whole world and how you were going to be leaving for a while but the two of you are trying to make it work and how this started at the wedding and how Trevor is totally smitten, and she is so excited."

"Whoa, take a breath."

"Please?"

"I passed on spending the weekend with Stephen's family and now this?"

"Like I said, it's not like with my family. There will be no strip poker or discussion of sex toys."

I giggle. "That's so good to know."

"Oh," she says, "I need to go. So I'll tell Duncan that you and Trevor will be here Sunday at three. Love you. Bye."

"Wait—"

Pulling my phone away from my ear, I look at the screen. "Bitch, you hung up." Of course, she doesn't hear me.

There's a number by my text message icon. I must not have heard the notifications when I was talking to Kimbra. I tap the screen.

Trevor: **"MY LADY, IF YOU DON'T ARRIVE SOON, YOU'LL MISS THE OPENING ACT."**

I shake my head.

Me: **"I'VE ALWAYS BEEN MORE OF A HEAD-LINER FAN."**

Trevor: **"THE OPENING ACT IS FOOD."**

My stomach growls as I recall that I only ate some of my salad today for lunch.

Me: **"ON MY WAY!"**

They say the way to a man's heart is through his stomach. I'm pretty sure that works for women too. I quickly fold everything I have on the bed and place it in my suitcase, making room for toiletries and my little black and white bag.

Leaving my work clothes on the floor of the closet, I slip into the tight jeans I wore Saturday night, a comfortable long top, and my tall boots. Running a brush through my hair, I secure it in a low ponytail and pull the length over my shoulder.

This is supposed to be my escape weekend. Looking at the clock, I see it's almost seven on Friday night. That gives me until Sunday at three. I plan to enjoy every minute.

*Goodbye, Ms. Price, professional fashion buyer. Hello, Shana, someone looking for an escape.*

I may have told Stephen I was going to use this weekend to assess my mess of a life, but as I'm turning off the lights to my hotel suite, I decide that assessment isn't what I need. Instead, for once, I want to simply enjoy. I want to forget about whatever is going to happen with my job, not think about Stephen's secret, and even put off thinking about Sunday's dinner at Kimbra's. For the next forty-plus hours, I want to relax and enjoy.

# CHAPTER
## Twenty Four

*Trevor*

ou would think I'm seventeen on my first date.

Since leaving the bar with Max and receiving Shana's text that she was done for the week and wanted me to take her mind off work, I've been in planning overload. It's what I do. I plan, probably excessively. After all, a structure doesn't become a fifty-story building without planning. First there are specs. What will be needed to secure the foundation? A building or a bridge, no matter how well constructed, won't stand without a strong foundation. After that, preliminary plans are developed. The investors' desires are taken into consideration but always with safety regulations in mind.

Once the basics are formulated, a model is constructed. While I loved Legos as a kid, these models are different, being built to scale for a very specific reason. If the model can't stand or withhold the stresses placed upon it, neither will the structure.

It's the way my mind works.

Of course, things are different for creating a weekend with the woman I'm falling for. I know it's true. Then again, maybe Kimbra was right and I've already fallen. That morning in Indianapolis, when Shana woke in my bed, I was a goner.

I'll never forget the way she looked at me. With her

beautiful blue eyes wide, wearing my button-down shirt, her expression filled with surprise and wonder. I admit I had fun teasing her and stretching out the explanation for our situation.

Through it all, she remained calm and innocent.

Oh, I wanted her that night. I wanted her that weekend, but not taking her has made what we've shared this week so much better.

I stop and look around my apartment. It isn't a bad apartment for New York. When I first moved in, I had Eric as a roommate. That helped with expenses. Now that he's getting married and living with Cynthia, I can't imagine downsizing. Not that it's large, but two bedrooms in Manhattan—unless you're my brother—is like a mansion in other areas.

Since I've taken Shana to many of her favorite spots this week—last night we went to Gaston's—I decided that this weekend would be different. No fancy restaurants—she has to dress professionally all week. No crowded venues. No fuss.

I remembered something Duncan told me once about Kimbra. He said that one of his favorite times is when they hide out all weekend getting lost in one another, movies on Netflix, and comfort food.

Shana and I may not have the jet-set life of Duncan and Kimbra, but I like what he said. It shows me that despite what he does, my brother is still the down-to-earth guy that our parents raised. We didn't always have a lot growing up, but we always had home.

For one weekend, I hope I can give that to Shana.

I take a look at my phone, hoping there'll be another

message from her, but instead there's one from Max and one from my mother.

Great.

I open the one from Max first.

## "EVERYTHING WAS CONFIRMED RECEIVED AT THE MAIN OFFICE. I'LL KEEP YOU POSTED."

I don't know if this is the best career move I've ever made. I've always been the guy who went where he was needed and picked up the pieces of whatever was given to me. This is the first time I've pursued a project with this much vigor. It could either work or backfire.

I scoff at my limited options.

"Yes, Trevor. You'll either succeed or fail. There's no gray area in that."

It seems like my options are a lot like Shana's. She did her best for that damn fashion show, the one I didn't want to attend. She put herself on the line and according to her, the sales have been successful; however, the decision she made to walk on that stage, to put aside her insecurities for others, could be her undoing in ladies' lingerie.

Nothing worthwhile comes without risk.

I decide to bite the bullet and open my mother's text.

Mom: **"DAD AND I ARE COMING TO THE CITY**

# FOR A CONCERT ON SUNDAY. I HEARD A RUMOR THAT I'D LOVE TO HEAR FROM YOU. MAYBE YOU COULD GIVE YOUR MOM A CALL?"

*Fuck!*

My damn brother is closer to our mom. It's not an issue for me. I'm a thirty-three-year-old man. I don't need to have dinner with her once a week. Yes, I think he still does that even now that he's married.

But just because he has dinner with her doesn't mean he has to tell her about me.

I look again at Shana's text.

With Friday-night traffic, she should be here soon. Shaking my head, I decide to rip off the Band-Aid and face my mom.

Her phone rings only once. "Trevor!"

"Hi, Mom. I just read your text message."

"So? Tell me..." Her voice is filled with excitement as if I'm about to divulge some Christmas secret.

"I can't talk long. Did you say you'd be in the city?"

"Yes, your dad and I have tickets to the Philharmonic. It's a rare Sunday evening show, Tchaikovsky and Elgar. I can't wait."

"I'd love to see you two, but I have plans this weekend."

"Trevor," she says, the elongation of my name meaning more than what she's saying.

"Mom, I'm going to guess you heard a rumor from Duncan."

"No, I heard a rumor from Kimbra."

I scoff, shaking my head. It's so much easier to be mad at Duncan than Kimbra. "And what did Kimbra say?"

"She said you are seeing someone. Oh, please, tell me it's true."

The intercom on the wall near my door buzzes.

"It's true, Mom, and I need to go."

"I want to meet her."

The intercom buzzes again.

"Mom, I need to go. I'll see what I can do."

"Okay, see you Sunday at Kimbra and Duncan's at three o'clock."

Before I can reply, she is gone.

No. Just no. This weekend is about hiding from the world, not taking my girl to meet my parents. That's like taking her from a bearskin blanket in front of the fire into the fire itself.

I push the button on the intercom. "Hello."

Shana's voice rings through the speaker. "Hi, it's me."

"Hi, me. Come on up."

# CHAPTER

Twenty Five

**Shana**

*B*efore I can knock, the door of Trevor's apartment opens and the doorway fills with Trevor Willis. In worn blue jeans riding low on his hips, bare feet, and no shirt, I can't take my eyes off of him. Tunnel vision doesn't seem to be affecting only me.

Trevor's gaze is zeroed my way.

Without his saying a word, my body is consumed by the hunger of his stare. His green eyes sparkle with explosions of golden flecks as he scans from my boots to my hair. With each second, it's as if his gaze touches my skin moving upward, the heat disintegrating my clothing in its path until I'm bare in the hallway, waiting for him to bid me entrance.

The tips of his lips move upward until his smile shines with the intensity of his gaze, "Welcome, my lady." He steps to the side, allowing me just enough room to enter. Still, our bodies brush against one another's as I wheel my suitcase inside.

"What is this?"

"I thought if I were spending the weekend, I might need a few things."

Slowly his head shakes. "I believe I told you it was a clothes-free zone."

I take another look at him, also scanning upward. I cock one eyebrow. "You're wearing jeans."

"For now."

As the door closes and I release the handle of my case, Trevor's large hands frame my cheeks, pulling my face toward his.

I let out a soft moan.

The heat of his gaze and tease of his greeting can't compare to the passion of his kiss. With a soft, sweet start, I'm lost as he pulls me closer, tempting my lips to open and rewarding me with the promise of his tongue.

I already know how talented he is with his lips and tongue. And while he can take me to ecstasy when he uses it on my sensitive parts, even with a kiss he has my insides twisting.

The spicy aroma of pizza causes my stomach to rumble, ending our kiss with his soft laugh. "My lady, are you hungry?"

I inhale the scent of his cologne encompassed in garlic and oregano. "For so many things. How about you?"

"Famished. Let's satisfy one hunger at a time?"

"I guess there's no rush. We have all weekend."

"Yes," he says, tugging me toward the kitchen.

Though it isn't my first visit this week, I take in his apartment. It reminds me a little of the one Kimbra and I shared, but bigger. In New York City, space costs money. There are few people I know who have a place like Duncan and Kimbra's. That's all right by me. I like the feel of Trevor's apartment. It opens from the hallway into his living room. There's no balcony, but there is a fire escape outside the window. On a night like tonight we could move out there and enjoy the night air.

His kitchen is larger than the one Kimbra and I had. His is remodeled, as the building is too old for the stainless-steel appliances and white and gray decor. The way it is designed, there isn't room for a table, but instead, there's a breakfast bar with three tall stools.

I know from past visits that there are also two bedrooms. Trevor told me about plans to turn the room his friend Eric had used into a study or an office. Right now, that one could be classified as a storage unit with boxes, a bicycle, and I think I even saw some snow skis.

Admittedly, I've spent more time in Trevor's bedroom. The bathrooms are small in comparison, again showing the age of the building. However, I can happily report that we both fit into the shower and yes, Trevor can sing.

My memories are a tad foggy, but I'm pretty sure he made me sing the last time I was in there with him. That is more exciting when you realize that I can't carry a tune in a bucket.

"We do have all weekend," Trevor says, peeking at me over his broad shoulder as he leads me to the kitchen. With a glint in his eye, he adds, "And rushing is not on the itinerary."

His words twist my insides, reminding me of the first night we came together, not the crazed passion against the wall, but the slow torture once we made it to my hotel bed. "Maybe we could find a happy medium?"

Trevor laughs as he pulls out a bar stool at the breakfast counter. "For you."

As soon as I climb onto the stool, I see the source of the fantastic aroma. Across the bar, on the other counter is a large white box, the edges discolored with grease, and I know I've met the man of my dreams. "I see you have been cooking all day."

"Hey, I found a lady who likes pizza as much as I do. I'm taking advantage."

"I do love pizza. Anything else?"

"Wine."

"My favorite combination."

Before he walks over to the food, Trevor bends down and kisses that spot behind my ear, sending chills through me, tightening the twists inside, and leaving goose bumps along my skin. His large hands skirt across my shoulders, lifting my ponytail. "T-Trevor..."

"Oh, you can't wear your hair away from your neck and expect me to behave."

I reach for my ponytail. "Would you believe me if I said that I didn't even think of that when I did it?"

"Yes..."

He kisses my exposed neck once again. This time the chills cover my entire body, making me glad I'm wearing a padded bra because I don't have nipple tape in my suitcase. I close my eyes as his warm breath tickles my skin.

His deep voice rumbles through me. "It won't happen again."

I lean back. "You won't kiss my neck?"

"No," he says with a grin. "I will definitely kiss your neck and your collarbone and..." His grin grows as his finger teases the neckline of my top. "You won't fix your hair this way...ever...that you don't think about my lips on you."

I reach up and run my fingers through his messy mane. "As long as you think of me whenever you forget to comb yours."

"I always forget to comb it."

"Then think of me—always."

He twists the stool until I'm parallel with the counter,

and he's in the space between my thighs. "My lady, since last May, you're all I think about."

"Is that why you forget to comb your hair?"

"It's why I can't think of anything else. Are you sure you're hungr—"

We both laugh as the rumble from my stomach interrupts his question.

"I'm sorry," I say. "I didn't eat much lunch."

With a kiss to my cheek, Trevor backs away. "Sustenance first. With the plans I made, you're going to need it."

"I like the way that sounds." As he steps around the counter, I ask, "Can I help you with anything?"

"Your job is to relax. This weekend is our *no-plans weekend.*"

"So...what do you have planned for our no-plans weekend?"

As he places two large wine goblets on the counter, he glances at me through his lashes. "Do you think I planned something?"

"Yes, Trevor Willis. I think I'm starting to figure you out."

"You are?"

"Well, you just said that with your plans I need sustenance. And besides, you're not a seat-of-your-pants kind of guy."

Trevor twists around and looks at the back of his jeans.

"Don't be so damn cute. Yes, you have a great ass. I like the seat of your pants. What I mean is that you plan your breakfast before you go to bed. I'd put money on the fact that we have plans."

His brows rise and fall. "First, breakfast is the most important meal of the day. What if you don't plan and then when it's time, you're out of eggs or cereal? The possibilities are numerous and would have lasting effects on the entire day."

"See. I'd win the bet."

"How much are you willing to bet?"

I feel the warmth in my cheeks. "Me."

"So if you're right, I can't have you all weekend?"

"If I'm right, I get to decide when and how you get me."

His chest grows as he inhales. The stream of wine coming from the bottle he's pouring grows precariously close to the rim of the glass as the muscles in his arms tense, bringing forth a beautiful array of bulging tendons and veins. Once he places the wine bottle on the counter, he exhales and replies, "Sorry, my lady."

"You won't take my bet?"

"Not for this weekend."

"Then you do have plans."

He hands me a glass of red wine. "I do but for more than a weekend. I understand that we don't know what the future will bring, but, Shana Price, my goal for this weekend and beyond is that no matter what I do, how I ravage you with unbridled passion or torture you with slow and thorough lovemaking, that you are in full agreement." He clinks our glasses. "You have my word, I'll never do anything you don't decide is right, but I will do my damnedest to convince you to let me give it a try."

I bring the rim of the glass to my lips as I think about his toast and take a drink. Once I sip, I place the glass back on the counter and say, "I'm not very good at giving up control."

"You don't have to. I'd never expect that."

"I don't? You wouldn't?"

"No, my lady, you have all the power."

"Then tell me our plans."

He reaches for two paper plates and grins. "See, I like it when you're bossy."

I take another sip of the wine. "You may like it, but you suck at obeying."

He hands me a plate overflowing with a warm slice of pizza. "Yes, I do. We can work on sucking later. First, we eat."

"And then sucking...?"

"And then...you trust me to keep my word."

I wake to the soft sound of Trevor's breathing. The window in his bedroom is open, allowing the soundtrack of city noises to float through the warming air. Cars and horns and brakes and voices have been our background music for the last incredible night and day and into this night.

I roll toward him, making out his features in the dim illumination. My fingers itch to comb his hair back and feel his soft, short beard. I marvel at the slope of his nose and the way his forehead protrudes. It's a comforting combination as if he's still planning and thinking in his dreams, yet relaxed and content.

It isn't often that I'm the one awake. It seems that when we're together, I'm the one who wakes to his sexy smile. The few moments of seeing him at peace gives me a strange sense of satisfaction.

I can't deny that he makes me happy, and with all my heart, I believe it's mutual. I'm not sure a man can fake the gratification he's shown.

Our plan-free weekend has been filled with marvelous options that I never expected. It has consisted of everything and nothing—from pizza to shower concerts, to wrapped-in-towels Netflix marathons, to dressed in his shorts or maybe just his T-shirt and sitting on the fire escape, to long torturous, thoroughly gratifying sexual encounters and finding sustenance. Except for accepting deliveries, the door to his apartment hasn't opened, and we mutually decided to turn off our phones.

After the mess that has been the last three weeks of work, I had no idea how much I needed a do-nothing-but-sleep-eat-screw-and-relax weekend. It's been perfect and yet as I lie here beside him, my chest aches.

If I were smart and sensible, I wouldn't wait. Instead, I'd ease my way out of his bed now and slip out of his apartment and his life.

I just know that this time next week I'll be back in London. I also know that it won't be to pack.

Don't ask me how I know.

I do.

And yet I can't pry myself away from this man.

It's an attraction like I've never known. From his warm, naked body beside mine and his plans for our plan-free weekend, to the knowledge that I'm supposed to meet his parents tomorrow...or is it today?

I search for a clock.

Two in the morning.

It's today.

As much as I don't want to hurt him when I tell him I'm moving back to London, I can't make me hurt myself by giving up one minute we could be together. Even if it is the smart thing to do, I can't pull myself away.

I'm beginning to wonder if I'll be able to make myself step onto the plane next Friday.

I've never before considered a relationship over my career, and I find it puzzling that the thoughts are even occurring. Yet they are.

# CHAPTER

*Twenty Six*

**Trevor**

*I* wake to my dark bedroom and reach for Shana, but she's not there. All at once, I'm sitting up and straining into the darkness, scanning my bedroom and listening for anything. The sounds of the city that never sleeps are just beyond my window while everything within reach is silent. Well, except for my heart. It's now beating within my ears.

"Shana?"

I call out once and then again, louder. "Shana."

My feet hit the floor as I make my way toward the attached bathroom.

The door is wide and she's not there.

I race toward the hall to the second bathroom.

Empty.

An unfamiliar sense of panic bubbles from deep inside me.

*Where is she?*

*What happened?*

I'm not losing her again. Not after the time we've had together. I won't.

"Shana."

It's as I turn from the hallway to the living room that I remember to breathe and my heart slows to a healthy pace.

Outside the window beyond the open pane is her silhouette upon the fire escape. For only a second, I stand and watch.

Her long unrestrained hair is blowing around her as she sits upon the windowsill. Step by step with my bare feet upon the wood floor, I slowly approach, not wanting to startle her and at the same time wondering how she didn't hear me.

"Shana?" I say softly, lifting the sash higher.

"Trevor?"

Though she turned away after saying my name, it wasn't before I saw the glistening tears on her cheeks or heard the emotion in my name.

I reach out my hand. "Baby, please come back in."

She shakes her head, but nevertheless, she does as I ask, gripping my hand and stepping over the sill and back into the apartment. Neither of us mentions my total lack of clothing as her long legs bend, toes point, and feet come into contact with the hardwood floor. As she gracefully navigates the window, I'm reminded of her on that runway. With as beautiful as she was that afternoon, I find having her here with nothing on but my T-shirt even sexier.

"I didn't want to wake you," she says, wrapping her arms around my torso and burying her face against my chest. She's chilled against my skin.

Wrapping her in my arms, we stand before the window, neither of us speaking. From the way she's trembling, I'm afraid the source of her shaking is from more than the cool night air. From the dampness on my chest, I believe she's crying. Although I've never been good at women's emotions —is any man?—I slowly rub a circle upon her back until she takes a deep breath.

"Shana, what is it?"

When she looks up, her blue eyes glisten with unshed tears. "I bought something. I brought it here and forgot to wear it."

"What?"

She pulls away. "It's Sunday. We're going to your brother's for dinner. I have to go back to the hotel and then...then..." She turns away.

Reaching for her hand, I pull her back to my embrace. "And then we'll handle what comes next."

"But you don't understand. I forgot about the nightgown. Now it's too late."

I shake my head trying to figure out what she's saying. "My lady, you are the most stunning woman I've ever seen. I personally think that Saks should consider a boyfriend's T-shirt line. I mean, I know they'll charge ten times as much as the real T-shirt, but damn, seeing you in mine and nothing else—it's hot."

She cranes her neck upward. "But I bought it for you. And now..." Her forehead drops to my chest.

Slowly, I release her and take a step back. "I'm still here and so are you."

"No. It doesn't work like that."

"What doesn't work like what?"

"I'm supposed to surprise you and come out of the bathroom all sexy, not a snotty mess with tangled hair like someone who's been sitting outside crying."

I palm her cheek as she tilts her head toward my hand. "Shana Price, you're sexy every minute of every day and night." I tease her hair with my fingers. "And I know how your hair got like that, which makes it the sexiest hairstyle you could ever wear."

"But..."

"Yes, I love your butt and your tits. If you bought me a surprise, I don't want to miss it."

"Now, it's not a surp—"

I touch my finger to her lips. "Should I wait out here or in bed?"

Her tits push outward as she inhales, yet her blue eyes never leave mine. Finally, she replies, "It's the middle of the night."

"No, my lady, it's the middle of our weekend. You tell me, bed or here, or I'll decide."

"Bed...but give me a minute first and promise me that you won't fall asleep."

"There's not a chance."

Shana slips through my fingers as her smile reemerges.

While I give her the minute she requested, I close the living room window. Before I do, I glance out and up. The space between the buildings isn't large, yet up in the sky is a full moon. I think of an old childhood story about wishes. I'm not sure what makes me think of it, but with my hands on the windowsill I look up to the moon. My mind tells me it's children's fables, that I used up my quota when I was young.

For the first time, I'm not listening to my mind.

My heart wants another one. I speak softly. "If wishes can come true, I want to fulfill every one of hers...and I don't want mine to end."

When I reach the bedroom, I hear Shana in the bathroom as light seeps from under the door.

Instead of thinking about why she was really out on the fire escape crying, I concentrate on whatever she has for my surprise. Each thought returns blood to my cock, reviving the erection that has been perpetual since she arrived here

Friday night. I reach for the sheet, not wanting her to think that sex is my only thought. As I do, she calls out to me.

"Trevor? Are you there?"

"I'm always here."

Slowly the door opens. With the backlight surrounding her, she reminds me of the pictures they show you of angels. That's what she is to me, and yet the negligee she's wearing would probably prohibit her from entering heaven's gates.

"Holy shit..." I mutter as I sit taller, completely unaware that the sheet I used to cover me is now lifted like a tent ready for camping.

Her cheeks rise as she comes closer, and her gaze goes from my lap to my eyes. "I guess that means you like your surprise?"

"You're fucking gorgeous." Forgetting my effort to cover myself I reach for her hand and stand. Lifting our hands, she slowly spins as her beauty is displayed from every angle. "I'm glad you didn't wear that one onstage."

"It's only for you."

"My favorite kind of fashion show with my absolutely favorite model."

Letting go of my hand, she walks to the end of the bed and stops. Turning she continues around to the other side.

"Where are you going?"

"I'm giving you your own show."

"Oh, I've seen enough. Come back here."

"Are you telling me what to do?"

"I am. Are you in agreement?"

Her smile broadens as she does as I said and comes closer. Looking first at my erection and then back to me, she says, "Yes, Trevor. I've never been in more agreement in my life."

"What do you want right now, my lady?"

"I want you."

"You've got me. Tell me more," I say.

As her cheeks grow pinker, she does. She tells me more.

Reaching for my cock, she runs her hand up and down my length. "This time, I want to be on top. I want to be the one who decides when you..."

"When I come?"

"Yes."

"Under one condition."

"What?" she asks.

"Don't take off my surprise."

Her blue eyes twinkle as she leads me to bed, directing my arms behind my head, I wait through the most exciting anticipation of my life. Staring at the ceiling, I expect her to climb on, to straddle and ride me until we're both over our mountain and stars erupt.

She doesn't.

When I lift my head, Shana is at the foot of the bed, crawling between my legs. Each movement ends with a kiss or a nip as she moves closer and closer.

*Fuck!* It's agony how fucking slowly she's moving.

"Shana."

Her tongue laps over my thigh and then the other. "Have I told you how sexy I think your thighs are?"

*Thighs.*

"I-I...goddamn it." I grip my own wrist, fighting my need to pull her up. "You said you wanted to be on top. Get on top."

Her soft laugh sends electrical shocks straight to my dick. I look up, but all I can see is her golden hair as she's inching closer. And then her lips take me in.

"Oh fuck."

Her hands move in sync as she sucks and licks. My balls grow painfully tight.

"I'm fucking serious, Shana."

"Not yet, baby," she coos. "I want you to remember I've been here."

She's using my words. My girl is using my words, and I've never been so damn turned on in my life.

"Baby, it doesn't work that way for men. You need to jump on...now."

Rolling my balls in her grasp, she takes one more long suck. The pressure is building, and I'm doing everything I can think of not to blow.

I'm constructing bridges, doing math equations, counting from 100 backwards.

100

99

98

97...

Nothing is working and then...

*Yes!*

"Fucking...yes..."

Her lips pepper my neck with kisses as her tight pussy grips my penis and I'm propelled by catapult straight through the pearly gates.

"Trevor. Trevor." Her soft hand cups my cheek. "Open your eyes."

I don't think my body has ever been this tight. I'm not sure I can control my eyes and cock at the same time.

"Trevor."

Slowly, my eyes open to the most beautiful vision.

Shana. Her hair is veiled over her shoulders, and her tits are covered in the white lace and right before my eyes.

"Please, move your arms and hold me tight."

I will my arms to respond, reaching for her hips. As I do, she rolls herself forward and then back. "Baby, this is..."

"Hold me," she says as her movements grow faster. "I think we may be in for a rough ride."

*Holy shit!*

The friction is...like nothing...

My grip tightens as my fingers press against her hips. I can't take my eyes off of her. The ecstasy of her expression as she moves, the way her hair teases my face when she leans down, and her hard nipples tenting the silk of the negligee...

"Trevor...Oh, Trevor..."

"I've got you."

# CHAPTER
## Twenty Seven

### *Shana*

Kimbra meets us at the door of her apartment, eyeing me up and down, her smile growing as she scans.

Looking down, I take a peek at the skirt and top I'm wearing, the ones I packed after talking to Kimbra. The skirt is long and flowing and the top is simple, yet chic. My shoes are a gladiator asymmetrical wedge, the soft straps fitting around my ankles. My hair is down with soft curls at the end and my makeup is minimal—especially compared to the day on the runway. And yet the way she's looking at me, I feel exposed. Her grin makes me want to blush, as if she's seeing beyond my well-thought-out outfit and knows every intimate thing Trevor and I have done since our last visit to her apartment.

Maybe that's what friends see when they look at you. They see what your words haven't had the chance to share. It's why Stephen knew I was having bunny-rabbit sex without my saying a word.

As my other best friend briefly crosses my mind, I recall a few of his subtle hints that I've recently been too preoccupied to notice. Now that I think about it, if I didn't know better, I'd say his sex life has improved too.

"Come on in, you two," Kimbra says with a wave. "Beth and Christopher are here."

Trevor's hand warms the small of my back, giving me confidence as we move forward.

The moment we enter the living room and his parents come into view, my anxiety wanes. Trevor told me that his parents were in their early sixties. I should have known that the couple who donated their genes to Trevor and Duncan Willis wouldn't be the epitome of grandparents in the making. No white-haired people with rocking chairs.

Beth, Trevor's mom, is absolutely beautiful in a comforting but not overpowering way. She's petite yet curvy. Her hair is a mixture of Duncan and Trevor's, not as dark as one or as light as the other. And right away, it's her eyes that I notice, the same stunning green as her sons'. What makes them even better is the way they're smiling at me, sincere and loving, with little fine lines crinkling their corners.

"Shana, it's so good to meet you again," she says.

I fight with the *again* in her sentence, and then I recall Kimbra's wedding. "Yes, Mrs. Willis, it's nice to see you again too."

"Oh, dear, my name is Beth," she says as she wraps me in a hug. Over her shoulder I notice Duncan's and Kimbra's smiles. When she pulls back, she looks me directly in the eye. "Now, I want to hear all about how you caught my son's attention." She lowers her voice. "And I can't tell you how happy we are that you did."

I glance over to Trevor, who comes to the rescue, securing my hand and tugging me back toward him. "Mom, yes, this is Shana. Can you please let her breathe?"

Beth laughs, reaching for Trevor and giving him a hug. "I can't believe that I had to learn about this beautiful—and from what I hear, successful—woman from someone besides my son."

Trevor's gaze goes to Duncan and back to his mom. "Yeah, I was surprised about that too."

"Hey," Duncan says, "I didn't say a word."

Without shame, Kimbra raises her hand. "It was me. It was all me. I just couldn't contain myself, and well, Duncan got tired of listening to me go on and on, so I called Beth."

A handsome man, an older version of what I decide is more Trevor than Duncan, steps forward offering me his hand. "It's always the dad who's the last to know. Nice to meet you, Shana. Since no one is introducing me, I will. I'm Christopher Willis."

"Hello, Mr. Willis."

"And that makes you, Miss Price?" he says with a wink.

"Christopher," I correct. "It seems like you all know all about me."

It's Kimbra's turn to speak. "First and last name. Occupation. Current job status as well as the possibilities for the future. Most sharable information from our living together." She smiles my direction. "With emphasis on your affinity for shoes. I love the ones you're wearing, by the way. Oh, and I didn't mention cannoli."

"Oh, do you like cannoli?" Beth asks.

Duncan, Kimbra, Trevor, and I all turn her way as the blood drains from my cheeks. I feel faint as the life-giving circulation seems to still. If it weren't for Trevor's hand returning to my back, I think I may fall to the floor.

"If you do," she goes on, totally oblivious to my discomfort, "I have the best recipe. Do you bake?"

Letting out a breath, I answer with a nod, "I-I love to bake, but honestly, I don't do much since I live alone."

"Oh, let me send you my recipe. The best part is you can freeze them, and then you don't have to eat them all at once." She laughs as we all find seats around Duncan and Kimbra's living room. "I know for me personally, if I don't use some self-control, I can overindulge on cannoli."

Kimbra leans back in an oversized chair—or maybe a baby loveseat, I'm not sure—next to Duncan and grins. "Death by cannoli. Not a bad way to go."

"So, Dad," Trevor says, trying to change the subject, "how's work?"

"Should I share with the competition?"

"Dad and I work for different engineering firms," Trevor explains.

A few minutes later when Kimbra stands, I do also. "Maybe I could help you in the kitchen?" I ask.

Beth stands too. "I'm all for letting the men do the cleanup—well, your men," she adds with a laugh. "Christopher and I will be off to the Philharmonic. But for now, we can help Kimbra get the dinner ready." She puts her arm around my back. "So you and Kimbra lived together here in New York and now you live in London? I've always wanted to visit London. What should I see first? Buckingham Palace? The London Eye? Big Ben? There are just so many options."

We step into the kitchen to the wonderful aroma of whatever Kimbra is cooking.

"Kimbra, this smells divine. What is it?"

She waves me off. "It's just a pork loin. We have potatoes and some vegetables."

"Honey," Beth says to me, "I brought an apple pie. However, if I'd have known you loved cannoli, I would have brought my homemade ones."

Shaking my head, I look past Beth to Kimbra's smile, and it takes all of my restraint not to break out laughing.

"Beth," Kimbra says, "I left my glass of wine in the living room."

"Oh," I say, "So did I. I can go get them."

"Nonsense, girls, I'll go get them." Before Beth makes it to the door, she turns back. "Shana, I promise, I'm not always this overwhelming. It's that I'm so happy you're here and that you and Kimbra are friends. It's every mother's dream."

"I'm happy to be here."

Once she's gone, I turn to Kimbra. "Death by cannoli?"

"Technically, we've already tried her homemade ones." Her eyebrows dance.

My nose scrunches. "Oh my God, will you stop?"

"She is their mother. She made them."

I shake my head, wondering how long it will take for Beth to return with our wine.

"Fine," Kimbra says. "How was your no-plan weekend?"

"It was wonderful."

And then reality hits me like a subway train, and my laughter disappears as tears prick the back of my eyes.

Kimbra reaches for my hands. "Babe, I'm sorry if I made you uncomfortable with the cannoli. It's just that Duncan is still giving me a hard time about it."

"A hard time? And you're complaining?" I shake my head as I look down with a sigh and continue before letting her speak. "No. It's not that. It's that I really like Trevor. I like him a lot."

"If that's a secret, you're not doing a good job of hiding it."

"I think he likes me."

"You think?" she asks.

I take a deep breath and wipe away a renegade tear that escaped down my cheek. "Five more days and it's over."

"Stop. It's not. According to Stephen you killed that fashion show. Even you have told me that the numbers have exceeded speculation. I know enough about the running of a business to know that numbers speak louder than anyone's opinion. Have faith."

"I want to."

Before Kimbra can reply, the kitchen door swings inward and Beth enters with three large goblets of moscato. I move toward her, trying to ease one from her hands.

"Oh, don't worry about me," she says, "A long time ago, I was a waitress."

"You were?" I ask, surprised.

"Working my way through college, I could carry three platters on one arm."

"Wow," I say, impressed.

Kimbra bumps her shoulder into mine. "I told Beth all about you, but I didn't have a chance to fill you in on Beth. Did Trevor?"

My cheeks warm. "We didn't get the chance to talk..."

Beth and Kimbra laugh in a way that makes me blush while at the same time feel like I'm talking with two friends instead of just one.

"I'm not that exciting," Beth says.

"Don't let her fool you. Beth is a teacher. She works for a public-school system upstate, specializing in reading comprehension." Kimbra gives her mother-in-law a knowing smile. "When it comes to patience, she's right up there with Job."

"My boys gave me all the practice I needed."

*Her boys.*

Earlier she'd said *your men.*

It's funny to think they're the same.

While the three of us talk and laugh, I realize that Duncan's success and wealth isn't the status quo of how and where he and Trevor were raised. In many ways, the Willises are similar to the Prices or even Kimbra's family, hard-working and loving, wanting nothing but happiness for each other.

As Kimbra fidgets with the last of the dinner prepara-tions, Beth fills me in on some stories about Duncan and Trevor as children. She mentions how they coexisted but were never as close as she'd wanted. Being two years apart in age, they were more competitive than she would have liked.

"Christopher and I did our best to keep the competition to a minimum. It was pretty obvious early on that they had different interests and strengths. We tried to promote those strengths in each one."

"Trevor is more like his dad," she says after refilling her wine glass.

"He's quieter than Duncan," Kimbra explains.

Beth shrugs. "The thing some people don't see, espe-cially if they're around people like Duncan and me, is that men like Christopher—and Trevor, I would presume—save their words for when it's important, for when they're with the person they truly want to have hear them."

Her observation returns my smile. I'd heard for over a year from Kimbra how quiet and shy Trevor was, but from our first meeting, my assessment was completely different. In Beth's words, that makes me the one person for whom he's saved his words.

Beth smiles at Kimbra. "And then there's Duncan, who

does take more after me. Sometimes people like us don't know when to be quiet. It could be said that we talk too much or are too demonstrative."

"I like demonstrative," Kimbra says.

"And, honey, we're all glad you do.

"I'd guess that you're talking too much now."

We all turn as Trevor enters the kitchen. Putting his arm around me and pulling me to his side, he asks, "Has my mother scared you off yet?"

I smile at Beth. "Actually, the opposite."

Before we know it, all three men are in the kitchen and everyone is carrying plates and platters to the dining room. The talking and laughing barely ceases, despite the fact that we're all eating the delicious meal.

It is as Trevor and I are leaving their penthouse that he gives me a kiss. "I'm sorry you had to put up with my family."

"I like your family."

He shrugs. "You know, after thirty-three years, they're starting to grow on me too."

# CHAPTER

### *Shana*

*E*merging from the subway tunnel near Rockefeller Center, I squint as the sunshine fills the street. As the crowd pushes forward, I'm like a salmon in a stream. Thankfully, we're all swimming the same direction.

Looking at my watch, I calculate that if I can walk the rest of the way at a swift pace, I'll make it to the tenth floor of Saks with over three minutes to spare. Considering that Trevor and I woke later than planned, my decision to take the subway instead of aboveground transportation may have saved the day.

When I went to Trevor's apartment Friday night, I didn't intend to stay until Monday morning, but plans change. That's my new attitude.

Adapt.

After spending the afternoon with his family, I didn't want to leave him and go back to my hotel alone. Continuing our no-plans weekend, we went back to his apartment, laid a blanket on the living room floor, picnicked with cheese and fruit, and continued our Netflix marathon with a few intermissions for exercise. Thank goodness we had the cheese and fruit for needed nourishment.

*Who knew watching television was so taxing?*

I giggle to myself as I make my way over to Fifth Avenue and up toward Fiftieth Street, trying not to think about how easy it would be to get used to spending my time away from work with Trevor or how nice it would be to go home to him each evening. Nevertheless, as the ideas creep into my thoughts, I find myself relishing them instead of dismissing them.

Maybe it's a new attitude for a new week. Kimbra is right. Numbers are what matter in sales and after all, that is the essence of what I do. I sell.

"Good morning, Shana."

"Good morning."

I smile as I make my way back to the temporary office Stephen and I are using. As soon as I enter, Stephen's expression takes away my newly obtained optimism. "What's up?"

"Check your email."

"That sounds ominous," I say as I fling my purse into the bottom desk drawer, turn on my computer, and notice the steaming grande cup of cappuccino sitting in the middle of my desk. Prying the lid from the tall white cup, I say, "You're the best."

"I am."

The screen before me comes to life, displaying too many unread emails. I guess that's what happens when my phone is turned off. "Before I jump into whatever this is, how was your weekend with your parents?"

His expression lightens. "It was fabulous. I got to see my sister's kid. He's this giant baby."

"Giant?"

"Well, he's something like months old. You know how parents never use years. I think I figured I'm now nearing my 361st month birthday."

I laugh, thinking how right he is. I have Facebook

friends that post pictures of their children with little month signs on the baby's tummy. For only a second, I imagine Stephen holding his sign. "So are you a giant baby?" Before he answers, I add, "And what do you want for your 361st month birthday?"

"Nothing. I'm not a giant baby. I think it's somewhere over 30 months when you cease to be a baby and become a kid." He points at his chest. "I've moved into man status."

"Yes, I'm glad to hear that."

"It's my nephew, Landon. He's this little football player." Stephen lowers his voice. "He's only like ten or eleven months—not quite a year—and he has all these adorable wrinkles on his chubby arms and legs. His dad thinks he's going to be an offensive lineman. But little Landon and I had a talk."

"Oh no."

"Yes, girl, we did. He wants to take after Uncle Stephen. He's already interested in the arts. He kept pushing the button on this toy and playing the same song over and over. I see show choir in his future. Then of course, the costumes will instill a love for fashion. In fashion design he's going to be king. We'll start our own design company."

"Should I ask about your brother-in-law's thoughts on this?"

"He'll get over the offensive line thing. Too many injuries. Fashion design is safer."

"How does your sister feel about the change of plans?"

Stephen waves me off. "We didn't include her in the conversation. What mothers don't know won't hurt them."

I smile, looking at my screen and seeing an email from Beth Willis, subject line: Best Cannoli. Yes, sometimes it might be better to keep mothers in the dark. I mean, I'm sure her recipe is good, but I personally believe I've found the best.

It's then I see the email from Neil Butler, our supervisor in London.

My stomach twists as my cursor hovers over his name. "Is it the Neil email you're talking about?"

Stephen nods.

"What does it say?"

"Who am I? Your assistant?" he asks.

"Well, technically, yes."

"The email is to both of us. He wants to have a conference call with us and HR in London tomorrow. He needs confirmation that we can both be on the call."

Instead of opening the email, I lean back in the chair. "Do you think this is good or bad?"

"I guess it depends on your definition of those evaluations."

When Stephen turns his chair with his back to me, I remember the text I sent him. "Hey, you never returned my text message."

"Yes, I did."

I pull out my phone and see that the sound is still muted from Trevor's and my no-plans weekend. Scrolling, I find Stephen's response:

**"MY MOM SAYS HI BACK. SHE SAID SHE MISSED SEEING YOU. WHAT SECRET?"**

The time stamp is this morning.

When I look up, he's staring at me from the corner of his eye.

"You finally replied...this morning?"

"I've been a little busy. You just read it...this morning."

"What aren't you telling me?"

He spins my direction with an exaggerated exhale. "A lot and it's killing me. I'm sorry. But your plate is a little full, and I wanted you to concentrate on your weekend with Mr. Sexy, you know, when you aren't thinking about here. You don't need to think about me."

"Stephen, that's not how friendship works. You know what's happening with me."

His eyebrows dance. "Bunny-rabbit sex." He sits taller. "How did he like the negligee? He didn't think it was too forward, did he? Oh, do tell."

Warmth fills not only my cheeks but my body as I recall Trevor's private fashion show and what came after it. "He thought it was okay."

"No way. *Okay* was not that man's assessment."

My grin grows larger. "He seemed to like it, a lot."

"And not too forward?"

I shrug. "The negligee wasn't. I might have been...that time."

He picks up a small tablet from the top of his desk and begins to fan himself. "Save the details for lunch. Give me something to look forward to."

"No details. Use your imagination."

"I'll save that until lunch, too. Otherwise I won't be able to concentrate."

I turn back to my computer screen. "Are you free tomorrow at nine? That's a good time for both time zones."

After Stephen checks his schedule, we both agree on nine-thirty, and I reply to Mr. Butler.

"Stephen," Vicky says, leaning her head through the doorway. "We need you in conference room four."

"What's happening in conference room four?" I ask after she's gone.

"If I'm lucky, it'll be an announcement that Saks is expanding into men's lingerie." When he stands, he goes on, "You know...Speedo-esque, G-strings, and thongs for men."

"Those are on the market."

His grin grows as he grabs his tablet to leave. "Preaching to the choir."

Once he's gone, I sit back and spend the next three hours replying to emails and fighting fires across the Atlantic. While Stephen and I have been in New York, our positions have remained vacated in London. It isn't like the junior department ceased to exist simply because we were on another continent.

Some of the emails deserved one response while others create a complicated string with attachments and multiple copies.

As the last fire begins to sputter out, I lean back and sigh. It's a strange sensation, or should I say a recently unfamiliar one. It feels good to make decisions and be in charge. I didn't realize how much I missed what we'd accomplished in juniors. In the two years we've been in our positions, Stephen and I have made a name for ourselves. For a few hours on Monday morning, I was reminded of what that was like.

I look up toward the door as Stephen returns with Vicky by his side. "Shana, don't forget," she says, "meeting at one-thirty with purchasing."

I click on the folder on my desktop to retrieve the data I've prepared. "I'm ready. See you then," I say, trying my most un-bitchy voice.

"I won't be there. I'm sure you can handle it."

And with that, she's gone.

"That woman hates me."

"I think she's scared of you," Stephen offers.

"What was your meeting about?"

"Well, it wasn't about branching into men's sexy attire." When I don't respond, he continues. "It was about the sales website. They want to spice up the way customers can see the products online."

"You know, we don't have to be a team. You have so much to offer beyond me."

"Are you trying to get rid of me, just as we're about to go to lunch and discuss our crazy-sexed weekends?"

"I'd never want to get rid of..." I process his words. "Wait. What did you just say? You had a crazy sexed-up weekend at your parents' house?"

He tilts his head toward the door. "Come on. I'm starving."

The clock on my computer says I have an hour and fifteen minutes until my meeting. "I need to be back a little after one."

Stephen nods.

"If we don't have time for all your details, this conversation is extending to after work."

"Sorry, boss lady, you only get me during working hours. Tonight, I have a date."

# CHAPTER
## Twenty Nine

**Trevor**

Shana stares at me pointedly as we sit across the table from one another at a quaint little pub near my apartment. Truth be told, I've exhausted my repertoire of cooking skills and people can only eat so much pizza. Thankfully, we had Kimbra's cooking yesterday, and Shana has offered more than once to cook, but my cupboards are bare. And I'd rather spend time with Shana doing things other than shopping for groceries.

"He said you knew. Why didn't you say anything?" she asks.

"Why didn't I say anything?"

Shana's lips come together as her eyes widen.

"You're asking me why I didn't say anything to you about Max still being in town."

"Yes, Trevor, that's exactly what I'm asking. Now that we have that cleared up, could we move on to your answer?"

I grin as I take a small drink of my beer. It's a local craft with a dark color and a surprisingly non-hoppy taste. After I swallow, I look again at the feisty lady staring me down. If I thought she was really upset, I wouldn't take this so lightly. The way she started the conversation with *Oh my God, wait until I tell you what's happening with Stephen...* is what has given me this pass. "You know you're cute when you try to be snippy?"

"I'm not trying to being snippy. One of my best friends had a relationship crisis—"

"Which—may I interject—was never explained to me. All I knew was that the two of you ran out of the bar after you got more than snippy with Max."

Shana takes another bite of her French fries before answering. "It wasn't up to me to tell. I couldn't betray his trust. After all, you were a friend of the enemy."

"Max and I are still friends," I say.

"The difference is that apparently now he's no longer the enemy."

I think about how Max hasn't called me today, how I'm waiting to hear from his investors and his firm about McCobb's proposal. Maybe now he is my enemy? I need to give that some more thought. "Okay, can you tell me now?"

"First, tell me why you didn't tell me he was still in town?"

"Shana, when did we discuss Max and Stephen before tonight? I asked what happened the night we met at that bar. You mentioned pond scum, and then said you couldn't talk about it. Yes, I met with Max last Friday, but how was I to know that you didn't know he was here? He and I talked mostly about business. And, if I need to be perfectly blunt, from the moment you arrived to my apartment last Friday night until you rushed out this morning, talking about business or Max or even Stephen wasn't high on my agenda."

Her cheeks rise as she leans forward.

I do my best to keep my eyes on hers. After all, they're bright and blue and beautiful. It's just that if I move my gaze slightly down, her blouse has a great neckline that gives me a hint of her perky breasts below. When our eyes meet again, she shakes her head at me.

"What?" I ask innocently.

"If I didn't know better, I'd think your agenda hasn't changed."

"I confess, Shana Price, I'm crazy about you, and if we follow my agenda, after we finish this meal, we'll go back to my place and continue not talking about anyone else. I'm okay with not talking at all. Personally, I like those noises you make when you're too consumed to talk."

With each word I say, pink fills her cheeks until they're both as red and rosy as my grandmother's—who used to wear way too much rouge. It's not that I'm an expert on makeup, but I remember the term *rouge* because my mom always thought it was funny.

"Trevor, I can't stay at your place tonight. All my work clothes are at the hotel." She looks down. "As it is, I wore the same outfit I wore to Kimbra's to work today."

"Would it be too forward to offer to pack my own bag and accompany you to your hotel suite?"

"I guess I do owe you one night for the night in Indianapolis."

"Best night of my life," I say.

"Really? We didn't do anything."

I reach for her hand and lift it until her knuckles reach my lips. "Yes, we did, my lady. We met."

She lets out a long breath. "Of course, you can stay. I need to gather all my things in your apartment anyway. I'm afraid some of my clothes may have gone MIA."

"The case of the missing panties," I say with a scoff.

"If you're thinking of writing romance, I suggest another title."

"That was a mystery. Speaking of mysteries, will you tell me what's happening or happened with Max and Stephen?"

Shana sits back, her expression a multitude of emotions as she explains how Max and Stephen met nearly a year ago in London. It was through a mutual friend. That friend was Max's assistant. The assistant and Stephen were friends since college. The assistant—his name is Charles—moved to London a few years before Stephen and Shana.

"Wait, Charles Mills?" I ask.

"Yes. How do you know that?"

"I met Max through my work. His investment company has financed projects I've been directly involved with for McCobb Engineering. I've spoken to Charles before when I've called Max."

"At work?"

"Yes," I answer suspiciously. "I have Max's cell phone number but not a number for his flat."

Shana leans across the table. "You're a smart man. Do you see where this is going?"

"Charles set Stephen and Max up. They hit it off. Charles wasn't happy?"

Shana shrugs. "When the incident happened, I didn't think to question. I mean, if you were to walk into my apartment and my assistant was in my shower, would you stick around to ask him why or his intentions?"

"Intentions," I say, remembering that Max had used the same word when we'd spoken. "What were his intentions?"

"Whose? Max or Charles?"

I savor the question, enjoying the puzzle Shana's created. "Let me guess," I say. "From Max's point of view, he had honorable intentions for having Charles at his flat. But...Stephen didn't take the time to find out."

"So it now seems," Shana confirms. "I don't know Charles's intentions. All I know is that Max fired him.

There's no sexual harassment suit pending, so that in itself speaks for Max's intentions. Charles told him a sob story about a broken pipe at his place. He then purposely set up a message that appeared to come from Max to Stephen."

I nod my head. "For the record, I'd wait for him to get his ass out of your shower, but then I'd question him. I don't think he's your type."

"Who?"

"Stephen. You asked me what I'd do if I found him in your shower."

Shana giggles as she finishes her glass of wine. "He's not. I'm not his type either. Max is." She sighs. "That's the thing that made their breakup so upsetting. When they were together, Stephen was so happy. I guess it is the bunny-rabbit sex."

I tilt my head. "Do I want to know what that is?"

"Just go with it. I promise, you aren't complaining."

"Now they're back together?"

"They are so back together," Shana says, "that Max went with Stephen last weekend to meet his parents and sister. Stephen's phone is full of pictures with Max and Landon."

"Who's Landon?"

"Stephen's baby nephew."

"Max Cantel held a baby?"

"According to Stephen," Shana says, "he held him a lot. And the baby loved him. If you ask me, Stephen has baby fever."

I can't stop my grin as I take in Shana's excitement for her friend. "You know, you really are a great friend."

She shrugs. "I have a lot of people who I consider friends but only a few really good friends. When someone makes it to that level, I want only the best for them. Even if that means it's not the best for me."

"What do you mean?"

"Stephen and I have a telephone call in the morning with our boss in London. I've decided that if by some miracle I get this job here, I'm giving my full support for Stephen to be hired in my previous position in juniors. I'll miss him like crazy, but he's good. He's very good at what he does. I'm not sure how I'll manage without him. The most important thing is for him to be recognized for his talents. And if you add Max to that mix, my best friend will be happy."

"What makes you happy, Shana?"

"Right now, it's you."

"I like that answer." I leave cash in the small folder with our bill and reach for her hand. "Shall we find those missing panties?"

Her eyes grow wide as her head moves from side to side, checking to see if anyone heard.

"Think of it as a mystery," I say in a stage whisper.

"I'd rather think of it as a romance."

I lean close to her ear. "Is there a lot of sex in those books you read?"

"It depends on the book."

"With a title like *The Case of the Missing Panties*, I think there should be sex."

"I agree, Mr. Willis. How else would they be missing?"

# CHAPTER
## *Thirty*

### *Shana*

"*I* can't believe they're taking this to the final buzzer," Trevor says through my phone.

Though his sports reference isn't lost on me, I'm too worried about what is about to happen to reply right away. Unable to sit still, I grip my phone tighter as I pace about Stephen's and my temporary office that is no longer.

All of our things are packed and ready for our flight. According to the people with Saks who organize our travel, with the royal wedding about to occur, there is no turning back on our pre-booked flights. If we did, we wouldn't get another flight for over a week—which doesn't sound bad to me—and the increase in cost would be astronomical—which sounds bad to them.

Even my hotel room is packed. "I know that I'm leaving," I say to Trevor, "but I wish I knew if I were coming back."

"Listen, I know you've worked for Saks for a long time. I know you love the company, but in my opinion, the way they've treated you on this is shitty. They flew you over because they needed someone to save the day and *you* did it. You and Stephen took what they gave you and made a kick-ass fashion show. Not only did you tweak it and make it a grand production but when it was needed, you did what that woman Vicky could never do. You put yourself out there as a model."

Despite the way my temples are pounding with this tension headache, the tips of my lips turn upward. "Are you a fashion-show connoisseur?"

"And a self-appointed model connoisseur. As luck would have it, I've been witness to two fashion shows in the last two weeks. The first one was definitely kick-ass with music and a stage and many stunning models. But the second one..." He lets out a long hum as if he's reminiscing. "...it had music from the window, no stage, and the most sensational model I've ever seen. That one was phenomenal."

"I'm glad you liked it. However, if fashion shows are judged on sales, the first one sold more."

"That's okay, my lady, the second one sold me."

Vicky's assistant taps on the open door. "Miss Price, they're ready for you."

"Trevor, I need to go."

"I love you. You can do this."

My mouth goes dry and my entire body freezes.

*Did he just say that he loves me?*

I can't respond.

"Shana, you can do this."

"Trevor?"

"Call me. I'll be waiting." And the line goes dead.

*Holy shit.*

Dropping those three words on me isn't what I need seconds before walking into this meeting. As if I don't have enough things to think about...

And then I let his words sink in and for a moment, take time to smile.

He did it. For only a split second, Trevor took my mind off this job. He reminded me that there's more to life than what is going to happen in this meeting. I'm not sure if that was his intention; nevertheless, it worked.

As I walk toward the conference room of my destiny, I remember the call Stephen and I had with Neil Butler. Our boss in juniors made his case clear. He wants us back. He wants both of us, and he's even worked out the numbers to put the money where his mouth is.

He's heard the rumors about us moving to lingerie and worked to receive authorization to increase our salary to match what we would make in lingerie. The kicker is that it would be in London. We'd be going back to stay.

During the phone call, I broached the subject of Stephen returning on his own and hiring his own assistant. While Stephen still scoffs at the idea, Neil didn't reject it.

Now it seems that the only factor separating the two positions is location.

*Or is it?*

In London, I'll report to Neil, the man who went out of his way to facilitate our return. In New York, I'll report to...

"Hello, Vicky..." I say, greeting everyone around the table as I enter the conference room.

Stephen hands me a small-stemmed glass and a tiny wine bottle as our plane reaches cruising altitude over the Atlantic Ocean. "You can't regret trying."

"That's what they say," I reply, my eyes still puffy, and my damn nose running like a faucet.

"You made the right decision."

I turn his way. "I don't know. You could have had juniors all to yourself. You'd be in London with Max, and if I'd taken what she offered, I'd be in New York." The words are like the twisting of a knife in my heart. I'm not in New York and it's my fault.

"It was a bullshit offer."

I finish pouring the contents of the small bottle into my glass and nod. "It was worse than a bullshit offer. Move to the children's department with the title I had before I left for London, including a twenty-percent decrease in salary and loss of my PTO—paid time off." I turn his way, my voice growing louder. "What kind of bullshit offer is that?"

Stephen's arm comes up and around my shoulder. "It's a suck-balls bullshit offer. It's worse than that. It's a sucking-hairy-balls bullshit offer."

"She couldn't deny the numbers," I say. "She wanted to, but there they were in black and white. In the room full of people, she couldn't kick me out after all we accomplished. So, instead, she came up with the shitty, hairy-balls offer."

"And you told her what to do with it."

"For a moment," I admit, "I was so flabbergasted; I couldn't comprehend what she had said. It didn't make sense. I started in juniors. Juniors is ahead of children's on the hierarchy of departments. She wanted to demote me to children and decrease my pay."

"Because you scare her. She sees your passion and talent. She's intimidated."

I set my glass within the indented circle on my small tray and let my face fall forward. "For a second, I almost took it."

"I know, honey."

Tears fill my eyes as my shoulders shudder.

"I wanted to stay..."

Stephen waits until I've quieted a little before offering me his napkin. "Here, your impersonation of a raccoon is getting too real. I think there's some TSA regulation about wild animals on planes."

Though I don't give a damn about my mascara, I take his napkin. In two dabs it's covered in black. "I-I barely got to see him," I say between sobs. "I had tried so hard to have hope. And when Vicky said she had an offer...before it was laid out...I did. It was all right there."

Stephen isn't holding my shoulder any longer, but his hand is covering mine. "What was all there?"

"You know? The dream. The whole entire picture. I never realized how badly I wanted it. I never let myself think about it. My goal has always been my career. I've worked my ass off to get where I am."

Stephen nods as he hands me my wine. "You have. It's like it's nearly totally gone."

"What?"

"Your ass. You don't even have one." He nods. "Legs straight to back."

I shake my head. "It was there. I could see it."

"I find Pilates helps."

"Stephen, I'm talking about the dream—the career *and* that someone special. I could get used to spending all my nonworking time with him. I did. In two damn weeks, I got used to it. Falling asleep and waking. Simple things like standing side by side when we brushed our teeth, having morning coffee...I know it's dumb, but it was..."

"It *was*..." I go on. "As in past tense. It's over. I gave it up to not lose twenty percent in salary and my paid days off."

"No, you didn't. That decrease she offered you was based on your current salary. It's not based on the increase Neil offered. By not accepting her offer, not only did your income not decrease by twenty percent, but also it is going to be increasing another fifteen."

"And besides the money," Stephen continues, "you're back on point in juniors. Your title hasn't changed for the worse. And one more thing, you're working where you're appreciated."

Suddenly, I have a thought. "Vicky talked to you first. Did you know what she would offer me before it happened?"

"No, not exactly."

"What does that mean?" I ask.

"Boss lady, before you went in there, I told her what I've told you: we are a team. I'm not upset about the way this went. I'm moving back to London, we're still together, and I too am getting that fifteen percent increase that Neil offered."

"He obviously didn't know what was going down in New York. He could have had us—"

"Or he did," Stephen suggests, "and he was afraid Witch Vicky might turn you against the company as a whole, and he didn't want to lose you."

"How can you always make me feel better?"

"It's in my job description," Stephen says with a smile. "And for the record, I know that this time with Trevor, this time leaving for London, it will be different."

"I want that. It's just that as I was leaving, he seemed so...I don't know the right word... distracted."

"Maybe he was holding out for the same dream. You know how those macho men are?"

I scoff. "Like you?"

"Yes, exactly like me." Stephen covers my hand again. "No, macho men want to fix everything. Your man is a planner and a builder. My guess is that he seemed distracted because that was what his man-mind was doing. Instead of giving you his full attention, he was figuring and contemplating. You know, like with the bridges and roads."

I sigh, recalling how Trevor kept looking at his phone instead of at me. I know that's a modern-day issue with everyone, but we were standing at JFK outside of security. Our kiss goodbye was about as romantic as a brother kissing a sister. Okay, it was a little better than that because it was on the lips and that would be...Eww.

"May I get you more wine?" the flight attendant asks, looking my way.

"Oh, the answer to that question for the entire flight is yes," I say. "And even if you have to wake me, it's still yes."

"She'll have *one* more for now," Stephen interjects, lifting one finger to emphasize his point.

"And for you, sir?"

"One also, for now. Thank you."

"You're not my babysitter," I remind him after she walks away.

"No, I'm your assistant. We're not in a hotel room with pizza. We can't exactly follow your mother's rule with pretzels and peanuts. It's my job to keep you in a state that will allow you to walk off the plane because we're not losing our new increase in salary or giving Witch Vicky ammunition to point fingers."

Leaning my head on Stephen's shoulders, I close my eyes. "I love you."

"I love you, too."

It's then I remember Trevor's words on the telephone and I reach for my purse, grabbing my phone.

"What are you doing?" Stephen asks. "You can't call or text from up here."

"No, but I can send an email. The airline has internet."

He covers my hand with his. "Maybe we shouldn't drunken email from fifty thousand feet."

"It's not drunken emailing. It's saying what I should've said this afternoon." I squint my eyes, but the letters and icons on the screen are still blurry. Thrusting my phone toward Stephen, I say, "You're my assistant. Connect me to the internet and find Trevor's email."

"Shana, is this a good idea?"

"My assistant."

A few minutes later he hands me back my phone. "You're connected to Wi-Fi. I have Trevor Willis's email. Are you sure you want to do this?"

I take my phone and with one eye closed carefully type out my message.

*Trevor,*

*I didn't want to leave you. I hope we can do this long distance.*

*No matter what happens. I heard you this afternoon. I'm sorry I didn't say it too. My silence wasn't because I don't but because I was shocked that you said it.*

*Just so you know and never doubt...I love you, too.*

*Yours,*

*Shana*

I hit send before I can change my mind and hand my phone back to Stephen. "Can you disconnect the Wi-Fi?"

"Yes, boss lady, it's very difficult. It's called *airplane mode*."

I lay my head back on his shoulder and close my eyes. "See, that's why we're a great team."

# CHAPTER
## *Thirty One*

***Shana***

*There's nothing like sleeping in your own bed.*

That saying is true. Since we landed at Heathrow Airport on Saturday morning and Ubered to our respective homes, it's what I've been doing. Of course, because it's all I've been doing, I have no food in my apartment—well, other than a few open boxes of cereal that may or may not be stale upon my return. The only thing worth trying to consume in the refrigerator—since I can't exactly drink condiments—is apple juice, and if I were a betting woman, I'd wager that it is close to fermentation at this point.

Basically, the only safe risks are the water bottles, but they don't do much for nourishment.

With the exception of the sandwich and chips Stephen brought over Saturday night, I haven't given eating too much thought.

Or...unpacking.

Or...shopping for food.

Or...doing laundry.

Or...showering.

As I snuggle under my covers, I give the last one—showering—more thought. With my nose scrunched, I move it back outside the blankets and I make myself a deal. The next time I wake, showering will be on the agenda.

In the meantime, I prefer sleep.

As my temples pound, I'm aware that this self-imposed reprieve from life can't last forever.

On Monday morning, I'll need to go to work. I'll need to face Neil Butler and thank him for his faith in me. Yes, I know if he stopped by at this moment, faith wouldn't be high on his list. Pity might have a higher ranking. That's why I'm staying put under the covers, just me and my stinky self.

Facing the shower means facing life, and I'm not ready to make that move.

I need some more time to wallow in my own heartache.

And headache.

*Does lack of food cause a headache?*

I decide to think about that later if I can come up with something to eat.

*Maybe I could add mustard to what's remaining of my house-plants and call it a salad?*

*Are houseplants edible?*

Maybe I should Google that shit first.

When Stephen and I first touched down at Heathrow, I turned on my phone long enough to see that I didn't have a return email from Trevor. I did have multiple voice mails from Kimbra and even one from Duncan, which seemed strange. I'm assuming that he's probably simply being a good husband.

Maybe one day I'll listen to them and find out what they say.

Right now, I prefer the company of dreams.

Dreams are truly magical places filled with memories and imagination. In dreams I can do things I could never do in reality. I can fly. I can transport myself back to New

York, to Trevor's apartment, to his fire escape. And then, in the blink of an eye, we're together in Central Park, at Serendipity 3, or in his bed. The possibilities are endless, and in dreams, the destinations aren't conscious. Each time I close my eyes, it's like an adventure waiting to happen.

When I first arrived home, I turned on the television. I'm not sure why. I think it was to hear voices. Truly, I should have thought of it earlier. There were banners and flags everywhere as I Ubered home. Of course, at that time, none of it was registering. I'll blame it on the flight or the wine. Either way... it has begun.

The royal wedding.

The greatest display of love since Romeo and Juliet.

The prince has finally found his princess.

Everyone is overjoyed.

And it's a *big* deal.

The guests, crowds, royal family, and state officials.

Streets are blockaded and the masses are gathering.

The festivities don't even start for a few days, but the entire world is abuzz with love.

*True love*.

I pull the covers closer to my chin.

Well, screw them.

It's a wonder that Stephen and I made it home. The lady arranging our flight wasn't kidding that changing our flights was out of the question. This place is a madhouse, complete with minute-by-minute coverage broadcast around the world.

Unable to listen anymore about the happy couple, I turned off the television. It doesn't matter. I'm sure I will be able to catch it later. There's no doubt that the live

coverage will be going on for days, and after that, it will all
be available on cable TV and YouTube.

My lack of interest in the impending nuptials can't be
blamed on my American roots. I'm actually a fan of the
royals. I always have been. I even love the history: King
Henry VIII, the Tudors and Windsors, the White Queen
and the Red Queen. My current disinterest stems more
from my melancholy mood.

I almost said bitchy, but truthfully, bitchy went out the
window as I walked out on Vicky's insulting offer.

The energy necessary to be bitchy dissipated by the
second as I bit my tongue, stopping all the words I wanted
to say, smiled politely, thanked Vicky for her consideration,
and told her that she and the entire lingerie division was
welcome, considering the fact that Stephen and I had trav-
eled to New York on a moment's notice, saved their show,
and increased their sales. I then stood, told everyone in
attendance that I would be returning to London and to
juniors since the counteroffer I'd received from Neil was
too good to pass up. I then bid everyone goodbye, leaving
Vicky's shitty offer sitting unsigned on the table as she
stared at me with her mouth agape. I did get the feeling she
didn't know about Neil Butler's counteroffer, which gave me
a smidgen of satisfaction.

I left so quickly that I didn't even have a chance to say
goodbye to Chantilly or others I'd come to like in the
lingerie department. The truth is that I had to leave while
my head was still high and eyes were without tears.

Needless to say, that all changed the moment I walked
out the doors and onto Fifth Avenue.

Now, without the adrenaline necessary to do more, I
once again surrender to dreamland.

Before I slip away, I contemplate checking the time, but if I do, my rational mind will tell me that people shouldn't be sleeping at four on a Sunday afternoon. I'm not ready to listen to my rational mind. Besides, my body still believes that four in the afternoon in London is ten in the morning in New York.

The tips of my lips turn upward and tears return to my eyes as I recall a week ago. Last Sunday at ten in the morning, I was still in Trevor's bed. After my little fashion show during the middle of the night, we were both out for the count.

Coma by cannoli.

We woke in time for another round of much sweeter lovemaking, bagels and coffee, and then a private shower concert before going to Duncan and Kimbra's. No wonder I was embarrassed when Kimbra brought up death by cannoli. I was possibly one more crazy sex round away from being a victim.

But not anymore...

Cannoli will only come in my dreams.

I close my eyes and recall...I'm almost to that place where sleep comes, erasing reality...

*Bang.*

*Bang.*

*Bang.*

"What the hell?" I ask, muttering to myself as I try to decipher the sound of pounding. "Is someone doing construction?"

*Bang.*

*Bang.*

*Bang.*

"On a Sunday?"

*Shit.*

*Bang.*

*Bang.*

*Bang.*

No, someone is knocking—no, pounding—on my front door. I consider my possibilities. If I hide under my blankets, maybe whoever it is will leave. It's not exactly like I'm up for visitors.

Another round of loud, annoying knocks.

Maybe it's the police? Someone reported the scent of dying.

I lower my nose under the blanket.

No, it isn't that bad.

Maybe it's Stephen with food.

*But wouldn't he call?*

It's then I remember my phone is still off.

For no other reason than the preservation of my houseplants and stopping them from becoming salad—because I remembered that I do have some expired salad dressing in my refrigerator that may work better than mustard if my plants aren't poisonous—I force myself to get out of bed and place one foot in front of the other.

Too occupied with the banging on the door and the pounding in my head, I barely notice my haggard appearance or wrinkled sleep clothes.

"Stephen, you'd better have food or you're fired," I yell toward the front door as I make my way down the stairs.

Since my front door is solid and the small-paned window to its side is frosted, it's a terrible combination to try to see who is visiting.

"Stephen, stop!"

The knocks begin again, but before they get to three, I open the door. "What is your pro—?"

*Silence.*

I can't believe my eyes. Standing on my stoop with two large suitcases is the most incredibly handsome man with stunning green eyes, staring at only me. Me, who is wearing shorts and a camisole with no bra, three-day-old hair, no makeup, and an aroma similar to rubbish that needs to be taken to the curb.

"Shana," Trevor begins, "I'm sorry to come unannounced. I tried your phone and couldn't get through to you. I seem to have nowhere to stay. There's some wedding or something happening, and I was wondering if maybe you had room?"

My eyes fill with tears as I wrap my arms around his neck. "Trevor? How are you here?"

After a kiss to my cheek, he asks, "Do you think that maybe we could go inside before your neighbors decide to watch?" He moves me to arm's length. "I'm good with this outfit, but I'd like to keep your lingerie to my eyes only, if you don't mind." He adds the last part with a wink.

My head is bobbing faster than I can think. "Yes, come in. How did you find me? How did you get here? There aren't any flights. Why are you here? What are you doing with suitcases?"

After the door closes, his finger touches my lips, stopping my questions. And then his head tilts as his gaze goes toward my hair and plucks something from its tangled depths.

When he brings the crumb into view, I shrug. "I think that's a chip."

"A chip?"

"Potato," I confirm. "I was eating in bed and fell asleep."

He nods. "Okay. I won't ask for more detail."

I look again at his luggage just before I tug him into the depth of my dark living room.

"Are you avoiding daylight? Did you suddenly become a vampire?"

"I sent you an email," I say as my heart tightens in my chest and I avoid his questions.

"And I'm replying, now, here, with me."

"With you?"

"Shana..." He reaches for my hands. "I didn't tell you that I love you because I was trying to help the situation at Saks. It slipped out. I didn't mean to say it. I know you had a full plate. But that doesn't mean it isn't true. I've known it since before I saw you on that stage. I think I've known it since the morning of Duncan's wedding."

"You do? Really?"

"I really do. I'm also not losing you again, ever."

I wrap my arms around my chest. "Trevor, I'm sorry I couldn't take that offer."

"I haven't made you one."

"No, the one Vicky made me. I wanted to stay with you. I wanted to stay in New York, but I just couldn't do—"

Again, his finger stops my words, followed by his lips and oh God, his tongue. I melt toward him, only to suddenly back away. "Oh goodness, I'm a mess. I've done nothing but sleep and not shower..." My hand covers my mouth. "...or brush my teeth..."

Trevor laughs. "You're the most beautiful woman I know. Now, Ms. Price may I propose my offer?"

"Propose? Your offer?"

He grins. "One step at a time. First, I would never want

you to compromise who you are for us. That isn't who we are or who I want us to be. I'm glad you walked out on her shitty offer."

"I didn't give you the details at JFK. How did you know about the shitty offer or that I walked out?" Before he can answer, I do it for him. "Stephen."

Trevor nods. "The thing is that McCobb has been bidding a job in Oxford. I may have seemed distracted before you left because I was hoping to tell you about it. I didn't want to give you false hope, and I was waiting on the reply. It didn't come until after you were gone."

"Oxford, England?"

"Yes, my lady. Oxford, *England*. I'll need to be on-site on and off during the week. We will figure all that out. But my weekends will be free. I was only one of the engineers who worked on the proposal, but after I learned how you were being treated in New York, I applied to my boss to let me supervise the project. Then, even before it was approved, I went to Max and pushed for the funding commitment. It was a long shot, but it worked."

"So you're here now in England?"

"I am."

And then I recall the royal wedding. "But how did you get here? Flights are booked. This city is a madhouse."

"I called in one more favor."

"From whom?"

"I called my brother."

The tears again threaten the back of my eyes. "You asked Duncan to fly you to England?"

"What good is it to have a hotshot brother with a company plane if I never use it?"

Forgetting about my lovely aroma, I reach up and wrap

my arms around Trevor's neck. "Of all the things you did, I get the feeling that call was the most difficult."

Trevor shrugs his wide shoulders beneath my grasp. "It would have been, but since you, it wasn't. Nothing is too big of an obstacle for me to get to you. I know we could have made this work long distance. Here's the thing, my lady, I don't want to be away from you."

I shake my head. "I can't believe you're really here. How long will you be here?"

"The spec on the project is for two years."

My eyes open wide. "Two years?"

Trevor reaches for my waist and pulls me toward him. "And after that, we'll see where life takes us. Who knows, there may be another project here?"

"Us? I like the way that sounds."

"So do I, and as for your email, I hope you meant it."

My head bobs up and down. "I meant it. I'm in love with you, too."

"*In love* with me?"

"Trevor Willis, I've never been in love before. I'm not sure exactly how it works. All I know is that leaving you Friday night was the hardest thing I've ever done in my entire life. Since that moment, I've been broken...until I opened the door and saw you. Your amazing smile, eyes, hair...and thighs," I say the last part with a grin. "In an instant you put me back together."

"Well, you've got all of me—even my thighs," he says, shaking his head. "Do you think I could possibly find a place to stay until my project starts?"

"I might have a spare bedroom," I say, running my fingers through his hair.

"I was thinking that sharing a room sounded more fun."

"I like the sound of that, too."

Lowering my chin, I lift my eyes to look through my lashes. "If you don't mind staying with someone who hasn't showered."

"Oh, I mind. Because you see, I have been traveling and well, I like showers. I was hoping that we could take one together."

"On one condition," I say, "only if you promise to serenade me."

"I will be glad to serenade you."

"If you're staying here for the future, I don't want just one personal concert."

Trevor gently places his palm on my cheek. "No, my lady, there will definitely be another one and another one after that."


THE END


*Thank you for reading my lighter side. I hope you enjoyed Shana and Trevor's story as much as I enjoyed writing it. For the record, this is the first completely "Aleatha" lighter one. My first two began as products of my alter-ego—no longer in existence—pseudonym, Jade Sinner. While my time as half of Jade was short, I'll credit her with my newer ability to look at romance from a fun and sexy point of view and thank her for the variety.*

*If you haven't read A SECRET ONE, the free novella about Shana and Trevor's first encounter, please be sure to download it today:*

*And if you haven't read Duncan and Kimbra's story, PLUS ONE,*
*it's ready and waiting:*
*The other lighter one of mine is ONE NIGHT, and while*
*completely unrelated to this story, it too is fun and sexy with more*
*than a side of sweet:*

*All of my "lighter ones" may be read as stand-alones and are*
*guaranteed to leave you with a smile on your face and maybe even a*
*bit hot and bothered.*
*Thank you for reading!*
*Aleatha*

# WHAT TO DO NOW

LEND IT: Did you enjoy ANOTHER ONE? Do you have a friend who'd enjoy ANOTHER ONE? ANOTHER ONE may be lent one time on Kindle. Sharing is caring!

RECOMMEND IT: Do you have multiple friends who'd enjoy this romantic comedy? Tell them about it! Call, text, post, tweet...your recommendation is the nicest gift you can give to an author!

REVIEW IT: Tell the world. Please go to the retailer where you purchased this book, as well as Goodreads, and write a review. Please share your thoughts about ANOTHER ONE on:

*Amazon, *ANOTHER ONE*, Customer Reviews
*Barnes & Noble, *ANOTHER ONE*, Customer Reviews
*iBooks, *ANOTHER ONE*, Customer Reviews
*Goodreads.com/Aleatha Romig

## STAY CONNECTED WITH ALEATHA

Do you love Aleatha's writing? Do you want to be kept up to date about Infidelity, Consequences, Tales from the Dark Side, Light series, her "lighter ones," and what's coming next?

Do you like EXCLUSIVE content (never-released scenes, never-released excerpts, and more)? Would you like the monthly chance to win prizes (signed books and gift cards)? Then sign up today for Aleatha's monthly newsletter and stay informed on all things Aleatha Romig.

Sign up for Aleatha's NEWSLETTER: (recipients receive exclusive material and offers) http://bit.ly/1PYLjZW

**You can also find Aleatha@**
Check out her website: http://aleatharomig.com
Facebook: http://www.Facebook.com/AleathaRomig
Twitter: https://twitter.com/AleathaRomig
Goodreads:

http://www.goodreads.com/author/show/5131072.Aleatha_Romig

Instagram: http://instagram.com/aleatharomig

Email Aleatha: aleatharomig@gmail.com

You may also listen to Aleatha Romig books on Audible:

http://www.audible.com/search/ref=a_mn_mt_ano_tseft_galileo?

advsearchKeywords=aleatha+romig&sprefixRefmarker=nb_sb_ss_i_0_7&sprefix=aleatha

# BOOKS BY NEW YORK TIMES BESTSELLING AUTHOR ALEATHA ROMIG:

## Aleatha's Lighter Ones:

Stand-alone "lighter" romances

**PLUS ONE**

**A SECRET ONE**

**ONE NIGHT**

**INFIDELITY SERIES:**

**BETRAYAL**

Book #1

(October 2015)

**CUNNING**

Book #2

(January 2016)

**DECEPTION**

Book #3

(May 2016)

**ENTRAPMENT**

Book #4

(September 2016)

**FIDELITY**

Book #5

(January 2017)

## RESPECT: A STANDALONE INFIDELITY NOVEL

(January 2018)

## THE CONSEQUENCES SERIES:
## CONSEQUENCES

(Book #1)

Released August 2011

### TRUTH

(Book #2)

Released October 2012

### CONVICTED

(Book #3)

Released October 2013

### REVEALED

(Book #4)

Previously titled: Behind His Eyes Convicted: The Missing Years

Re-released June 2014

### BEYOND THE CONSEQUENCES

(Book #5)

Released January 2015

# RIPPLES

A Consequences stand-alone novel

Released October 2017

## COMPANION READS:

## BEHIND HIS EYES-CONSEQUENCES

(Book #1.5)

Released January 2014

## BEHIND HIS EYES—TRUTH

(Book #2.5)

Released March 2014

## THE LIGHT SERIES:

Published through Thomas and Mercer

## INTO THE LIGHT

(June 14, 2016)

## AWAY FROM THE DARK

(October 2016)

## TALES FROM THE DARK SIDE SERIES:
## INSIDIOUS

(All books in this series are stand-alone erotic thrillers)

Released October 2014

## DUPLICITY: (COMPLETELY UNRELATED TO BOOK #1)

Release TBA

## THE VAULT

Sexy, fun stand-alone novellas showcasing the hot and steamy side of Aleatha.

## UNCONVENTIONAL

(January 2018)

(Originally appeared in THE VAULT anthology)

## UNEXPECTED

(Coming August of 2018)

# ALEATHA ROMIG

Aleatha Romig is a New York Times, Wall Street Journal, and USA Today bestselling author who lives in Indiana, USA. She grew up in Mishawaka, graduated from Indiana University, and is currently living south of Indianapolis. Aleatha has raised three children with her high school sweetheart and husband of over thirty years. Before she became a full-time author, she worked days as a dental hygienist and spent her nights writing. Now, when she's not imagining mind-blowing twists and turns, she likes to spend her time with her family and friends. Her other pastimes include reading and creating heroes/anti-heroes who haunt your dreams!

Aleatha released her first novel, CONSEQUENCES, in August of 2011. CONSEQUENCES became a bestselling series with five novels and two companions released from 2011 through 2015. The compelling and epic story of Anthony and Claire Rawlings has graced more than half a million e-readers. Aleatha released the first of her series

TALES FROM THE DARK SIDE, INSIDIOUS, in the fall of 2014. These stand-alone thrillers continue Aleatha's twisted style with an increase in heat.

In the fall of 2015, Aleatha moved headfirst into the world of dark romantic suspense saga with the release of BETRAYAL, the first of her five-novel INFIDELITY series that has taken the reading world by storm. She also began her traditional publishing career with Thomas and Mercer. Her books INTO THE LIGHT and AWAY FROM THE DARK were published through this mystery/thriller publisher in 2016.

In the spring of 2017, Aleatha released her first stand-alone, fun, and sexy romantic comedy with PLUS ONE, ONE NIGHT, and in 2018, ANOTHER ONE.

Aleatha is a "Published Author's Network" member of the Romance Writers of America and PEN America. She is represented by Kevan Lyon of Marsal Lyon Literary Agency.

Made in the USA
Lexington, KY
20 September 2018